Three of Us

Ann Grech

Edited by: Hot Tree Editing
Cover design: CT Cover Creations

Blurb

Two cowboys walk onto a ranch. The girl falls for both. But they're in love with each other, and she's stuck in the friend zone. Sounds like a bad joke, right?

Welcome to my life...

But I think I was wrong; my two cowboys are just friends.

It's been the three of us since the day we met. I've settled for friendship for over a decade, but I want more.

I've fantasized about getting between them, but they don't think I'm *that* type of girl.

It's about time these boys wake up and realize they're in love with me.

And each other too.

Hold my beer while I sort this mess out.

Three of Us is a standalone book in the Pearce Station universe. You'll meet new friends who become family and fall in love with Ally, Sam, and Craig.

To Scottie, Pete, Ally, Craig, Sam, Ma, Nan, Jono, Waru, Yindi and Den. Thank you for this last year. Being with you meant I could hide from the 'real world' when I needed it.

Acknowledgements

I have wanted to write another MMF for quite a while, but the characters have all been holding out on me. When Ally started speaking though, I knew I had to listen. From the moment I started to get to know her in Outback Treasure I, I was both in awe and inspired by her. She, Ma and Nan are three women who have gone through it all and not only survived but thrived. Living in the Aussie outback is tough beyond anything most of us who live cushy lives in the suburbs can imagine. So when Ally basically handed me her beer while she sorted her boys out, I followed along and wrote what each of them showed me. I feel privileged that they chose me to tell their story to.

Once again, a huge thank you to Robyn and Simon Corcoran and Luke Newton. Your advice on Pearce Station, auctions and bull breeders and everything associated with them, made up for my lack of knowledge. It's a whole lot more realistic than it was before your input, and I greatly appreciate that. Any errors or artistic licence I've taken are my own!

Susan Horsnell, I appreciate you sending me 'The Legends of Moonie Jarl.' It means the world that you'd gather information for me when touring Queensland while speaking with our Indigenous Australians. You helped me tell stories that resonated with both myself and my characters. It was important to me to properly honour our indigenous cultural heritage, so thank you.

Thank you to Kariss Stone for your feedback on the earliest draft of this story. It was very much appreciated.

My beautiful friends who make up the MM DreaMMers authors (Viva Gold, LJ Harris, JJ Harper, Angelique Jurd, Tracy McKay and Megs Pritchard), thank you for your advice, inspiration, daily pics, motivation and most of all, your friendship. I'm grateful every day for you being in my life.

To the team at Hot Tree Editing, thank you. Becky, my gorgeous editor and all-around story advisor, I couldn't do this without you. You and your team's advice made this story into something I absolutely adore.

Thank you to Clarise Tan from CT Cover Creations too. You managed to turn my supremely vague request into something that is both stunning and perfectly represents Ally, Craig and Sam. I adore this cover artwork.

Linda Russell from Foreword PR, your support, advice and encouragement to get this story into the world and for helping me work with my insane procrastiplanning is very much appreciated. I've loved working with you once again. Cheers, lovely!

To my hubby and kiddos, I couldn't do this without your support and encouragement, the cups of tea and the Byron Bay Cookies. I love you all to the moon and back.

My A-Team, thank you! You're my happy place.

Last and most certainly not least, thank you to you, the readers and bloggers, for your unending love and support.

Sharing, reviews, general shout outs and, importantly, reading our words means the world to every author. This is my thirteenth novel. It's something I never dreamed possible, but you've made that a reality for me. For that – the realization of a childhood dream – I'll forever be grateful.

Ann xx

GLOSSARY

This story is set in outback Queensland, Australia and uses Australian English. There are some terms that you may not have heard before, so a few are set out for you. If you come across more, please let me know and I'll try to explain. You might also want to take a peek at my website too – I'll add more there as they come up.

Arvo – afternoon.

Billabong – a pond or small lake filled from the offshoot of a river. It is often filled seasonally.

Bloke – man.

Bogan – an uncultured or unsophisticated person.

Bonza – great, awesome.

Bottle-O – liquor store.

Brisbane Broncos – a footy (rugby league) team in Brisbane.

Brissie – Brisbane. Queensland's capital city and location of the Ekka.

Bundy – Bundaberg Rum.

Caravan – a mobile home.

Coldie – a beer.

Cooee (within) – close, within reach.

CSIRO - Commonwealth Scientific and Industrial Research Organization, a government organization responsible for scientific research aimed at improving the performance of industry to enhance economic and social performance for the benefit of the entire country.

Dam (see Chapter 8 in the context of Spook) – the mother of a foal.

Damper – a form of bread traditionally baked in the embers of an open fire.

Dero – a social derelict. Possibly homeless, drunk or a tramp.

Dole – slang for unemployment benefits granted to out of work Australians.

Drizabone – a jacket designed to be worn by horse riders.

Dunny – toilet.

Ekka – a nickname for Royal Queensland Show originally called Brisbane Exhibition (Ekka is short for exhibition). It is an annual agricultural fair in Queensland.

Esky – a cooler.

Fair dinkum – for real, seriously.

Fella – bloke, man.

Footy – rugby league, a full contact sport played between two teams for two forty-minute halves where the objective is to score more than the other team by carrying the ball over the 'try line' and, after making a try, kicking the ball between the posts to add an extra two points to the score (called a conversion).

Fourbie – Four-by-four.

G'day – hello.

Golden Gaytime – a delicious toffee and vanilla flavoured ice-cream coated in chocolate and dipped in biscuit/cookie pieces.

Grog – liquor.

Hard yakka – hard work.

Jocks – underwear.

Kitchen bench – kitchen countertop.

Kays – short for kilometres, a metric unit of measurement. One mile is the equivalent of 1.6 kilometres.

Knocked (him) for six – reference to a cricket term where one hits a ball so hard it crosses the perimeter line of the pitch without bouncing. In the context of a person being knocked for six, it's a very hard hit.

Longreach – a town in outback Queensland.

Maggoted – drunk.

Metre – a metric unit of measurement. One hundred centimetres equals one metre, which is approximately three feet.

Milo – a chocolate powder that you can drink warm or cold in milk, or on ice cream as a dessert.

New South – New South Wales, a state in Australia, forming part of the southern border to Queensland.

Old codger – affectionate term for an eccentric old man.

Paddock – a corral for livestock.

PJs – pyjamas.

Poofter – a slur for gay men, equivalent to faggot.

Queenslander – a style of architecture for houses built in Queensland to suit the varied climate in the state (sub-tropical to desert). Traditionally, the houses are constructed on stilts to allow for ventilation and flood waters to pass under the house, with wide verandas and windows all around the house. Painted in a light colour, the combination ensures cooling shade and cross ventilation.

Roo – kangaroo.

Sanga – sandwich.

Scone – a sweet biscuit (i.e. American-style biscuit, not a cookie) that you traditionally eat with jam (i.e. jelly) and whipped cream.

Schnittie – chicken schnitzel.

Semi-trailer – a transport truck, big rig, eighteen-wheeler or articulated lorry.

Servo – gas station.

Sick as a dog – very unwell.

Spag bol – spaghetti bolognaise.

Spewin' – very upset.

State of Origin – rugby match between the mighty Queensland Maroons (the Cane Toads) and the meh at best New South Wales Blues (the Cockroaches). Usually the Blues have the blues because even though the stubborn bastards will never admit it, Queensland is by far the better team. Go Queenslander!

Starkers – naked.

Station – equivalent to a ranch.

Swag – a canvas sleeping bag.

Tea – depending on the context, either a hot beverage or dinner.

Tele – television.

Trackies – sweats.

Tucker – food.

Undies – underwear.

Uni – university.

Ute – equivalent to a pickup truck.

Veggie patch – vegetable garden.

CHAPTER 1

Craig – Aged 15

The shed was dry and dusty, much like everything else around here. We hadn't had rain in at least four years. I wasn't even sure I remembered the sound of it on our tin roof. Or the smell. It seemed like a long time ago for us teenagers. It was even longer for our parents.

We'd grown up on Hayes Horse Farm in southern Queensland, but since we'd been in high school, we'd attended a boarding school in the city during term. It was good to be back home, but our time there was coming to an end. It was late summer and school was going back in just a few weeks. Soon my mate, Sam, and I would get our gear packed and his dad or mine would make the five-hour trip into Brisbane to begin our next year. Goondiwindi was less than an hour east of us, and they had perfectly good schools there, but our parents wanted us to have a good education. So that meant leaving for ten weeks at a time to be stuck in the city, before returning home. By any description it was a hundred kays past the middle of nowhere, but we wouldn't have it any other way. Until we were forced back to school, we'd spend every minute we could here.

With the shed doors thrown open, the late summer sun cast dust motes in the air. Long shafts of light pierced the shadows in the shed where there were gaps in the rusty iron roof. We had plenty of light to work with but enough shadow to make our jobs bearable at this time of year. The heat was so thick it could be cut with a knife. At over forty degrees Celsius, most of the life on the farm was wallowing in the shade. But Sam and I were still at it, trying to get our chores done for the day. We were motivated to get in our parents' good graces, not that we'd been especially rowdy of late, but we had something to ask and it was better to do it while the folks were in a good mood. Sam's dad, the owner of the farm, and my dad, his head farmhand were the go-to men, but our mums ruled the roost. So we had to impress both.

We were already considered men when it came to work, but not where it mattered. While we loved it here, we wanted off the farm for just one weekend. Our sixteenth birthday weekend, so we could party in town with friends. Goondiwindi wasn't exactly known for its nightlife, but girls, grog, and a pizza was about all we wanted anyway. But until we could work our way up to asking, we had chores to do.

Stacking hay bales was physical work, the heat sapping the energy out of us almost as much as tossing the rectangular cubes of feed. I wiped sweat from my brow, using the back of the yellow suede gloves I was wearing. My forearms were scratched and in some spots dots of dried blood littered my filthy skin, but it didn't bother me. I'd grown up out here, crashing and tumbling around. I barely noticed the few surface-level scrapes.

A gust of heated wind blew into the shed, sending the fine dust pluming into the air. Sam sneezed and I coughed, taking in a lungful of red-dirt-laced air right at the wrong time. "Shit," I muttered, spluttering. I lifted the hem of my sweaty tee and wiped my face. Grit had filled my mouth, and I took a swig from the water bottle hooked over the back of the ute before spitting it over my shoulder.

"Bloody dusty, hey?" Sam complained as he hefted a bale above his head, carrying it from the ute over to our neat stack. His lithe muscles bulged, his faded navy blue T-shirt riding up and showing a strip of pale skin and a dimple on his back just above the waistline of his low riding jeans. Those jeans hugged him in all the right places. He managed to look good, even covered in dirt, hay, and sweat. Sam didn't even strain as he tossed it to the second level while butterflies swooped in my belly as I watched him jump up onto another bale to position it properly.

I could watch him work all day, but he'd kick my arse if I did. So with a smile, I followed him, lifting the bale off the tray and taking it over to where he stood. We worked as a team, stacking them three bales high in neat rows.

Feed didn't grow of its own accord anymore. No water and blinding heat ensured that any grasses that sprouted were quickly burned to a crisp. The Macintyre River that ran along the boundary of the farm had run dry, no more than puddles in the deepest parts. Our horses were healthy—

well looked after—but at the toss of a coin, they could be desperately clinging to life. They moved between the shade and the bore. We took the feed to them, so they'd keep up their energy levels. After the endless hot summer, dehydration was a real risk.

Taking the feed to them was the easy part. Getting it out to the farm was harder. Dad and old man Hayes, Sam's dad, moaned about it all the time.

From my spot on the second layer of bales, I looked over to my best mate, admiring the way Sam didn't stop working, no matter how hot it was. I caught the bale he tossed, saving him from jumping up, and positioned it ready for the next one.

I knew Sam stood next to me before he even said anything. It was as if we were tuned into each other so closely that we didn't even have to speak to communicate. We'd grown up together, learning to crawl and walk holding onto each other, riding our bikes, then our horses. In the last few years, our parents had even taken it in turns giving us driving lessons along the dusty trails of the farm.

I couldn't imagine being without him. We were still as inseparable as we had been as kids. Everyone knew that where one of us was, the other could be found too. But it wasn't only that we spent all our time together. Our skills complimented each other's as well. Where I was better at arts, English, and history, Sam was a numbers and science whizz. Around the farm, we were evenly matched, even to the experienced horsemen Sam's dad hired. We could hold our own against any one of them in terms of riding skill and training.

Sam nudged his elbow into my arm, and a tingle of awareness shot through me. "Whatcha thinking about?"

"Just looking round at the paddocks," I lied, steadfastly refusing to admit I was thinking about the way he moved. "Summer's hot." I pointed to the copse of gum trees swaying in the breeze that looked like a mirage. The heat shimmered off the dusty ground, masking the line of the horizon in the distance. Blue skies and reddish dirt where the lush green grasses had once grown created a stunning contrast. Nature in all its glory.

"We can stay out here once we've finished up if you want? Be a bit cooler by then. I've got this new book that Ma picked up for me. It's supposed to be good. We can read it together if you like."

"Yeah." I loved reading—could bury my head in a book all night. And I loved being out here in the summer evenings—the sunsets, the way everything seemed to move slower in the heat. But it wasn't really what I was thinking about. We stood there, the quiet enveloping us. Even the cicadas, which could deafen you on a summer day, were silent. The land was lying in wait for the rain, waiting for new life to be born. Waiting to breathe again.

"You gonna tell me what you're really thinking about?" Sam kicked my foot and grinned at me, sitting down on the edge of the bales. I followed him, getting comfortable on the prickly surface.

"Dunno," I answered as truthfully as I dared. My feelings were all over the place lately. It was as if I was a spring coiled under pressure, ready to burst free and bounce away. I was crawling out of my own skin.

"You think we'll get the parentals to agree to let us stay in Goondiwindi?" Sam thankfully changed the subject.

"Not unless it's at the pastor's house." I huffed. That was the last place I wanted to stay—there would be no chance of hooking up with anyone if we were there. "And he's gonna want to have us doing youth club activities."

"Mightn't be so bad." Sam shrugged. I looked at him incredulously, my eyebrows hiked high. "Hear me out. Youth club in Goondiwindi is gonna have most of the kids around town there, right? There's got to be a couple of girls who'd be up for doin' it."

"S'pose." I nodded. "Maybe I should check the flyer that Ma always collects when they go into town."

"You ever wondered what it's like to make out with a girl?" Sam asked quietly. His body language oozed confidence, but I heard the uncertainty in his voice. He was nervous. "Dunno if a girl'd go further if we don't know what we're doing."

"What are we supposed to do? It's not like our hands can kiss us back." I used the same sarcasm-filled tone that Ma hated, but usually made Sam laugh. He didn't though. This time, he looked at me like he wanted to be sick. His eyes were filled with doubt. Sam sucked in a breath and I waited. I wasn't sure what he'd say, but the words that came out of his mouth weren't what I would have expected in a million years.

"We could practice? On each other?" His voice was tight. Higher pitched than normal. "You know, so we aren't clueless when it happens for real."

With his justification, he gained confidence, or maybe he was just winging it. He was one for logic. If he saw a problem, he'd work on it until he came up with a solution. That's what this was. It was Sam coming up with the answer to a problem we'd talked about endlessly.

His suggestion made my gut flip. The kaleidoscope of butterflies that had taken flight before swooped again, doing tumbles in my belly. A pang of something shot through me—what I had no idea—and my dick filled at the prospect of learning how to pash. Even if it was with my best mate, not with a girl. He was right though. It was better that we knew what we were doing than coming off totally clueless. We were already at a disadvantage not having any girls our age out here.

The last thing we needed was to be shitty in the sack too.

"It's not like we're poofters or anything," I hedged thoughtfully. The blokes out here always went to pains to make it clear that it was okay to be anything, as long as we weren't poofters. "I mean, we'd only be practicing, right?"

"Yeah, course. Means to an end." He nodded and turned to me. "You wanna?"

"S'pose." I shrugged, ignoring the urge to adjust my half-hard dick.

"Stack the next set of bales up at the front. We can hide behind there so we don't get busted. It can be our practicing hideout." He grinned and I barked out a laugh, the tension between us broken. We'd had practicing hideouts our whole lives. One for making mud pies, one for growing seedlings, and another one when we got older for whittling sticks. We even had one for smoking until we'd tried it. That'd ended real quick. The latest one was drinkin', but it was hard to try when the only grog we had on the farm was a few bottles of cheap red wine which Ma used for cooking. It'd given me a headache that'd lasted for three days, and I'd sworn off the stuff after only half a bottle.

We got to it, hefting the bales into place and creating an alcove where we could get comfortable. The whole time my mind raced, my body pulsing with anticipation. I wanted to burst out of my own skin with excitement, but at the same time, I knew I shouldn't be as keen as I was. It wasn't like it was for real. Like I'd said to Sam, it wasn't like we were gay or anything. We were practicing so that we could be better at it when we did it for real with a girl.

I knew if I kept Lindsey, the cutie from church, or the blonde girl from *Dawson's Creek* that Sam always had a wank over in mind, I'd be right. I'd be able to push past the fact that I was practicing with my mate.

Twenty long minutes later, we were done moving the hay. The space we'd left for ourselves was tight—one bale wide and four bales long. There was just enough room for Sam and me to sit comfortably in it. I looked at our handiwork and hesitated. Sam saw it and gripped my arm.

"We don't have to. I just thought we should practice if we wanted to get to second or third base, or even go all the way on our birthdays. It's not like a girl's gonna give up her v-card if we can't look after her." He pulled a piece of hay from the bale and snapped it in half. "I don't want to be one of those arses who gets a shitty rep because he got off and didn't look after his girl, you know?"

"Yeah. Yeah, I'm totally with you." I didn't want to be that kind of guy either. "Yeah, nah, we're good. You wanna get in first?"

"Practicing your manners already, huh? What am I, the girl?"

"Shut the fuck up, idiot." I laughed. He always knew what to say to lighten the mood, even when he was just as nervous as me. We crawled in and knelt in front of each other. I hesitated, not really knowing what to do. "Do we hug each other or something or just go for it?"

"Should try to make it as legit as possible, shouldn't we?" he asked, his brows dipped questioningly. I nodded and leaned in, realizing I was still wearing my gloves. Yanking them off, I dropped them to my side and reached for him, running my hand up his forearm.

The dark hairs there stood on end as his skin prickled with goosebumps. He was watching me, wide-eyed, as I shuffled forward and reached for his shoulder, wrapping my hand around the back of his neck. He came willingly, and we met in the middle, both up on our knees until our bodies touched. When Sam slid his arm around my waist and brought his hand up to my face, my heart stuttered. "You're so pretty." He leaned forward and I bit back my laugh, but when our noses bumped and we went cross-eyed looking at each other, I couldn't help it. The laughter bubbled up from my chest and I rolled my eyes.

When he pulled back, looking playfully wounded and added, "Hey, I was serious," my cheeks heated. I honestly couldn't tell whether he was being corny or genuine, and that made me shift awkwardly.

"This is weird. Is this weird?" I turned to hide my embarrassment.

"Yeah, totally weird." He gently cuffed me on the chin. "Whose idea was this?"

"Yours." I poked him in the chest, giving him shit. I couldn't help my grin at his smirk.

We were so much closer physically than we'd been in years, probably since we were kids and had insisted on sharing a swag when we camped out by the fire with our dads. Sam's warmth seeped into me, and I leaned into his touch. His fingertips dancing along my shoulder had my muscles going all jelly-like, quivering from the energy he radiated. His firm body, hardened from years of physical work even though we still had a ways to grow, was pressed against mine. His cheeky smile turned soft as we gazed at each other. Hugging him was nothing like what I imagined a woman's body would be like, but in that moment, I realized how much I liked it.

Or maybe it was just being with Sam. I didn't know.

I loved curves. I loved the idea of being with a woman. I'd seen tits and bush and they were beautiful. But my body was reacting to Sam. Then again, maybe I was just worked up from the thought of getting close to someone and getting off without using my own hand.

The thought of getting off had my dick hardening and begging for friction. If only I could get closer. Press harder against him. But I couldn't. I mean, how would I feel if he started riding my leg, using me to get off? What would it be like to touch him? To wrap my hand around his dick? *No!* That's something a poof would do, and I wasn't one of them. I'd heard the stories. Hell, there was even one about a boy at school who'd killed himself. They still called him Priscilla in the hallways. There was no way I was one of them.

But my body ignored the fucked-up monologue in my head. All my dick wanted to do was get out and party. It wanted to grind and rut against bare skin. Feel what it was like to blow with another person. I tried to focus on Sam instead of getting off. On what was before me. *Who* was before me. He was my best mate, not a girl I wanted to hook-up with. I needed to keep that in mind.

I took a breath and focussed. Concentrated like I would when getting near one of the more skittish horses. Holding Sam close, I looked into his eyes. Brown with hints of green, they were as familiar to me as my own. This time it was my heart that reacted. It flip-flopped in my chest. I loved my best mate. Not *love* love but love, and I knew I wouldn't want to kiss anyone else.

My thoughts screeched to a halt. *Practice. It's just practice.*

I ran my thumb along his throat, touching the soft skin there and feeling him swallow. My eyes slipped closed as I leaned in and rubbed my cheek against his, just breathing him in. His breath, hot on my cheek electrified every nerve ending. His stubble, still soft like mine, had me doing it again, rubbing against him like a cat. But then I moved my mouth and my lips touched the corner of his. On a gasp, he tightened his grip on my back, digging his fingers into my flesh. Liquid fire travelled down my spine. My restraint snapped. Any doubt, any confusion dissipated.

I wanted this. I wanted him.

I kissed him.

My mind whited out.

Every thought, every uncertainty, every justification for whatever this was fled, and I was left with instinct. My body took over, my mind surrendering to my first kiss. That first press of my lips at the corner of his mouth was everything I'd imagined. As if I'd been lassoed by an invisible rope, I was drawn closer. I couldn't resist Sam's pull. Another gentle kiss on his mouth, his lips soft and full beneath my own.

I was kissing my best friend. I wanted to laugh and cry at the same time. I couldn't deny that it felt right being in his arms. Safe, like I could be me with him. I knew I belonged there, but I also knew I couldn't have him. No matter how much I wanted to keep kissing him and to let go and see what it would feel like to have him pressed against me naked rather than someone else, I had to keep my wits about me. I did like girls. There was no doubt of that.

But then there was Sam.

Another press of open lips, this time Sam leading. He slid his tongue into my mouth and my brain short-circuited. I couldn't help my needy moan.

Our tongues tangled together, teeth clashing and lips sliding. Exactly like we'd watched on the tele. I dove in deeper, taking and giving in equal measure. Pashing was perfection. But I still wanted more. Needed more. More of Sam. I tangled my hands in his hair, loving the way the short silky strands slid between my fingers. The musky scents of our bodies surrounded me, and I knew without a doubt that I could get off with both girls and blokes. But how could I want both? It was as if my body couldn't make up its mind. I knew wanting Sam was wrong, so why did it feel so right? I imagined kissing a beautiful girl and it was just as appealing.

I pushed the thoughts aside. This was my one chance to be with him. There was no way I was going to take our time together—practice or not—for granted. Tugging gently on his hair, I angled Sam's face and licked into his mouth. Dipping my tongue in as far as I could reach, I tasted him, savoured him. Running my tongue up his own, I drank him in, getting high on every part of Sam I could touch. He tasted sweet like the gum he chewed, with something underlying that made me hard.

I shifted, pressing my iron-like dick against his hip as stealthily as possible. I got an erection from a gust of wind, but this was no coincidence. I wanted him. I wasn't entirely comfortable with that nugget of truth, but I couldn't stop either.

Sam brought his calloused hand around to my front, and I wished I could feel him skin on skin. He thumbed my nipple, cupping my pec like it was a breast. Like he'd do to a girl. The added sensation sent me spiralling, getting me so close to coming that I had to pull back and gasp for breath.

I didn't want it. But I did. And I still couldn't stop.

I ran my hand down his back, delighting at the flex of his muscle as we kissed. Slipping my work-roughened hands under his shirt, I touched his heated skin for the first time and knew without a doubt, I never wanted to stop.

This was supposed to be a practice round. I wasn't supposed to discover this thing about me, but I had. I didn't quite know what to do with it until he kissed down my throat, sucking gently on my pulse point. Then I knew. I needed to touch every part of him. To experience this like it was my one and only time, because we couldn't do this again.

I couldn't risk it.

I couldn't risk falling for my best friend or getting caught. Especially getting caught.

Running my hands lower, wishing I could reach into his jeans, I palmed his arse with both hands and pulled him tight against me. Our mouths met again, and we dove in, all sloppy wet kisses filled with tongue. For two inexperienced blokes, we were good at this.

Sam moved his hand away from my pec, and I missed his touch immediately, but when he slid his hand down, I gasped.

Finding the edge of my tee and lifting, he pulled back but didn't let go of my waist. With a handful of my shirt in his grip, he pushed against my shoulder, making me arch back until I was pressed against the bales behind me. He leaned down, blowing against my nipple, and I bit back a cry, my hips thrusting instinctually. Cupping my pec again, he swiped his tongue out and licked the flat disk. It pebbled immediately and he closed his lips over it and sucked. It was as if he had a hotline to my dick. I was straining and soaking my jocks with pre-cum, grinding on him. Sam rolled his hips, letting me feel his hardness against my leg, and I moaned like a porn star.

"Shh." He laughed, pulling me in for another kiss. His movements were urgent, trying to cover any sounds we were making. Neither of us wanted to explain to our parents or any one of the other farmhands what we were doing.

When Sam moved his hand down to my waist, I nearly cried. I wanted more of his mouth on my skin. More of his hands on me, and for one horrifying moment, I thought he was pulling away. My head was telling me that I should only want a girl to do it to me. Dad had given me the birds and the bees talk years ago. I'd seen it in practice in nature enough too. It wasn't that I didn't want girls. I did. But I also wanted this boy in front of me.

Maybe I was being greedy. Maybe I couldn't make up my mind. Whatever it was, I was acting on instinct. My body knew what it wanted.

And I wanted Sam.

But when he thumbed the button on my jeans, I froze. Sam dove in deeper, alternating between giving me more tongue and sucking on mine before he pulled back and whispered against my lips, "It's okay, baby. I'll look after you. Lemme touch your clit. I'll send you flyin'." I jerked my head back, shock rendered me momentarily speechless at his words. Jesus fucking Christ, I'd forgotten for a moment that we were practicing. That he was pretending I was the girl he wanted.

I'd been thrown off-kilter. Flung so far out of myself that I was burning up on re-entry. My traitorous body wished he was speaking directly to me, that he was telling me how much he wanted to feel my cock in his hand. Knowing he still had his head in the game, that he was still practicing, pulled me out of the tornado of my mind. Switching my brain off was easier said than done, but for a moment, the uncertainty fled, and I melted into his touch.

Gods, his touch sent me flying.

The flick of the button on my jeans made me shudder. As he walked his fingers down my groin to my leg, it pushed me to the edge. I was so close to coming. I was treading a line—a dangerous one—but somehow that made me want him more.

I had everything to lose. His friendship, his respect. It'd kill me if I lost either, especially if he was disgusted because I came apart from his hands. It wasn't what we'd agreed, but I couldn't help it.

Desperation for his touch clawed at me. I wanted his hand wrapped around my length jacking me off. I wanted to feel him play me like a fiddle and see how my body responded in kind. And for a moment, I wanted him to want me too. I didn't want him pretending I was a girl. I wanted him to whisper my name against his lips. But I had to shove the thought down. I had to bury that dream.

There was no way we could ever be together.

Sam bypassed my dick, walking his fingers down the outside of my jeans near my hip while I squeezed his arse, kneading the globes and internally cheering when he rocked his hips into my grasp, straddling my leg and riding it. I sucked in a breath through my nose and thrust my tongue into his mouth. When he slipped his hand between my legs, rubbing higher up my leg and getting closer to my nuts, my mind spun. Like that coil being compressed again, my body ratcheted up, energy whizzing through me.

I edged closer as he ran the back of his thumb over my inseam. Tingles exploded in his wake, coiling me tighter. Sam pressed his thumb down a little harder, shifting a little further back to the sensitive spot behind my nuts. He kissed me, all hot and hard as he rocked his hips, and I hit the point of no return.

One. More. Touch and I'd be gone.

He did it then. Cupped me. Rocking his hips forward, he pressed the heel of his hand behind my balls and I grunted, a shudder passing through me as I lost my load in my underwear. The first time it'd happened with another person. My cock flexed, endlessly shooting stripes of cum without ever having been touched. My nerve endings buzzed, the high overtaking me as I sucked on his tongue and shook through my orgasm.

When Sam groaned, I froze, barely able to heave in the breath I needed. Shame washed over me, tinged with fear. What had I done? I couldn't go there with him. I couldn't do it. I couldn't want this. It was... wrong.

I never thought for a second that the insults that were casually thrown around by virtually all of us would apply to me. When the drunks in town fought, or the boys at school taunted the geeky kid, the first go-to insult was that they were a limp-wristed poofter. And I was one of them. My sticky jocks were proof. The wet patch no doubt forming on the front of my jeans, the smoking gun. My heart hammered and my vision swam. I blinked back tears because that's apparently what little faggot girly-boys did.

They cried.

Lightheaded and disgusted with myself, I pulled back and dropped my hands. I shifted away from Sam. I fought my instinct to stay close to him, but I needed distance.

"So, yeah," I squeaked, clearing my throat before I continued. "We're all right at this. Good idea practicing. I think... I think we're good to go. We're good, aren't we? I've gotta—" I hooked a thumb over my shoulder. "Tea'll be soon. I've gotta go and wash my hands. Ma'll have a shit fit if I sit down this dirty. So, yeah. Um. I'll see you later, yeah? We can, um... Yeah? Good." I stumbled out of our hiding spot, nearly landing on my arse as I tripped over my own feet, before sprinting to my house.

CHAPTER 2

Sam – Six months later

We'd arrived home from boarding school at the end of term. Dad had picked us up and listened most of the way home while Craig and I complained about the end of term tests and planned our two weeks of winter holidays.

"Your mum and dad'll be at our house." Dad stepped out of the fourbie, his shoulders hunched and his lips turned down. He looked to be carrying the weight of the world. I hadn't noticed until that moment, but there was an impossible weariness hanging off him. My dad was larger than life, but with the dullness in his eyes, it was as if all the fire and vitality had been sucked out of him. Why? What had happened? Was someone sick? Was it him? Ma?

Craig furrowed his brows and followed silently. As I trailed behind, every step I took was like walking to the executioner. I stepped over the threshold, waiting with bated breath for the news. What greeted us was completely different to my fears, but just as dire.

Our parents were gathered around the table drinking a cuppa. A Christmas-themed biscuit tin lay open, the empty white patty pan papers off to the side. Weary gazes met our own, and sadness radiated from everyone. Then I looked around the room, expecting to find the comfort of home. But my world came crashing down around me.

Instantly, I knew that the news we were getting was something that would irreversibly change our lives. Boxes were stacked neatly along the back wall, taped closed with ugly brown packing tape. Pictures had been taken down and the floral antique china dinner set that Ma proudly displayed in the glass-fronted cabinet was missing, its shelves stripped bare. She loved that ugly dinner set. I swallowed the lump in my throat and prayed I was wrong. That I was misreading the situation.

But I hadn't.

I reached for the chair, eased myself onto it when my legs wobbled underneath me, threatening to give way. I met Craig's startled gaze from across the table. Fear had stolen away my teen bravado, and he was pale and wide-eyed, his hands shaking as he balled them into fists. I was sure the look on his face mirrored my own.

The letter had been delivered a week earlier, Dad said. The bank gave us three more weeks to clear out our personal belongings. Dad thumbed through the paperwork and explained it, painstakingly going through every option the bank had given them and why it wouldn't work. Why it couldn't. The bank's refusal to extend the line of credit meant that we needed to come up with some cash and fast.

"What about the horses? We can do it. Sell them all off except one or two of the mares and stallions. That'll reduce down the debt. There are other things we could sell too. What about logging the trees closer to the river? Couldn't we get some money from them?" The panic bubbled through my veins and bled into my words.

Ma's smile was impossibly sad, but patient. "No, son. We're out of options. I'm sorry, but this is our only way forward. We've kept the farm running as long as we possibly could. But all of us need to eat, and if we stay here any longer, that won't even be possible."

"But they can't just kick us out like this," Craig interjected.

Craig's dad reached out and grasped his shoulder sympathetically. "The bank offered to keep us on. I'd continue as lead horseman, but our new bosses would be the bank's agri-managers. But would you want that, Craig? Sam and his parents wouldn't be here."

"What? No!" Craig's panic made his voice ratchet up to a squeak, his eyes darting around the room. "No, they have to be able to stay."

Craig's ma sat on the other side of him and she reached for his hand, squeezing it tight. "We haven't advised the bank yet, but we've made our decision. We wanted to run it by you and you agree. None of us are staying."

"Who's going to look after the animals? You can't just leave them here without anyone to feed them. We need to be able to stay." I balled my fists and slammed my hand on the table. Injustice and impotence stole over me. This wasn't fair. It wasn't the way things were supposed to go. They should be staying. All of us should be.

This was our land. What right did the bank have? They were some dickheads sitting in suits in the city signing off on things they didn't understand. No one understood what it was like to be out here. They wouldn't survive a day, and we'd been here for generations. This was my home.

"Why don't any of you care?" I yelled. "Why can't you all just stay until we can come back? Surely we can go talk to someone higher up. Surely this is just a mistake. They don't get how hard it is here. If we talk to them, we could make them understand. I could get a job. I could help pay it off. Quit school and work full-time. We could save up enough if they'd give us time."

Dad's chair scraped on the scuffed timber floors as he shifted and came to crouch next to me. His knees popped and ankle cracked as he moved, but he was still fit as ever. "Son, we've tried. The one thing we no longer have is time." He covered my still-clenched fist with his own much bigger hand. Callouses decorated his palms, his hands veined and weather worn. "I'm sorry I failed you. This place was supposed to be your future, and I know how much you wanted it to be. I'm sorry I can't give it to you anymore."

I opened my mouth to interrupt him, but the words were stolen from my mouth when I saw the tears tracking down his face. He was blaming himself?

No, this was the bank's fault. Not his.

Over the next fortnight, we watched the winter mists roll over the plains and be burned off once the sun began to rise in the sky. And just like those mists, my carefully constructed plan of eventually taking over and running our farm as my own, with my best friend beside me, dissipated into thin air. My whole future—every dream I'd ever had—evaporated into a great void of nothingness right before my eyes. Three generations of my family before me had called Hayes Horse Farm home. I was supposed to be the fourth. But it was all over.

We'd lost everything.

Our home. Our legacy. Our livelihood.

My hands were freezing as I helped haul the last of our furniture into the rented truck. I hated every minute of it. We should have been caring for the horses in the stables, riding our own along the dusty paddocks and slowly starting to train the foals. We usually camped out too, coming back a couple of days before we returned to school. It was my favourite time of year. Sore after days on the saddle riding upriver, we'd bundle ourselves up in heavy jackets and sit around the campfire toasting marshmallows and listening to stories of adventures and tall tales so exaggerated they were impossibilities. Instead, I stood outside and watched as Dad hitched up the horse float, my new reality crashing over me.

I hadn't had time to think about what it would be like to leave the farm for the last time. Until I suddenly had to.

Dad moved his fourbie slowly, driving in a Y-shape to back the float into the big shed. That moment was one I'd never forget. It dawned on me then—or maybe I'd known and had refused to acknowledge it. But with the clanging shut of the sliding door to the shed, it was as if the death knell sounded. I couldn't deny it any longer. Our horses weren't coming with us. We were leaving them. My girl, Eadie, was staying behind. Same with Craig's horse, Delilah.

My heart beat faster, and my breaths became short and sharp. Dizziness washed over me. Panic surged like a violent tide. My heart broke. No. I couldn't leave them. I wouldn't. Our horses were family. They weren't the bank's. They were more than dollar signs. More than numbers on a page.

My legs were carrying me to the stable before I even realized I was running. Heavy footfalls behind me spurred me on. The door to the stable stood closed, protecting the horses from the cold air outside. I skidded to a halt, wrenching the door open on its slider. The familiar smells hit me, and a surge of melancholy threatened to drown me. Hay, leather, fresh manure, and the horses were as familiar a scent as Ma's fresh-baked bread.

The last few steps to her stall felt like a lifetime. It was as if I was sinking in quicksand, each movement becoming increasingly difficult. When I finally reached her stall, Eadie stamped her foot and huffed, shaking her head. Her dark mane flitted over her snow-white back as she moved. Her whinny made my already broken heart crack like the spidering across a windscreen. She knew something was up.

Agitated and confused, she could sense the tension and disappointment in the air, the powerlessness making us move like automatons. I hadn't cried up to that point, but I had no hope of stopping the tears now. A choked sob tore from my throat, and I scaled the timber slat fence in two moves, needing to comfort my girl. Her head next to mine, I soothed my hands down her long neck and cried. Damn near shattered into a million pieces. Wishful plans formed in my head—smuggling her out, keeping her at the new house, running away to keep her safe—all of them more ridiculous than the one before.

It was hopeless. Impossible. This was goodbye.

I heard the rattle of the gate as someone climbed it behind me. I refused to look. Anger, sharp and fierce spiked, making me want to tear the world to shreds. I wanted to rail against the unfairness of it all. Why us? Why this farm? Why not the one next door? Why not the ones who had no hope? I shook off the hand on my shoulder, pushing away from the gentle touch. I didn't want anyone's sympathy. I wanted my dad to fight like he used to. I wanted him to tell me that we weren't giving up, that we didn't have to leave. But it was too late. The world had moved on and I was left grieving something that had already slipped out of my grasp.

I wasn't expecting Craig to slip his arm around my shoulders and take my hand in his, squeezing it as he pulled me into his arms. "It's so unfair," he whispered. "So fuckin' unfair that we have to say goodbye to them."

His hand on my nape did me in. It was the first time he'd touched me since we'd pashed. It had been awkward between us those first few days, but as time went on and neither of us brought it up, I'd resigned myself to acting as if it'd never happened. I never wanted to forget, but he seemed determined to ignore what went down between us.

So that's what we did—we turned a blind eye to the elephant in the room.

But I would forget about the kiss if it meant that he would keep offering that solid strength, his comfort and friendship without hesitation. I turned into him and buried my head against his shoulder. Fisting his shirt, I sobbed, pouring out all of my heartache and frustration. I clung to him as he held me tight, never letting go.

I didn't know how long we stood there, but when my tears finally dried and I was left a hiccupping, snotty mess, he pulled back and gazed at me with such sadness in his eyes that the waterworks nearly started again. I wiped my nose on my sleeve and rested my head on his shoulder again.

He kissed my forehead and wiped my cheek with infinite gentleness. "We'll be okay. We may not have Delilah and Eadie anymore, but we have each other. We make a pact, here and now, that we'll stick together no matter what."

I nodded, not letting him go. "Deal," I breathed, as it finally sunk in that I'd never see this place again.

That it was no longer our home.

✲✲✲✲✲

Sam – Aged 25

We crossed the border into Queensland, and I sighed in relief. We were home. Well, not quite home. But near enough. My heart still ached with the memory of that night we'd found out about losing the farm. Now, with the benefit of another decade under my belt, I knew Dad was right. It never would have been possible. You couldn't get finance to buy back a farm that you'd already lost. The debts we'd accrued from the force of Mother Nature in all her violent glory had made Hayes Horse Farm our unicorn.

But even knowing that a new manager had moved into the homestead the very next day and the place was sold to a foreign conglomerate a week later, it was still a bitter pill to swallow. Our parents had moved on, but the grief in their eyes remained. Craig and I had stopped by to see them as we'd travelled north through central New South Wales to the Queensland border. We'd been on the road since the end of our final year in high school, travelling in a beat-up ute, camping under the stars and doing odd jobs to buy fuel and keep food in our bellies.

We didn't want for anything, but both of us were sick and tired of living like nomads. When we'd decided to settle back down, we didn't even discuss where it'd be. We both just motioned north and nodded, feeling the call of Queensland.

Now, as Craig drove through Goondiwindi, I wondered whether he'd stop, or keep going. We didn't have any plans, or even anywhere to go, but people around these parts remembered us, so we knew we'd get work somewhere.

When Craig pulled into a car park in front of the old pub, I raised an eyebrow at him. One side of his mouth tilted up, and he shrugged. "Figured we'd put the word out with the locals. It's Saturday arvo. Where else are they gonna be?"

"Good thinkin'." I yawned, exhaustion washing over me. "Be nice if they had a room we could get for a few nights too. I'd kill to sleep in a real bed. Everything hurts."

"Yeah, I'm aching everywhere too." He stretched and twisted his back, his vertebrae cracking like it always did when he'd been sitting for too long. He was so familiar. We'd spent every day together for years. The only times we were apart was during hook-ups, but most were nothing more than a quick roll around in the back of the truck. Anything longer came few and far between.

I stepped out of the ute and leaned up against the tray, closing my eyes and tilting my head back as a four-by-four rumbled past along the wide street. The winter sun washed over me, its rays warm this far north. The weight that'd been on my shoulders for the better part of a decade lifted.

I sensed his presence next to me before he'd said a word. It was like that with us though. We could read each other, often communicating without having to say a word.

He was smart, shy sometimes too, and more stubborn than anyone I'd ever met. Above all else, he was loyal. The best friend I'd ever had or would have, and I respected the hell out of him. He cared about his work. He cared about his family, and he'd do anything for someone he loved. I was lucky enough to be counted in that small group of people.

Craig ruffled my hair, then gripped the back of my neck, his big calloused hand squeezing gently. "You okay?" he asked, his voice as soft as his touch. He was an enigma. A rough and tumble type with everyone but me. Most people thought he was a bit of a smartarse and an even bigger arsehole. But it was a front. He showed me his more sensitive side. Like now. Instead of charging in and downing a coldie, he'd stand outside with me for as long as I needed.

He knew it was hard for me to come back to the town where we'd all come to stay after Mum and Dad had lost the farm. We'd driven in with the trucks piled high. Word quickly spread that we were homeless and jobless. We soon realized we weren't the only ones. Two days after we'd arrived, our neighbours had also pulled into town, the same conglomerate who'd bought our property snapping up theirs too.

I knew it was difficult for Craig to come back too—he was just as conflicted about it as I was. We'd roasted marshmallows over our campfire the night before and confessed how nervous we were to be crossing that invisible line from New South Wales into Queensland. So we'd nutted out a plan to stay in town for a week and make ourselves known. Until something more permanent for the both of us came along, we'd take a breather, sleep indoors and enjoy food that didn't come from a can.

Neither of us wanted to stay in Goondiwindi for good, but if we found work that lasted for more than a few weeks, we'd take it. We'd helped with the winter muster at the last station we'd worked at. We could find temporary work—that was never an issue—but something which gave us more than a week or two in each place was harder to come by. I had faith that eventually we'd come across the right job though.

I nodded and opened my eyes again, surveying the street that hadn't changed a bit in the ten years we'd been gone, and yet was somehow completely different. "It's good to be home. I've missed it here."

He hummed quietly, his hand shifting to my shoulder. "It was time to come back." He kicked at a lone piece of gravel on the bitumen road, sending it skittering towards the centre median strip. Goondiwindi was a border town. The intersection of a few major highways dissecting the country. Trucks and cars of every description passed through, and peak hour was often represented by kilometres' long convoys of semi-trailers and the odd tourist with their caravan or camper trailer.

"Let's get maggoted," I mumbled, as memories of this place and a past I'd rather not relive continued to slam into me.

CHAPTER 3

Craig

Pearce Station was nothing like I'd imagined when we'd taken the jobs. We knew where it was, of course. We'd had the map open in front of us when Scottie, the manager, had given us the address. He'd warned us that it wasn't like anywhere we'd been before. Remote, harsh, and unforgiving. But I hadn't truly absorbed his words until about the three-quarter mark of our trip. We'd driven the twelve hours north-west of Goondiwindi. I'd mistakenly thought Goondiwindi was an outback town. I was so wrong. It was country, sure, but it was easily accessible via paved roads. It was absolutely bustling compared to so many of the progressively smaller townships we'd travelled through on the way to the property.

By the time we'd reached the road bordering Pearce Station, we hadn't seen another car or truck in hours. It was like a ghost town compared to the main drag in Goondiwindi, and yet everywhere we looked, life was flourishing. I was captivated by the scenery—the colours, the big skies, and vivaciousness of the red. It changed by the hour, despite the endlessly flat plains.

The kilometres had bled into each other, time seemingly interminable as our tyres ate up the road. He was right—it was nothing like I'd ever experienced before. Dirt roads passed for highways and the wire fences strung between sturdy timber posts were the only other signs of occupation.

Of everything though, it was the sky that had captured my attention so completely. We'd set out before dawn, getting a jump start on the day. We wanted to do the trip in one hit and with both of us driving, it wouldn't be impossible, just exhausting. As the sun crested the horizon for the first time that morning, we'd watched the glowing fiery ball grow and fill the sky with a gentle warmth. It wasn't hot, but it was bright, as if we'd been in a darkened room and suddenly stepped outside to brilliant sunshine. As the morning progressed, the sky had steadily grown from the blackest of night just before the dawn to greys, pinks, mauve, and finally the most pristine royal blue that I'd ever laid eyes on.

It was a wonderland for the senses.

The red of the dirt was so deep, so intense. Combined with the equally brilliant blue, it created the richest of contrasts. There was green everywhere too, a sprinkling of lush new vegetation in the form of soft grasses that rippled in the light breezes flowing over the plains. Resplendent in its sheer scale and magnificence.

"It's beautiful after the rains, isn't it?" Sam spoke reverently, wanderlust in his eyes. "Think you can handle living out here?"

"Do you?" I side-eyed him as I concentrated on navigating down the corrugated dirt road wishing I could keep looking at him. His smile set something alight in me, and I loved watching it break across his face. The bumps had everything vibrating and the old ute pulled to the side wanting to slide right off the road.

"I dunno." He was quiet, his nerves on full display. I reached out, needing to touch him and gripped the back of his neck gently, the skin at his nape soft under my callous-roughened hands. His short hair tickled my fingers and I shot him a small smile when he responded. "But I'd like to try. The bloke we spoke to seemed like a decent fella and I liked that he's near our age."

"He did seem like a good bloke, and from what that old codger in the pub said, their family knows what they're doing. I'm looking forward to meeting his ma." The bloke from the pub wasn't overly complimentary of the station's former manager but went on and on about how Scottie had the goods that were needed. I'd rolled my eyes and let him rant about how women shouldn't be running stations; he was a lost cause. As far as I was concerned, anyone who could keep a station afloat, man or woman, had my respect. It wasn't an easy life.

And that was before I'd seen how remote Pearce Station was.

"That's it." Sam pointed up at the timber sign swinging from an L-shaped post in the distance. As we got closer, I saw the rusted drum sitting sideways on the fence post just off the road, noticing the slit cut in it as I turned the corner. The makeshift letterbox, the greyed timber of the weathered sign, and the long tufts of yellowed grass growing around its base, against the rich red dirt carpeting the ground created the most Aussie of pictures around. The bright green shoots of new growth grass seemed almost out of place there.

I sucked in a breath and eased the battered ute over the cattle grate so I didn't fishtail the car. Anticipation bubbled in my veins, excitement warring with nerves. I'd never experienced it before. This felt big. Momentous somehow. It was so much more than just arriving after a long journey.

I looked across at Sam and the wonder in his eyes as he ducked to look through the windscreen had me smiling at him. "There's an eagle up there that's gotta be the size of the ute. It's huge." He looked out, wide-eyed before dragging his gaze away and smiling so genuinely that his whole face lit up.

Moving onto new stations was something that we'd done a hundred times before, but I really wanted to get this right. To fit in and find our place in the universe. The desire to stay at Pearce Station seized control and I hadn't even seen the place. I was tired of moving, but it was more than that too. Part of it was desperation—to help my best mate find his home again—and part of it was the yearning to make something for myself too.

Sam had been rudderless for years. Truth be told, I had too. We'd struck out, travelling from place to place as we were needed. I'd kept a promise I'd made as a teenager, and now I hoped to be able to fulfill it here. Had we found our safe harbour? Our deep water port? Ironic that we might have discovered our haven in one of the driest parts of Australia.

I pulled the ute up to the homestead and stepped out to stretch my legs in the cooling late-afternoon sunshine. The air was fresh and crisp, a cool breeze floating around me. With one foot still in the ute, a sense of calm washed over me and settled in my gut, as if the very land itself was welcoming me, wrapping me in its arms. A holler sounded and I looked around to see who it was, but all I saw around me was history and family.

A legacy.

A few of the buildings looked to be at least a hundred years old. The most recent addition was obviously the house itself. Painted white with a corrugated iron roof and set apart from the other buildings, it was big but understated. No frills. There were no finials or timber fretwork decorating the gables or the underside of the awning. There was no fancy balustrade encircling the veranda either. But it was beautiful. Raised off the ground on stilts, the wide veranda wrapped around at least two sides of the two-storey house. Instead of its height being imposing in the wide flat landscape, it was inviting. Homely. Rocking chairs and hollow bamboo wind chimes decorated the space, and the smells of fresh baked goods permeated the air.

There was a much smaller home off to the side that needed some TLC. It was getting it though; I could see the renovations in process. Building materials were stacked up alongside it, parts of the classic post and rail balustrade along the veranda unpainted. Across the other side of the driveway, the veggie patch dwarfed both the houses combined. Fruit trees and vines grew along trellises and one raised garden bed after another were all full of growth. Black piping ran like a snake above the beds, suspended from timber posts. It was a watering system fed by the water tank that stood as tall as a building next to it. Two sheds, one probably used as storage and the other a barn for the horses that were grazing in the paddock next to it, were built next to a series of smaller buildings. Each was the size of a large shipping container with a lean-to roof and brightly painted doors in cheerful colours. They were likely the workers cottages, one of which Sam and I would be calling home if things worked out here. Beyond the buildings, the fences converged. Loading yards and paddocks filled with red dirt had me itching to explore. To get on a horse again and ride off into the sunset to experience everything that this fascinating land had to offer.

There was definitely something magical about Pearce Station, and I'd already fallen for its charm.

"G'day, fellas," a friendly voice called as they sauntered over to us with a natural swagger that came from years of experience. He was older than us, probably our parents' age. "The name's Jono. I'm the lead stockman here."

I shook his hand. "Craig Williams, and this"—I motioned to Sam— "is Sam Hayes. Good to be here."

Sam walked around the ute and shook Jono's hand as well, the two of them trading pleasantries as Jono motioned to the house. "Scottie or I will take you on a tour and introduce you to the others after you've had a cuppa. Ma's got some scones fresh out of the oven. Come on inside."

A woman, who had to have been in her sixties but acted like she was half that age, met us halfway, shaking our hands with a firm grip and insisted we call her Nan. She was the oldest generation of Pearce ladies living out here, long retired. I desperately wanted to meet her daughter—apparently, she was known as Ma around the place—but I knew within a moment of meeting Nan that she was the cool grandparent I wished I had around growing up.

Another lady, this one carrying a tray loaded with afternoon tea, managed to slip out the screen door without it slamming behind her. "Welcome to Pearce Station, boys," she called as she set down her load on the coffee table under the veranda. She made her way over to us and I knew she was Ma. I was a little star-struck and it showed. I stuttered my introduction and my face was aflame when Sam chuckled and slapped me on the back.

"Thanks for the opportunity to be here, Mrs Pearce," Sam added after we'd introduced ourselves and ascended the steps to the veranda.

"It's our pleasure, but none of this missus or mister here. Scottie'll get a big head if you call him Mr Pearce and God knows what Ally will do if you try to use "miss" on her.

I'm either Ma or Lynn. You've met Nan, or if you'd prefer, Karen." Lynn fussed with the cups and saucers, setting them out. "Tea, or would you like a cold drink?"

"Tea would be great, thank you."

I shook my head when Karen motioned to the rocking chairs. "We've been sitting all day. You sit, please." Sam leaned against the post, and I reached for the cup and saucer Lynn handed me. It was all incredibly polite and straight out of the 1950s in a weird way, but they were warm and welcoming, brushing off my awkwardness with a smirk or two.

"So where are you boys originally from?" Jono asked.

I hated that question because I knew it always brought up mixed feelings for Sam, but we needed to get it out of the way. At least people who'd experienced station living usually stopped asking about it once Sam told them the basics. "My parents owned a horse breeding operation just outside of Goondiwindi when we were teenagers. We lost it after the drought. Spent a few years in town after that. Then, when we finished school, we travelled to wherever we could get work."

"Sorry to hear that, Sam," Jono replied. "I respect anyone who's made a go of it like you boys. When Scottie showed me your work history that you'd emailed through, I was impressed. You'll fit right in here with your experience."

"We're looking forward to getting started." If I could get out there that second, I would. It'd only been a couple of weeks since I'd been on a bike, but I'd been shooting the

shit with people far more than I was used to, and I was peo-
pled out. I turned my attention to the paddock where the
horses were grazing and sighed wistfully. It'd been years
since I'd been on a horse. Most stations used bikes nowa-
days and Sam avoided horses whenever he could. It'd torn
him apart to lose Eadie, not that he'd ever admit to that being the reason he didn't ride anymore. I missed Delilah
every day too, but Sam took Eadie's loss the hardest. I suspected that losing the farm would have been bearable if
he'd been able to keep her.

"G'day" came a deep voice from behind us and on cue,
Sam and I turned to see a bloke about our age walking up
with an aboriginal couple. The woman was wiping her
hands with a rag and all three of them were dusty from
head to toe. I recognized his voice, but even if I didn't, I
would have known instantly it was Scottie. He had this presence, a natural leader that left no one in doubt he was in
charge. But it wasn't arrogance that radiated off him. It was
something else. A magnetism that made me want to hang
off his every word. How the hell he did it, I had no idea. He'd
literally said one word and I was in awe of him. It was a great
start, me being star-struck over his ma and going bloody
googly-eyed over the station manager.

I gave myself a mental slap to the head, shaking myself
out of my thoughts, and watched as Sam took the stairs in
a couple of steps to land in front of Scottie with an arm outstretched.

The two of them were cut from the same cloth, and I
smiled at their matching grins as they checked each other's

get up. Both in trackies, old boots and footy jerseys. Sam wore one from the Brisbane Broncos and Scottie wore a Queensland State of Origin one.

They laughed as they shook hands. "Nice to meet you, mate." Sam motioned to me. "This is Craig. I'm Sam."

"Scottie, and this is Yindi, our resident genius with anything mechanical, and Waru, our horse expert." Sam repeated the action with Yindi, the lady, and Waru, the other man. I exchanged hellos with them too and Scottie told us all about the problem that Yindi had managed to fix in the big tractor. Honestly, I was impressed as hell already, with every single person I was introduced to. And it wasn't lost on me just how capable the women on the station were. Remarkable really.

Conversation moved onto a tour of the station and when tea would be served. It'd be a while yet, Lynn and Karen wanting to wait for us to arrive before they put the pies in the oven.

"When you've finished your cuppa, I'll take you round." Scottie motioned to the buildings. "Won't get time this arvo to get on the horses or bikes, but we'll do that tomorrow."

By the time we'd finished the tour of the immediate grounds, I was both in awe and jealous of Scottie. Not so much for me, but for Sam. Owning a station had never been on the cards for me. But the farm had been a possibility for Sam, and Scottie was exactly where Sam should have been at our age. Our parents would be ready to retire, and Sam and I would have been running Hayes Horse Farm. It wasn't until Sam knocked his elbow into me and shot me a look, that I snapped out of it. "What's gotten up your arse?" he hissed, brows furrowed and teeth clenched as Scottie shut the door to the shed that we'd just walked out of.

"Nothing, sorry I'll…." My trail of thoughts disappeared, vanished without a trace when I saw her. Slim with long brown hair, she had a husky laugh that had my dick taking notice. I nearly swallowed my tongue when she raised her hand and waved, rocking gently with the sway of her horse until she lithely slid off the saddle, opened the gate for her mount, and closed it again after the big mare had pushed through.

"What?" Sam followed my line of sight and his eyes widened before he turned to me blinking a few times. "Fuck. She's gorgeous."

"Need a hand?" I offered as she walked her mount towards us.

"No thanks, boys. I've got this." She petted the big mare affectionately. "This here is 'Tella and I'm Ally." We shook hands and I got lost in her eyes—an incredible ice blue with a darker blue ring around the outside, that had me mesmerized. She squeezed my hand and narrowed those beautiful eyes at me when I held onto her a touch too long. Her grip outmatched her brother's, and it was just as calloused. My initial assessment of the women of Pearce Station had been spot on. Except for one thing. I'd forgotten to add breathtaking; she was nothing short of it.

Scottie clearing his throat had me spinning towards him again as I readied myself for an arse whooping. I knew enough men so protective of their sisters that they'd fire a bloke on the spot if he was caught looking, never mind flirting or making out with that sister. "So, ah, yeah…," Sam began.

Scottie laughed and shook his head. "She'll eat you two for breakfast. You fellas are probably exhausted from driving straight through. Ma and Nan will have tea sorted in about half an hour, so you've got time to freshen up if you want." I nodded, still waiting for Scottie to chew me a new one. Sam scratched the five o'clock shadow that was darkening his cheeks and winced, obviously waiting for the same. "Alrighty," he continued. "Let's go get you sorted in your cottage. Head on over to the main house for six-thirty tea."

Our cabin was the one with the bright blue door. Rustic rough-hewn timber planks were laid vertically down the side with the door and window. The lean-to's corrugated iron roof changed angles at the edge of the cabin, and the protrusion provided some shade over the door and double-hung windows. Iron sheets were fixed to the side of the small building that I could see, and I worried about the heat that the boxy little cabin would hold. I needn't have. When Scottie held the door open for us, we entered into a small kitchenette with a two-person table crammed into the corner of the room, a two-seater sofa, which had no leg room and a small TV sitting on the kitchen bench. From there, there was a short hallway, big enough for three doorways. One led to a tiny bathroom with a shower stall, sink, and dunny, and the other two were bedrooms, each with a single bed and a small cupboard in it with a large opening window facing south. Ceiling fans were in every room, and there were wide eaves that ran the length of the front and back of the cabin. Heavy curtains hung in both the bedrooms, and flyscreens covered the windows to keep the bugs out.

"It's not much," Scottie said, "but we have plenty of room in the main house to spread out and watch tele in or relax. You're always welcome in there. You can take the table and chairs outside if you like, and we have a firepit and stools out near the main house that we sometimes sit around in the evenings. Make the place yours, however you like." He paused for a moment, his eyes flitting around the room. "Keep the outside of the building the same though. Nan's pop built these cabins so they're historic."

"No worries, mate. This is great. Heaps bigger than we've had in the past, hey?"

"Yeah." I nodded, excitement making my pulse spike and a smile break out on my face. "This is brilliant." I wasn't even sure whether I meant the cabin, the job, or the sister of the man we were speaking to.

CHAPTER 4

Sam

I snagged the spot next to Ally at the dinner table and sat down before Craig could even think to muscle his way in. Even a blind man could see how besotted he was with her. The thing was, I was too. The moment she'd slid her work-roughened hand into mine to shake it, I'd wanted to pull her close and feel the contrast between her hands and the flawlessly smooth skin on her face and the rest of her body.

Knife and fork in my hands, I breathed in the delicious scent of good tucker. Homemade chunky meat pies with mushy peas and mash potato was one of my favourites, and the flaky pastry on top of the pie had me salivating. "S'good, Ma," Ally spoke, her mouth shielded by her hand as she swallowed down a bite of the pie. I turned to her and nodded my agreement, sucking in a breath as she licked her lip, chasing a drip of tomato sauce. Dear God, she smelled like sensuality personified. Soft and warm with a hint of a citrusy spice too. I wanted to breathe her in and get drunk off the heady scent. I'd smelt those same notes before. No, they were matching, but still slightly different. Not quite identical.

I closed my eyes, concentrating on the smells and trying to follow the scent with my nose. All at once, memories slammed into me and I bit back a groan. Mint and that familiar citrus spice hit me, and I was transported back to the barn with Craig in my arms. My best mate used an aftershave with the same blend of notes that I'd just breathed in like a drug. Which one of them was I smelling? Was it the stronger splash of aftershave, or Ally's gentler fragrance? I couldn't be sure, but there was one thing I knew—I wanted to get intoxicated off it. Breathe it in and immerse myself in it. Rub it all over me until it was part of me. My body knew that scent. I was drawn to it, like a pheromone designed with my DNA in mind. I wanted more of it.

I blinked open my eyes when the nudge to my foot landed, and I realized it was harder than the first I'd been too absorbed to register. Craig. I turned to him and the disquiet in his eyes slayed me. He inclined his head ever so slightly and asked a silent question. I blinked slowly, barely nodding. The crease in his forehead lifted, but his eyes darted to the door asking me an unspoken question. I shook my head, the slightest of moves to reassure him that I didn't want to leave. I knew him. If I gave the word, he'd walk out, no questions asked. No explanation. But there was nowhere else I wanted to be. This right here was everything I'd ever wanted and nothing like we'd managed to experience since we'd lost my family's farm.

My movement was enough for Craig. He smiled tentatively and I grinned back, digging into my dinner. I only noticed everyone was finished when the conversation started back again a moment later and I was still eating my first mouthful of food.

"Is it okay, Sam?" Karen asked me, a little uncertain.

"It's delicious. It feels like an age since I've had home cooking this fantastic. My brain short circuited on how good everything smelt."

The answer obviously pleased her. She smiled and nodded at me, pointing the last piece of pie crust at me. "Good answer. You two can stay." I laughed around my latest mouthful and looked over the table, taking in the new faces that were laughing and talking. The friendly faces that already had us eating at their table like family. The same people who'd waited for us to arrive so we could all eat together and had welcomed us by giving us a place to bunk and telling us to make it our own. The one who'd ridden a horse across a driveway and stolen my breath, shaking my very foundation in the very best of ways. Yeah, staying. That sounded just about perfect. My gaze landed on Craig last of all and I playfully knocked my shoulder into his.

"Hear that? We can stay." When his answering smile lit his entire face, I knew we'd made the right call. I knew dialling the number we'd been given after the most random of conversations we'd had with a bloke, who said he knew a bloke who knew someone else who was looking for permanent stockmen, that we'd made the right decision. The drive out here cemented the feeling of rightness that'd swept over me when, less than twenty-four hours after we'd sent through our work history Scottie had telephoned us back with an offer to do a trial run with him. We still had to prove ourselves, but that was the one thing I knew we wouldn't have a problem with. This property, this place... it was as if we'd worked for so long, sometimes in the shittiest of conditions, just so that when home called us, we'd know.

With dinner done, Karen excused herself to the recliner and Lynn cleared the dishes away. I offered to help, but my gesture was waved away. "No, love. You'll be out there like the rest of them soon enough. The kitchen is our job. We all contribute here."

"But we've just shown up and eaten tea—" Craig chipped in.

"Treat it as the welcome it was." Lynn smiled and patted our shoulders warmly. "Everything here is swings and roundabouts anyway. You'll get your chance to help out. Now, why don't we get you lot sorted with some marshmallows you can roast outside."

"You trying to get rid of us?" I smirked, already incredibly fond of her.

"Too right! You'll just make a mess when I'm trying to clean up."

Scottie walked around the table and kissed his ma on the temple. "Thanks for tea. I'm gonna get the bonfire set up. Let us know if you and Nan want to come out. We'll move the rocking chairs for you."

"No, love. We're watching a new series on the tele. You young ones go and enjoy yourselves."

Scottie went to the pantry and grabbed out a container of marshmallows and a lighter. "Come on, you two, let's go get a fire on." We followed him outside into the darkness, only to find Ally already out there, swinging an axe to chop timber by the light of a spotlight on the side of the house. Waru and Yindi were carrying an armful each, with timber of different sizes ready to be tossed onto the fire pit. Jono was breaking up small sticks and twigs and scrunching a couple of pieces of paper, ready for Scottie with the lighter.

"You do this often?" I asked.

"As often as we can, but we don't have enough trees out here to chop down, so we buy firewood. We've pulled a lot of rotted-out timber off the old homestead though, so anything that's not painted and can't be reused is being used for fuel."

The crackle of the fire started, and I watched as the flames curled and danced, licking over the timber and setting it alight. "All right, boys, pull up a seat and get comfortable." The seats he was talking about were cut logs about a foot and a half high. They'd be uncomfortable as fuck to sit on for any length of time, but it didn't matter right then. They'd done this for Craig and me, and I was more than appreciative of the welcome party they'd given us.

"So what's your first impression?" Ally took a swig of water from a bottle she was carrying with her.

"Pretty bloody amazing." I thoroughly agreed with Craig's answer. "It's picture perfect. The colours are so intense. I kept thinking that someone had dialled up the saturation on the filters, but I was seeing it through my own eyes."

"I've never seen anything like it. In all the places we've been in Queensland and New South, there's none that compare," I added.

Scottie smiled and looked around, seemingly seeing the land even under the guise of darkness. "I can't imagine wanting to be anywhere else. It's a pretty special place to call home."

I saw Ally flinch from the corner of my eye, and her reaction drew my attention. Lips pursed, she shook her head and huffed out a breath, before snapping the twig she held in her hand and tossing it into the fire. "On second thoughts everyone, I'm out. Night." Ally stood and stalked away without a backward glance. The abrupt change in her sent me reeling. What had prompted it? I thought back, trying to figure out what could have upset her enough to make her leave, but without really knowing anything about her, I was grasping at straws.

"Scottie," Jono chided gently.

"Yeah, I know," he muttered, rubbing his forehead wearily. "Sorry, boys, I'll be back."

Jono smiled at us, silently apologizing for the hosts walking away from our gathering. "He'll be back in a minute." Jono opened the marshmallows and added three to the end of the stick he was holding before passing the container to Craig. "Help yourself." Craig did, swapping my empty stick for a loaded one. After we were done, we passed them onto Waru, sitting next to Ally's empty spot.

I roasted my marshmallows on the fire until the outsides were blackened and picked up on the earlier conversation to stem the awkward silence hovering over the group. "It's hard to believe the colour of the dirt is for real."

"The dirt wasn't always red," Yindi responded. "Us black fellas tell the story of Wyju the Traveller. It's how the ochre came to be."

Jono tilted his head, as if thinking about a long-lost memory. "I haven't heard that story, Yindi. What's it about?"

She looked to Craig and me. "These boys probably don't want to hear our stories."

"I'd love to," I answered quickly. "I don't know much about Aboriginal history, but I'd like to find out."

Yindi smiled and Waru nodded at me. Whatever I'd said, it'd made them happy. I just wanted to know the story of how the land came to have such a spectacular colour. No, it was more than want. It was as if I needed to know. I couldn't explain why but I needed to learn about this place. To know everything I could.

Yindi started speaking, her voice scratchy and melodic at the same time. The light from the flames danced on her dark skin and I watched, hypnotized as she passed her marshmallow stick to Waru and began speaking. "Wyju was a lone traveller. He moved from camp to camp, never staying in one place very long. On his travels, he came across a group who was in mourning. When he questioned them, asking if he could help in some way, they explained, 'The Great Snake came into our camp and swallowed our child.'

Wyju asked, 'Why don't you hunt the serpent down and kill it?' and the man responded, 'Because this serpent is magical. It controls the water. If we kill it, we will all die of thirst.'" Yindi stretched out her arms wide, and I imagined the lands running dry. Parched from drought. The animals dying one by one. The grasses tinder dry. Lightning and fire ravaging the bush. "Wyju knew of this being and others like it. He said, 'But even magical snakes may be killed. Do you know how to kill it without invoking the serpent's magic?' This time the child's mother responded, 'Yes. If the snake is stretched out in a straight line, it may be killed. But if it is coiled up, the rivers will stop flowing and the land will dry.'"

Yindi paused, looking around the campfire, building suspense as she let the meaning of her words sink in. A drought had taken my parents' land. We'd respected it, but maybe not enough. We'd taken from the land, not always sustainably. Was the drought nature's way of resetting the balance? Of weeding out those of us who didn't adapt? Had we taken too much, leaving none for the future? I'd one day hoped to be able to work at a station that held sustainability as a core value, but given that survival was sometimes the only goal, I'd seen first-hand how sustainability could become a pie in the sky ideal. An impossible dream.

"Wyju promised that he would help and that the child would be returned," she explained, her voice taking on a reverence for the traveller. "He set out, tracking the snake until he found it coiled up, sleeping under a tree. He was not a devious man, but a plan formed in his mind. He plucked the roots of a mallee shrub. Carefully, he climbed, making sure his movements were light and silent. Slowly he went higher and higher, until he found a sturdy branch above the Great Snake that he could perch on. He tipped the root, letting the water drip from it—"

"Dripping water from the root? Is it different to a normal root?" I asked, wondering why I'd asked a question of the root and not the existence of a magical serpent. Then again, it wasn't the first magical serpent I'd heard of. The brothers in the private school we'd attended as kids had harped on and on about the original sin and how we must atone for ours.

"The mallee root is like a straw; they hold water. If you cut the root, you can drink from it," Waru explained, toasting another marshmallow on the fire.

Yindi continued, satisfied I wouldn't interrupt again. "Wyju let the water drip from the root. Drip. Drip. Drip. Onto the serpent's head. Woken, the snake reached upward, seeking out the water to quench its thirst after feeding. Up, up, up it stretched, uncoiling itself as it balanced on the tip of its tail, its tongue flicking in and out to taste the water. Wyju reached out, gripping the snake below its head and slashing its throat with the knife he carried. He jumped from the high branch, running it down the length of the serpent's outstretched body. The child tumbled out, dazed but well, and Wyju helped the child, dodging the snake's falling body. They returned to the camp. The child's parents were overjoyed."

"It's a Red Riding Hood story." The amazement in Craig's voice was clear. "Imagine that. Cultures from opposite ends of the world tell the same story. Different animals, different interpretations, different centuries, but at its heart, it's a tale of caution. Be careful of the malevolent spirit—you don't know who is good or evil by looking at them. The snake is magical, it's a provider, but it's evil too."

"Yes, but that's not the end of the story." Yindi smiled patiently. "Wyju returned a hero. Men came from far and wide offering their thanks and asking if he would consent to becoming the husband of their nieces. Each time he turned them down. He was a wanderer, and it wouldn't be fair to a good woman for her husband to always be gone. Each time they responded with 'We will speak with Kirkin then.' Wyju wondered who this Kirkin was and he asked one of the men of the camp. The man explained that Kirkin was the handsomest of men with long golden hair that would glint like a halo in the morning sunshine when he combed it, but he was still unmarried. No woman had accepted their un-cles' suggestions that they marry him. You see, Kirkin knew that he was handsome. He was very vain, always wanting to look his best, and each of the women knew he spoke of nothing but himself." Yindi paused as Waru handed her a stick with freshly roasted marshmallows on it and she bit down, the snowy white of the treat contrasting against its toasted surface.

"Now Kirkin," she continued, "was frustrated. He wanted a wife of his own and yet none were interested in him. Kirkin's friends taunted him saying, 'Too bad no one wants you. They want Wyju.' He wondered who the man was, especially because he'd heard that Wyju had turned down every offer of marriage he'd received. Kirkin grew jealous of the attention that Wyju had been receiving and went to the camp in search of him, demanding to know why Wyju hadn't been to see him. Wyju replied with 'I have heard of your hair, but I didn't think I needed to visit you. The men here have told me so many good things about you.' Kirkin didn't know whether to take Wyju's comment as a compliment, but in his insecurity, he chose to believe he was being insulted. Kirkin was not a good man and he planned revenge against Wyju. He knew that the perfect way to exact that revenge was a hunting trip. So, he invited Wyju to hunt with him the next day, and after the traveller had agreed, Kirkin stole into the bush to dig a trap. He filled the bottom of the deep hole with stakes with their ends whittled into sharp spikes. Then he covered the trap with branches and leaves, hiding the hole."

I closed my eyes and the light of the flames danced behind my closed eyelids, the warmth against my skin warm compared to the cold air at my back. I could imagine the scene unfolding. The heat of the day and the dry air. The blue sky. The sticks, the cover, laying leaves and dirt over the top to hide the hole. But the dirt wasn't red in my imagination. Even in my head, I could see what it was like before the ochre was made.

Yindi continued, her voice hypnotizing, "Wyju met Kirkin the next morning and they went hunting for walliow together. They came to the trap Kirkin had set, and he instructed Wyju on how to hunt for them. It was impossible to catch the large rat with a spear or boomerang. To catch a walliow, the men would pounce on it as it exited its burrow. Kirkin tricked Wyju into believing there was an animal near the trap and encouraged him to lie in wait for it. Movement in the grass had Wyju pouncing. He fell into the hole, the stakes spearing his feet and legs, his blood staining the dirt red. In pain, and bleeding, Wyju begged Kirkin for help, not seeing at first that Kirkin had betrayed his trust. Kirkin laughed and walked away, but not before telling Wyju that he would be crippled from his injuries and no one would want to marry him anymore. That he would die alone.

"When Kirkin left, Wyju began to cry and he begged the great spirit, Baiame, the creator of the world, to help him. He pleaded for aid, like he had given to many whose paths had crossed his. Baiame heard Wyju's pleas and sent the Winjarning Brothers to his rescue. The Brothers lifted Wyju from the trap, but his blood had run deep into the dirt, staining it red, creating the place where we gather ochre."

"Did Wyju die?" Jono asked.

"No, the Brothers had Baiame's healing ability. They sealed his wounds and he lived."

We sat silently for a moment, listening to the crackling of the fire. Scottie had returned sometime during Yindi's story. I hadn't noticed him sit down, too absorbed in her words. Craig's question made me jump. "What happened to Kirkin?"

"After the Winjarning Brothers healed Wyju, he set off to Kirkin's camp, desperate for revenge. At first light, when Kirkin emerged to brush his golden hair in the morning sun, Wyju threw his boomerang, slicing Kirkin's throat. He built a pyre and heaped his body on top, burning it. Soon, all that remained of Kirkin was a small bird that fluttered out of the fire, eating the insects that were attracted to the flames."

"Do you see birds doing that?" My question surprised even me. Yindi's people believed that the dirt was red because of the blood of an innocent man. But in today's terms, he wouldn't be innocent. He'd be just as wrong for exacting revenge as Kirkin was. But that was today's justice. Today's world. Dreamtime stories had been passed down for thousands of years from generation to generation. The systems of justice were suited to the circumstances. Justice was swift and decisive. Commit a wrong against a person and you would face punishment.

"We do, but not always."

"I'd love it if one day you could share the stories of the other colours," Craig asked. "But not tonight. I'm wrecked." He yawned, his jaw cracking as he did and I followed suit, weariness washing over me like the incoming tide.

"Thanks for the welcome, Scottie." Words didn't seem enough. A simple thank you insufficient to communicate just how grateful I was for giving us a chance. For opening up the possibility that Craig and I could one day plant our roots again. "I appreciate everything you've done. And thank you, Yindi, for your story. I could picture everything you were saying. It's as if this place—"

"Is past and present combined," Craig finished my thoughts, putting words to something I couldn't quite express. "I closed my eyes, and I was watching Wyju kill the serpent and then be betrayed by Kirkin."

"Time seemed to disappear," I added. "The stories of the past came to life in front of me. It was uncanny."

Waru and Yindi traded a look. Their silent communication seemed loaded, and I didn't dare ask what it meant. But when they turned to Scottie and Yindi spoke, the weight I'd been carrying on my shoulders—the loss of the place I'd called home for over half my life—lessened. It was as if I could take a breath for the first time in a decade, and I knew my healing could begin.

"They're of this land, Scottie. They understand." Waru stood and held his hand out for Yindi before clapping his boss on the shoulder. Hand in hand, they nodded, bade us goodnight and wandered off in the opposite direction to the cabins.

Conversation petered out then as we watched them. "Aren't they going in the wrong direction?" Craig asked, voicing the question I didn't want to.

"They are, but they've lived on this land all their lives. They know it better than anyone and they'll often camp out, especially on nights like tonight."

"Is Ally okay?" I asked, unsure of whether I was stepping over a line that shouldn't be crossed. "She seemed upset."

Scottie nodded. "Me and my big mouth, s'all. I didn't mean to piss her off, but yeah...." He shrugged, but it was obvious that he was playing down his concern from the tense set in his shoulders, the crease in his forehead, and his lips pressed together. "You blokes right to make your way back to your cabin?"

We were. Even if we weren't, Jono was still with us. As the head stockman, I was pretty sure he wouldn't get us lost in the hundred metres or so to the workers' cabins. We said our goodnights and Jono expertly led us in the darkness to them.

As soon as we got away from the light of the fire, which Scottie was dousing, I looked up at the stars. A blanket of glimmering diamonds in the sky, and like the precious gems, there was an array of hues. Some pink, others red. Some more yellow and a few blue, all against the purest black backdrop. Untouched by city lights or pollution, the depth of night was all the more intense with the lack of a single cloud in the sky. Mother Nature was at her most perfect.

"God, look at that," Craig whispered reverently from next to me.

I turned to him and watched his Adam's apple bob as he swallowed and looked with wonder up at the sky. Warmth spread through my chest and the urge to take his hand into mine swept over me. I shook my head, startled at my thoughts, but the niggle of curiosity lingered. I dismissed it, knowing I was just happy he was having good vibes about this place too, because of every person in the world, he felt like mine. He'd been with me through every important step in my life, unconditionally supporting me. He'd walked away from every long-term job offer we'd had, putting his own life on hold—or at least it felt that way—when I'd turned down offer after offer. None of them had been right. But this land was speaking to me, telling me to stay. I didn't even have to ask Craig what he thought of it. His attention had been captured the moment he'd spotted the sign for Pearce Station hanging off the old timber post. He'd been utterly captivated the moment he'd seen Ally dismounting 'Tella.

We walked inside the tiny two-bedroom cabin, and I hesitated at the door to my bedroom. It was going to be strange to not share a room with him. I could count on one hand the amount of nights we'd slept in separate rooms. Most of the stations we'd worked at had two singles to a room and when we'd camped, we'd always either slept around the campfire or shared a tent. "So, I've been thinking," Craig hedged, hesitating until I'd acknowledged him. "Scottie said we were welcome to watch the telly in the main house if we wanted, but we could rearrange these rooms without too much drama. It'll give us a bit more space to watch TV."

"Whaddya have in mind?" I tried to picture the options but there was only one solution I could think of.

"Bedrooms are a little small, but if we had both beds in one room and the wardrobes in the other, we could use the spare room as a lounge room. Move the couch in there, pop the tele on one of the shelves in the cupboard. Might even be able to open up the room by taking out a wall. Could give us more space in the kitchen area."

"We'd be back to sharing a room."

"Feels kinda weird knowing we won't be in the same room to be honest. We've lived in each other's pockets for the last decade." He chuckled and rubbed the back of his neck. A flush rose, staining his cheeks, and I was charmed by his embarrassment. "And it's not like we're doing anything in there. Just sleepin'."

Those words... they lit a fire inside me, my curiosity igniting and morphing into something stronger. My hands itched to pull him to me, and I licked my lip, chasing the taste from the ghost of his kiss from all those years earlier. It may as well have been a lifetime ago, but the memory tingled through me like a current, electrifying me. I wavered, leaning closer to him without conscious thought and found myself reaching for him. Our eyes locked together and the heat I saw flare in his scorched me.

He blinked and startled, looking away. The spell I was under released its hold, the moment vanishing into the ether. Realizing I was still reaching for him, I dropped my hand, unsure whether I was grateful that I didn't get to touch him or disappointed.

I cleared my throat, shaking out of the pull my body had to him and willed my scrambled brain to come up with something—anything—to break the tension between us. "Yeah, I was kinda thinking it'll be strange not having to listen to you mumble in your sleep and snore from right next to me." I smirked at him, pleased I'd managed a coherent sentence, and he playfully punched my shoulder.

"Shut the fuck up, idiot." He laughed and I eyed the cupboards, motioning to the closest one.

"Think they'll be heavy?"

"Probably, but when has that ever stopped us?" This time Craig grinned at me and I couldn't help but laugh at him. He was absolutely right.

We tried to be quiet, but there was a lot of shuffling, grunting, a few stubbed toes, and a lot of swearing as we shifted the wardrobe into the smaller of the two rooms just off the kitchen, and moved the second bed into the bigger bedroom. By the time we'd finished, I was wrecked. Exhausted from the long drive, the late night around the campfire, then two hours of shuffling around lifting heavy-arsed furniture without punching holes in the walls or making so much noise that Jono would be in here wondering what the hell we were doing.

After we'd each managed a two-minute shower, and I was stripped down to my jocks waiting for Craig to finish brushing his teeth, I was ready to hit the sack. Craig was wavering too, half nodding off as he finished up his night-time routine. It sounded ridiculous, but having him next to me soothed something inside me that wanted to be close to him. Maybe it was borne of a decade travelling together, of always being in each other's pocket. Whatever the reason was, the need to consider it faded when I stretched out on the surprisingly comfortable mattress. Brand new pillows and soft bedding had me sinking into sleep.

I didn't even remember turning out the light.

CHAPTER 5

Ally

The two new blokes had arrived only a week earlier and so far, so good. Scottie had hired them after one phone call, and they hadn't disappointed. Their references were top-notch, and they didn't flinch when taking orders from Ma or me, even though we weren't technically in charge. They didn't even look to Scottie for confirmation either—a nice change after the last lot we hired, who'd lasted a week before we fired their arses. But I could see these two sticking around for longer. They seemed to fit.

Sam and Craig were a bit of alright too. Half a head taller than Craig, Sam was the dark-haired, dark-eyed quiet-type. He was wiry and seemed shy. He was a cool drink of water— beautiful, if you could call a man that. Looks wise, he was about as different to Craig as they came. But while they were opposites in many respects, they were equally as attractive. Craig's sandy blond hair and thick muscles made me want to strip him off and see just what was underneath those dusty clothes he wore. His blunt honesty had me initially sitting on the fence about him, but he'd proven his skill and his loyalty. That loyalty was all directed to Sam so far, but I was glad he had the other man's back. He'd told Ma that provided he and Sam worked side by side, he'd do whatever was needed of him. Sam had agreed, promising to be there for all of us if it meant staying on for the long term. We appreciated that promise. It wasn't exactly an easy life out here, and although I knew they'd both spent all their lives on stations, there weren't many they'd been on that were as remote as ours.

I watched them in the rear-view mirror of the tractor, keeping them in my sights as I turned the vehicle around, ready to pick them up and head back to the homestead. They moved together, completely in sync. They weren't talking, just moving around each other, dodging the too curious cows that were getting right in among them as they kicked at the rounded bale, rolling it along the earth. We were in the springer paddock that morning. Smaller than the others, it kept the cows close together during their gestation and allowed us to closely monitor them, an impossibility in the other larger paddocks. Our station was five thousand square kilometres of desert, unique and wild. Its untamed plains stretched out endlessly until red dirt met blue skies at the horizon. Normally the contrast between the two was stark, but today the earth was dotted with rich greens as new grasses sprouted after the rains earlier in the month. Not much of it remained in the springer paddock. The grazing cows had razed most of the ground bare, but there were still a few lone clumps that were growing. To give the vegetation a fighting chance of survival, we were adding hay.

I gazed out, looking to the west. I could see the ranges in the distance, changing colours with the desert as the day progressed. That afternoon as the winter sun reached its peak, they would look almost purple, but for now they were yellow. The grasses had already grown long enough in places to have begun drying.

It was still cool, even for a winter's day, and I adjusted my beanie before turning my attention back to Craig and Sam. I enjoyed working with them. There was an easiness between them borne of years of friendship. No drama, no conflict. Just the way I liked things.

"C'arn you lot," I yelled from the cab, grinning at them as they flipped out the last part of the bale. Faded-blue jeans hugged Craig's thighs while Sam's stretched across his tight high arse. Their footy jerseys hid whatever fineness was underneath, and I almost felt bad for perving on them both. Almost.

Craig leaped up onto the step of the tractor and grinned. "Couldn't wait to be near me again, huh?"

"Keep dreamin', mate." Sam laughed, chucking me gently in the chin from the opposite step. "She's head over heels for me."

"Oh, boys," I sighed, "If only you knew." Grinning at each of them, I floored the tractor and side-eyed them as they grabbed for the handrails to stop them from falling off.

The ride back to the homestead was bumpy, but the boys hung on tight as I manoeuvred us around the rutted paddocks. My heart lurched as I saw my brother on the roof of the oldest of the buildings—the original homestead—which was being converted into our new guesthouse. He was hammering away, replacing sheets of roofing iron with Yindi's help. Waru and Jono stood below. We were a motley bunch. A cobbled-together family of drifters, Australian Aboriginals, and generations of station owners. But even though we weren't all related by blood, we were all family, and this was our home.

The building they were working on was dilapidated—its roof had sagged and parts of the veranda rotted away. We kept it because of its sentimental value, but the idea to restore it and rent it out had been genius. City folk were looking for farm stays—an escape. We'd started pulling apart the damaged parts of the homestead and realized most of the rot could be fixed with a bit of hard yakka.

Now that we were restoring it, we could celebrate its history too. Pops had grown up in the two-room house, extending it to five when he'd married Nan, and their three girls came along. His parents and their parents before them had lived there, and they raised Ma in that house until she'd married Dad. Scottie and I had spent so much of our childhood sleeping over at Nan and Pops's house, especially when the fighting between Ma and Dad got bad.

When they'd gotten married, Dad had insisted building a new homestead, putting some space between them and Nan and Pops. I wondered sometimes if Ma would have married Dad had she foreseen that he wasn't going to last out here. I couldn't blame him for wanting to leave though.

He'd grown up in the city. Lived there his whole life. I thought I wanted the same thing—to go to Sydney and experience the harbour city and all it had to offer. I'd enrolled in uni, packed my bags and walked away from this place, determined not to look back. I hadn't even made it to the beginning of the semester before I realized that the red dirt and big skies were a part of me that I never wanted to give up.

I'd missed this place down to the very depths of my soul. The quiet, and the sense of belonging. Sydney was amazing. Incredible. The food and the culture and the excitement. But none of it held a candle to dusty plains and trees as old as our country. To blue skies unmarred by smog and planes and helicopters at all times of the day and night. To my family, even though only a few of us were related by blood, and so many species of animals that I couldn't count which survived against all odds.

"Whaddya need us to do now, Ally?" Sam eyed Scottie hauling the final piece of roofing into place. His words broke me out of my reverie.

"Let's go see if Scottie's got everything under control. If he has, I need to help Ma with a couple of the garden beds in the veggie patch. One of the dogs dug under the fence and destroyed a section of it."

"No worries," Craig answered, nodding.

With the tractor and trailer parked in the shed, we walked the short distance to the old homestead. Scottie was just getting down off the ladder and Yindi was already pulling her toolbelt off. She and Waru were only ten years older than me, but their life hadn't been easy. Like many of our Indigenous Australians, they had suffered through generations of systemic racism and class differences that had been etched into the very grain of this land like an ugly jagged scar. Yindi and Waru were mentors to many of the youth around Longreach. They lived on the station with us in the workers' cottages, but they continued their traditional ways too.

Visiting their ancestral lands, teaching their ways to the youth and preserving their culture, Waru and Yindi wanted nothing less than to educate every Aboriginal child in the area. It was a lofty goal and one that we were all in favour of helping with in any way we could. Usually that meant having groups of young people ranging in age from children to teenagers travelling out a couple of times a month to visit the places of cultural significance on the land and stay overnight as they hunted and performed ceremonies together.

"Scottie, you right, mate?" Sam asked. "Need any help?"

"Nah, we're wrapping up here, but Ma was in the veggie garden. If you could help her out, that'd be great."

"That's where we were headed next," I called out, detouring that way.

Ma had only just gotten started and she looked to be struggling already. "You right, Mrs P?" Craig took the shovel from her as she held a hand to her lower back, sweating and obviously in pain.

"I'm hurtin' all over already." She wiped her brow and groaned.

"Let us take over then, Ma," I encouraged. "Tell us what needs to be done and we'll look after it for you."

Sam didn't hesitate, holding his pointer finger up to indicate one minute, and he took off at a sprint to the house. Ma narrowed her eyes at his retreating form and shook her head. I had an inkling what he was doing, but Craig snared my attention when he picked up the crowbar and snapped the partially rotted sleeper away from the support post. "Mrs P, that dog did you a favour. This timber needed replacing anyway. It's full of termites."

"Craig, I'm only going to tell you this one more time. I'm not Mrs P. It's Ma or Lynn. Please." She glared at him waiting for him to react. She wasn't really annoyed with him though—the twitch in her lips as she supressed her smile made it obvious enough.

"Okay, Ma." His lips tilted up in a shy smile, and he nodded once. "Thank you. It means a lot having family again." I knew he'd moved around a lot over the last few years, and he didn't spend all that much time with his own folks. It wasn't as if they were estranged, but Craig's and Sam's parents had travelled where work took them, just like their sons did. I guessed it didn't leave them with much time to keep their relationship intact.

We worked together, breaking down the termite nest and letting the sunlight do its thing and kill off the pests. The dirt was rich and dark here, fertilized with layers of compost and dried cow patties. When Sam came back carrying one of the rocking chairs from the veranda, Ma huffed and tried to bat away his assistance, but even Craig stopped to help ease her into the chair before going back to checking the timber railway sleeper garden beds.

"These ones all look solid. It's just these few here near where the nest was that needs replacing." I knocked my foot into the three affected beds. It would take us a while, but we'd get it done together.

"Ally, where are the replacement sleepers?" Sam asked as I pushed back another shovel full of dirt.

"In the big shed with the other stores." I pointed. "Easiest if we load them onto the ute."

He took the shovel out of my hand and motioned me to sit.

"Take a load off while we get them." Craig reached out, taking my hand and leading me over to Ma so I could ease myself onto one of the solid railway sleepers. Sam ran his hand down my ponytail, smoothing it down, and I smiled to myself. It was nice to be treated like a lady every now and then, even if I hated the idea of being singled out because of it. Ma had put up with sexism all her life. So many people told her she couldn't run the station, because apparently women were meant to be barefoot and pregnant, not working the paddocks. What a load of shit. Ma had grown up out here. She was a fourth-generation station owner and more competent than many of the men around here. But apparently her lack of a dick was a problem for quite a few of the other station owners whose attitudes were better off being left in the 1950s.

"That self-satisfied smile you're wearing suits you. Which one of them are you interested in?"

"Nah, it's not like that, Ma. Although they're both pretty fine." I sighed. "I dunno. It's nice to be treated like a lady every now and then, but still be listened to when we're working."

Ma nodded. "Yeah, you hold onto the ones like that." She had a sad smile on her face, and she shook her head. "You have so much of your dad's personality, you know that? He had an adventurous spirit. Scottie only remembers him when he was staying inside working on his investments. But he wasn't always like that."

"What are you trying to say, Ma?" I was looking up at her, feeling like a little girl while she imparted her wisdom, and I listened with rapt attention.

"Don't make the same mistake that your dad did," she implored. "He stayed here far longer than he should have, trying keep us together. Trying to do the right thing by his family. You're just like him in that way." When I shook my head, she shushed me and continued, "You came back here because of me. You were set to start uni until the doc said it was osteoporosis, then you chucked everything in and came home—"

"Mum—"

"No, Ally." She stared me down. "I can't make the same mistake with you too. I won't. I was selfish with your dad. I tried to keep him here when he was never meant to stay, and we hurt each other more by dragging it out. If you want to leave, if you want to go back to Sydney to start uni, do it. With Craig and Sam here, we have enough bodies on board

to run the station. You'll always be my daughter. You'll always have a home here. But you don't need to live here."

My gut sank as dread washed over me. "Do you want
me to go?" I was unsure now where I stood.

"No, Ally." She reached out for me and I slipped my hand
into hers. She squeezed it tight. "I want you to make sure
you're staying for you. Not for anyone else." She looked
over her shoulder at the boys and I followed her gaze. Craig
was hefting the thick timber onto his shoulder and Sam slid
in behind him, sharing the weight as they placed the heavy
sleeper into the tray of the ute. "They like you. They both
do. You keep the good ones, but not at the expense of your
own happiness."

"I'm glad I came home, Ma. I was homesick." I huffed
out a laugh and toed the red dirt at my feet with my boot.
"Sydney was exactly how I imagined it would be, but instead
of being excited by the people and the chaos, it drained me.
I'd sit on the ferry as it crossed the harbour and just stare
out at the water and finally breathe. It wasn't until my last
trip, when I knew I was coming home, that I realized it was
the only time I felt at peace there. Being home... I fit here.
It's as if everything was telling me to come back. I just
hadn't heard the message until Scottie called me."

"What did he tell you to make you come home? You
never told me."

I shook my head. "He didn't say anything about me coming home. He told me you were in pain again and were weak
on your feet, so he'd taken you to hospital. He said that I

didn't need to worry because everything was under control, but he knew I'd want to know."

"Then what made you come back?"

I huffed out a laugh. "Dad and I had the exact same conversation that we just did." I looked up at her and bit down on my lip with a smile. "I hung up with Scottie and Dad told me that it was okay if I wanted to go home. He'd told me that leaving us was the hardest thing he'd ever done, but he knew if he stayed, he would have destroyed all of us. He couldn't ignore it for his own mental health. He said he saw himself in me when the initial wow of the city had worn off. He'd felt exactly the same being here as I did in Sydney— like a fish outta water." I shrugged, trying to play down the gravity of my homesickness. "By the time Scottie called, I was looking for an excuse to come home."

Ma didn't say anything for a time, and I gave her some privacy as she blinked the tears from her eyes. I watched Craig and Sam hefting the sleepers off the ute and onto their shoulders bringing them over to us. They were so in sync with each other. It was a thing of beauty. I wondered, not for the first time, whether they shared a bond beyond that of friendship. It would make sense—the two of them had been friends for a long time, and from what I could gather, they hadn't been apart since they were teenagers. It was oddly romantic if that were the case—them drifting around the country together, stealing nights in each other's arms as they hid their love from the outside world. It was also depressing as fuck. Hiding couldn't be easy.

"So where do they fit in?" Ma motioned to the men as Craig took the weight of the sleeper in his arms as Sam manoeuvred around and lowered to his knee. Craig inched closer to him and hefted the heavy timber off Sam's shoulder, dropping it on the ground by their feet.

I marvelled at Craig's strength and the way they compensated for the differences in their physical capabilities. I liked them. Probably too much, but I was hardly going to admit that to Ma. "They're eye candy, good workers, and nice blokes." Ma chuckled and my smile turned into a grin. "There've got to be some advantages of living out here. I count them as advantages."

CHAPTER 6

Ally – Four months later

Scottie sighed impatiently. "Ally, it's your birthday. Take the damn day off."

"Nah, I don't need to." I shrugged. "I'll be bored if I do and there's work to do, so I might as well get it done." I didn't want anyone to make a big deal of it; it was just like any other day. Scottie always worked on his birthday. There was no reason why I shouldn't do the same.

"Scottie, me, 'n Sam noticed that there looked to be a few weeds out near the billabong the last time we were there. While we've got time, I thought we could go out there and assess it."

It was news to me. I hadn't seen any. "What weeds?" I asked them both, my gaze swinging between Craig and Sam.

"Oh, yeah." Sam nodded, the look on his face serious. "Lantana weed."

"What the hell?" I asked, shocked to my core. "We don't have lantana out here. It doesn't even grow this far west. And why didn't you say anything when you saw it?"

"You blokes sure?" Scottie asked, his brow furrowed, disbelief in his tone. We'd had minor flooding down near the gully and rockpool a year or so earlier, but we'd never had too much of an issue with anything germinating from the waters. Most of the seeds and uprooted plants were light enough that they flowed with the floodwaters, and last summer had been a hot one. Anything like lantana, which usually grew in coastal areas where the climate was more temperate, didn't survive much past germination.

"Pretty certain that's what it was, but we'd better make sure, ay? I'd hate to not look for it, then find that it's spread." Sam was right. As unlikely as it was that we had lantana on the station, we needed to be sure. It was poisonous to cattle and although we had the gully and billabong fenced off from them, there was no telling where else it could be growing.

"Yeah. Yeah." Concern etched Scottie's brow. He scrubbed his hands over his face and rubbed his eyes. Dark circles under them spoke of just how tired he was. The tense set of his jaw and the edges of his mouth turned down in a frown had misery radiating off him. But whenever I asked him if he was happy, he'd brush me off with a non-answer. His standard reply was "I wouldn't be anywhere else." Whenever I asked if he wanted to join me for a night in Longreach—he needed to find a pretty lady and get laid—he'd always turn me down. I had no idea why he was determined to isolate himself out here. "We'll need to work out how to get rid of it. Ally, do you think you can make sure you know what it looks like and how we can clear it?"

"Yeah, no worries. I'll hop online and grab some pictures, then I'll go with the boys and take a good look around. We'll get a better idea once we've seen what's out there." How could I have missed it? Lantana was pretty easily spotted, especially out here. It would stand out like a sore thumb. But it wasn't impossible.

The trip to the billabong was about ninety minutes in the four by four. We'd be gone half the day. Not a bad way to spend my birthday, I supposed, especially if we could come away with a plan to get rid of a weed that had no business growing out here in the desert.

We tucked into brekkie and before I knew it, Sam and Craig were hustling out after Scottie and I were left to download some photos.

"Leave lunch with us, hon. We'll whip something up for you and the lads and pop it in an esky for you."

"Thanks, Nan." I hesitated, then sighed. "I can't believe I didn't see it."

"I doubt that it'll be lantana," Ma responded, her face serious. "And if it is, don't beat yourself up about it. You can't be expected to spot everything. Both you and your brother are perfectionists, but you can't control everything."

"But it's my responsibility."

Ma placed her hands on my shoulders and squeezed gently. "This is a big station. You can't be expected to know of every plant that's growing on it. Go and enjoy yourself. Think of it as a day with two good-looking blokes, a picnic, and a walk. Enjoy their company and relax." She smiled and added, "They're trying not to show it, but they do like you."

"Yeah, right." I rolled my eyes at her. If those boys were interested in me, they sure as hell didn't show it. A little flirting and playful banter in the early days was as far as it'd gone. Then it was as if a switch had flipped and both backed off. I'd been officially friend-zoned.

At six in the morning, it was already warming up. The day would be stinking hot, and the storms that had been brewing over the last few days made it muggy as hell. I was hanging out for summer's first storm, but we were still a few days away yet. By the time we walked around the billabong, I doubted we'd be wanting anything more than have the wind on our faces as we drove back. The food would probably get eaten in the fourbie rather than in the midday heat.

"We right?" Sam ducked his head into the kitchen.

"No, still got to download a few photos. Give me five. Grab the esky from Nan when she's done with it." I jogged up the stairs.

I worked fast, downloading a few images of lantana leaves, flowers, and the whole of the plant. I had no idea what variety it would be, and there were a few, so I needed to cover my bases. I packed my camera, sunscreen, and another shirt so I didn't end up with a rash from the leaves before I dashed down again and waved bye to Ma and Nan, who were tidying up the kitchen. Sam and Craig were already waiting by the four-wheel drive for me, and I tossed my bag in the boot, and held out my hand for the keys. Craig dropped them onto my palm and slid into the back.

The drive was bumpy and in places, slow-going. Some of the tracks had been damaged by cattle hooves sinking into soft ground when it'd rained and weren't much more than rutted areas of red dirt. As the sun rose in the sky and the heat intensified, I wiped the bead of sweat from my brow and navigated around trees that were older than the station. Some were around well before Captain Cook even sailed into Botany Bay.

I watched as the blue of the sky deepened, the red dirt seeing another summer's day. How many had passed before me? Too many to count. This land was ancient; its history intertwined with its present. The spirits whispered a soft breeze through the rustling leaves and the animals that embodied them. White man had come here and destroyed so much of this precious country. Climate change and natural disasters were changing the environment. Mining and development had obliterated so many sacred sites and cultural history going back sixty thousand years. It was up to us to protect it. We were graziers. Cattle station owners. But we were really caretakers, looking after the land for our lifetime so we could pass it onto our children to do the same for the next generation.

We were all quiet on the way there. My head turned over and over, the guilt of having missed the noxious weed on my visit to the gully only a few weeks earlier never leaving me. It weighed on me that I'd failed in my responsibility to protect the biodiversity of the desert from something as aggressive and invasive as a weed that could not only kill our cattle, but native animals too. I rubbed my forehead and let out a groan of frustration before thumping the heel of my hand against the steering wheel as the gully came up ahead. Only a few hundred metres in front of us lay the off-shoot of an old riverbed. Wide and shallow at its entry, the ravine narrowed and deepened as it neared the billabong, with it ending in a lake surrounded by a rocky ledge on one side and trees overhanging the water with a muddy bank on the other. It was our oasis in the desert. A secret place we'd come to as kids. It was where Dad had taught us to swim and Ma had laughed along with us as he'd tossed us in the air. This place held happy memories for us.

I pulled up the Landcruiser and swung open the door, but before I could get out, Sam grasped my hand and Craig rested his hand on my shoulder. "Ally," Sam started.

"There's no weed." Craig's voice from behind gave me pause. I was unsure whether to knock them for six or leave their arses out here and turn around and go back to the homestead. "We wanted you to have the day off," Craig continued, the truth spilling from his lips lightning fast. It was as if he needed to get the words out before I flattened him. It was a fair call on his part. "We spoke to Scottie before brekkie. Told him we wanted to do something special for you. That's why he was trying to get you to have the day off."

"When you wouldn't agree, this bloody fruit loop came up with the brilliant idea that we could trick you into coming out." Sam hitched his thumb over his shoulder.

"You were the one who mentioned lantana."

"You were the dickhead who said there was a noxious weed growing out here. Lantana was the first thing I thought of."

I took a deep breath and blew it out slowly, but my words had an edge to them that made Sam flinch. "So, let me get this straight. There's no weed. There's nothing that you're worried could poison the cattle. It was all made up?" I glanced at Sam. He nodded, his eyes downcast and shoulders slumped. I moved my eyes to the rear-view mirror, and Craig met my stare but couldn't hold it. He nodded too. "I don't do liars. I won't put up with it. Trust is everything to me; I won't accept anything but honesty. In saying that, I get what you were trying to do, and I appreciate it, even if it would have been just as easy to say 'grab your swimmers, we're going to the waterhole.' Got it?"

"Got it." Sam nodded.

"Sorry, Ally. Won't do it again."

"Okay then. So, no walking around looking for weeds. We've got a picnic, a billabong, and a few hours up our sleeves. Shame we didn't bring swimmers."

"Who needs swimmers? We'll swim in our jocks." Craig laughed as he got out of the four-by-four and made his way to the back.

"I'm not fucking wearing any," Sam muttered under his breath. I laughed at the irony of that. *Maybe, just maybe today might be the day that they finally get it through their thick heads that I don't want to be friend-zoned anymore.*

"Neither am I." I shrugged and slipped out too, going to grab my backpack. When I pulled it out, I noticed the folded towels that had been hidden by the esky. "You guys remembered towels, but not swimmers or undies?"

"Craig remembered towels. I was too stressed out about you nutting me for lying to you to get you out here."

I slipped my hand in his and squeezed. "Thank you. Means a lot that you wanted to do something for me."

"Always, Ally." Sam lifted my hand and kissed it. "You're like a sister to us."

My gut sank like an anvil had been dropped into it. My head spun, not because I'd had some delusional thoughts that I was irresistible, but because of how badly I'd misread the situation. They hadn't been flirting with me; they were apparently treating me like their little sister. And I'd gone and done something stupid like fall in like with them. It was bad enough that there were two of them.

God, what a mess.

There was a song that Ma and Nan used to play from the sixties or something that had a line in it about crying on your birthday. I was about to do it. Damn it, it wasn't bloody fair. I liked them and I'd been friend-zoned. By not just one of them, but both. I was a right muppet for even thinking that I'd had a chance.

I pulled my hand away from Sam's and smiled a smile that I was sure looked as brittle as I felt at that moment. One comment from him would make me shatter into a million pieces. I gritted my teeth and pulled my shoulders back. I would not let this get me down. I wouldn't. If I liked them more than either liked me, neither one was the right man for me. I deserved better than that.

By the time I'd trudged to the water's edge, Craig had set the esky down and his boots and socks were off. I raised an eyebrow at him, and he grinned, the larrikin in him showing. "Comin' in?"

I still needed to process my thoughts. Accept the fact these blokes just wanted to be friends when I'd hoped — and believed, maybe naively—that there could be more between us. "Yeah. Nah. I'll just sit out here for a bit."

Sam looked at me and visibly swallowed. "I'll stay with Ally." I waved him off, spread out the picnic blanket Ma had packed and sat down, wishing I had a book with me to disappear into. When I settled myself, I saw Craig running, his lily-white arse flashing us a full moon, as he whooped and cannonballed into the water. The bank fell away quickly from the small beach I was sitting on, into deeper water that you had to dive under the surface a good few metres to reach.

After he'd resurfaced, Craig shook his head. Water dripped from his blond hair, darkening it to an ash colour as the drops beaded down his face while he treaded water. "Come in, Sam. It's bloody beautiful."

"Nah, all good."

I shot a look at him. More like a glare. "I won't look. Wouldn't want you—"

"Ally—"

"Sam, just..." I blew out a breath that was more a growl and shook my head. My tone was clipped. I sounded pissed even to my own ears. I didn't want to be an immature, self-ish princess, but bloody hell, I didn't want to be babysat by my big brother either. Thankfully, Sam didn't need me to explain myself. He got the message and stripped off his boots and socks, followed by his shirt. I tossed him two towels that he slung over the low hanging branch of a tree growing at a steep angle over the water and looked away. I didn't see him take off his jeans, but I heard them land next to me as he gingerly toed towards the edge. He slipped into the water silently, the ripples in the water the only evidence that he'd just entered it. Where Craig was a loud-mouthed cheeky bugger, Sam was always quieter. More introverted.

I turned to face them when I heard thrashing and watched as I kicked off my RM Williams boots, toed out of my socks, and sat in bare feet. Craig was splashing Sam, while Sam shielded his face. Finally, Sam went under and within a moment, Craig went wide-eyed and was pulled under too. They broke the water together and laughed, Sam splashing Craig before shaking his hair out and treading water.

"Boys, try not to splash too much. The crocs tend to be drawn to you if you do." I smiled sweetly at them. I expected that they'd swim to the shore like they were being chased, but they didn't do that. Instead, the colour drained from Craig's face and within a split second, he'd launched himself at Sam. There was no playful splashing this time though. Craig's movements were short. Sharp. Urgent. He meant business. He thought I was serious. Both of them did. Within a split second, Craig had wrapped an arm around

Sam and used powerful strokes to shift them to the edge. Craig was pushing Sam, getting him out first, looking over his shoulder, ready to shield Sam with his body.

I was already on my feet, scrambling to them. Running to the water's edge to meet them. "I was joking. Shit, I'm sorry. It was a smart-arsed comment. I should have realized that... fuck. I'm sorry."

"What?" Sam now stood before me, starkers and breathing hard. He gripped Craig's hip and pushed him further up the bank, out of the way of the imaginary danger.

"I'm sorry. Scottie used to scare me, telling me there were crocs in the water. It became our inside joke. There aren't any crocs. It's perfectly safe. I wouldn't have let you get in if there was any danger." That immature, selfish princess I didn't want to be? Well, I'd officially crossed the line. It wouldn't have surprised me if they'd grabbed their towels and stormed off to the Landcruiser. Or if they left me there either. But I knew they wouldn't, not out here and not in summer. Get lost and they'd be recovering a body. Scottie would have made that clear to them the first day they were here—he rehearsed his speech with every new person on the station—and he wasn't wrong.

Sam and Craig shared a look. An intense stare that communicated so much more than words could say. Thank you. I love you. You protected me. I want you. It only lasted a millisecond, but it was as if the shroud over my eyes had been lifted. Everything slotted into place. I was right to wonder whether there was more between them. Their easy familiarity, their inseparability. Craig's protectiveness and

Sam's innate way of looking for Craig whenever they were apart. I understood now why they'd never like me the same way I was hooked on them. They were in love with each other. It was clear that they worked hard to hide their affection from the world, and I resolved to never out them. The knowledge settled and I fell a little harder for them, not in that "I want a gay best mate" way, but because they'd made their relationship work. They were solid. Made for each other.

I squealed when strong arms wrapped around my waist and lifted me off my feet. I'd spaced out and Craig had pounced. I was being carried to the water's edge. "No crocs?"

"Put me down," I yelled, laughing. "Yes, there are crocs. They'll eat us all if you throw me in."

"Too bad, sweetheart." Craig chuckled and fell backwards into the water, taking me with him. Fully clothed, my shirt and jeans would stick to me and take all day to dry off, but I didn't have it in me to care. Cool water surrounded me, enveloping my senses. The harsh buzz of the cicadas was silenced and I relaxed in Craig's arms, enjoying the water all around me. Sam pulled me to him a moment later, wrapping his arm around my waist and tugging me against him into deeper water. We broke the surface gently, Sam kicking to keep us above water.

"You had us going for a minute there." He tried to act all serious, his eyes narrowed into slits, and his brow furrowed, but the grin he was failing to bite back almost had me chuckling. Almost.

"I'm sorry for scaring you."

"S'all good." He popped my forehead with a sweet kiss. "But we need to get you out of these wet clothes, or it'll be an uncomfortable drive back." I nodded mutely and he began to unbutton my shirt, exposing my bare breasts to him. I knew he wasn't interested, I knew I wasn't his type, but my heart hammered in my chest nevertheless. His fingers moved lower in the water to the bottom button, the shirt suddenly loose around me. When I felt Craig's strong body behind me, reaching around to tug open my jeans, I nearly combusted on the spot. My nipples were hardened peaks, my clit sending shocks of electricity through my body as it rubbed against the denim, the heat of their bodies a shocking contrast to the cool water. Out here in the blistering summer I rarely wore underwear, and I wasn't sure if I wanted to be completely naked with them begging them to touch each other while I sorted myself out, or whether I wanted to run and hide myself so I didn't risk exposing how much I'd grown to want them.

Sam spread my shirt open, his gaze only flicking down for the briefest of seconds as he pushed it off my shoulders. When Craig took over sliding my shirt down my arms and Sam gently ran his hands down my sides to my waist and lower to my hips, submerging himself so he could push my jeans down my legs, my core clenched and a shudder rocked through me. Jesus H Christ. I wanted to be between these two, not just watching them.

They left me bereft as they swam to the edge, stepped out of the water and walked up to a tree, its branches in the sun. Craig wrung out my shirt as Sam did the same to my jeans and they hung them on the branches. I couldn't help but stare at them. The perfect lines of their backs, narrow waists and their grabbable arses. While Sam was taller and slimmer, his arse more of a bubble butt, Craig's was thick and muscular. When they turned, I nearly swallowed my tongue. Either they were both showers not growers, or they were half hard. My mouth watered and I wondered, not for the first time, what it would be like to be with them both at the same time. It didn't matter what that involved; I'd gladly have them both any way they wanted me. But I needed to remember that they were together, not with me. I'd keep their secret. I'd never out them and I'd always be their friend. But I was way beyond just wanting that, especially now that I'd seen them naked.

I had to remember that nothing else would happen that day, or ever. I had to take solace in watching from afar and enjoying their physical perfection.

CHAPTER 7

Craig

I startled awake in a sweat, breathing hard. My sheet was tangled around my ankles and a boner tented my loose boxer shorts. The shorts had been a gag gift from Sam—we did it every Christmas. This one had three horses on the back with *hind quarters* written across the butt. They were oddly appropriate; I'd been thinking about arse all night. My dreams had taken a turn for the weird lately and this time was no exception. Naked swims with the birthday girl would do that to any red-blooded man, especially one who'd had a hard-on for said lady since the moment he'd seen her. Her pale skin, glinting in the dappled sunlight dancing across the water had given me wood that I literally could have hammered nails with, but it wasn't only her in my dream. I'd been touching Sam too. Holding him and kissing him. Spreading his cheeks and sinking into him while Ally let Sam taste her.

My cock throbbed; my balls drew up tight. It wouldn't take more than a bit of pressure to set me off, but I couldn't do it, not with the vision of Sam writhing beneath me so fresh in my memory. It was wrong. He wouldn't appreciate it and I wasn't that kind of bloke. I was *not* a poofter. Those kinds of blokes couldn't handle it out here—that's what they always said. Years of the other boys taunting the fem kid at boarding school, of hazing him when he didn't act as uber masculine as the rest of us taught me that only the toughest survived. I could see why the gay kids at school enjoyed looking though—even as teenagers, some of the boys had been fine. The curve of their backs down to the elastic of their jock straps, which framed their arses like a damn picture, and the bulges in the grey trackies we all wore after footy matches were a sight not to forget. But looking and admiring didn't make me a pansy-arsed poof. I mean, if I was to do it with anyone, it'd be Sam who I'd feel most comfortable with. Yeah, nah.

Flashes of the memory of our fifteen-year-old selves fumbling in the shed teased my consciousness and I hard-ened even more. No. It was Ally who'd got me ramped up. Not Sam. The swell of her small breasts, the peak of her dusky pink nipples and how beautiful they'd look with Sam's lips wrapped around one. The heat of her pussy as I slid into it. Or watched Sam do the same.

I closed my fist around my iron-hard cock and fucked my hand, focussing on the beautiful woman we'd had in our arms. One stroke, two, and I was coming, my back arching off the bed as fireworks exploded behind my closed eyelids and my jizz coated my boxers. I sucked in a breath through my nose and choked out a muffled cry into my other fist as

I kept moving my hand, my grip around my dick loosening as the aftershocks had me twitching.

Exhausted, I slumped back and blew out a breath rubbing my chest as the buzz flowed through my veins. I watched the fan spin lazily, slightly off centre, and the heavy curtains pushed all the way to my side of the room ruffle in the breeze coming in from the open window above Sam's bed. My gaze shifted to him and I watched as he slept silently. He faced the opposite wall, his sheet up to his armpit as he hugged his pillow. It was good to see him sleeping peacefully like that. It hadn't always been that way. Our last couple of years of school had been torture for him. Insomnia had plagued him and when he finally slept, he had nightmares. But since we'd arrived at Pearce Station, since we'd realized this place was home, he was sleeping better. Now it was me tossing and turning.

I must have drifted off again after I'd cleaned myself up because I blinked open my eyes to the crowing rooster and Sam already moving around in what we'd turned into the loungeroom. I stumbled out of bed and got dressed in my standard jeans and tee shirt, throwing a couple of changes of clothes into a backpack. Today I was heading into Roma, to supplement the mob with a couple of bulls from a breeder that Scottie'd had his eye on, and then we were checking out the auctions in town.

The four of us—Scottie, Ally, Jono and me—would make the nine-odd hour drive. I was sure Scottie was still testing Sam and me out, separating us so that he could see where each of our strengths lay. Scottie had left Sam in charge.

Level-headed, fair Sam would make sure everything at the station ran smoothly while we were away. I didn't have as much faith in myself this time around. I had no business being there with them. I didn't know how to judge the pedigree of bulls, but maybe Scottie was planning on training me. Or maybe I was with them just to keep me out of Sam's way.

"You right?" Sam asked as he slipped on his boots near the front door.

"Yeah." I wiped my mouth after brushing my teeth and followed him out into the breaking dawn. The colours lighting the horizon would never get old. Seeing the sky turn from greys into such a vivid blue that somehow saturated the red and washed out the grey-greens of everything that managed to grow out here. The world was fresh and calm and so full of promise at daybreak. I wasn't one of those city suckers who survived on caffeine and stress, but even I could appreciate the peace that dawn brought with it.

We meandered over to the main homestead, Jono joining us as we made our way around the veggie patch and down the long driveway, greeting each other with a "mornin'" and a smile.

Before we knew it, brekkie was done and we'd been driving for hours, each of us taking turns at the wheel towing the big cattle float. The two-lane tarmac road stretched out before me as I drove, straight for as far as the eye could see. The white lines flashed by as the kilometres to our destination fell away. It was easy to get hypnotized by those dashes on the road. It was the only thing that seemed to change. The vast desert landscape was filled with nothing but scrubby trees and patches of green grass. The red dirt peeking through gave us flashes of colour to catch our eye, as did the odd mob of roos clearing the highway in a single jump.

Wind buffeted the Landcruiser as the road train passed us. It was only a small one—three trailers attached to the rig—but it was enough to push the four-by-four and our trailer around. I held the wheel, keeping it steady as I rode the edge of the bitumen, giving the truckie as much room as I could. These highways were designed for heavy haulage, but the two lanes always seemed narrow when encountering them at over a hundred ks an hour.

Scottie and Jono sat in the back, reviewing paperwork. They'd read every detail of the two Charolais bulls the breeder was selling, deciding whether they would get one or both. I soon learned that Scottie had planned to drop a good fifty grand that day.

Ally looked over her shoulder and added a comment here and there, but mostly she was quiet next to me. It was comfortable between us. It had been ever since our swim. Ally suddenly seemed to let go of whatever it was she had on her mind and really became herself with us. We'd joked and splashed each other until we were laughing so hard we couldn't breathe. Then Ally had walked straight out of the water, leaving Sam and I swallowing our tongues at the sway of her bare arse as she sashayed up the bank, stepping delicately over the sharp rocks and roots protruding from the dirt to get her towel. I'd wrapped my hand around my semi like a complete creeper, stroking myself as she moved. But I couldn't help it. She got her revenge though. When I followed her out, I wished I'd been prepared enough to bring the swimmers she'd spoken of so I could hide my arousal. She hadn't been looking, and neither was Sam—I'd checked him out just to see if I was alone in my predicament, and I definitely wasn't—but I'd still been self-conscious as fuck. It'd been a relief to get the towel around my waist and be able to sit down, my knees bent and feet planted on the picnic rug just to hide the boner I was sporting.

Ally had stretched out and closed her eyes, a small smile playing on her lips as the warm summer air dried the droplets on her arms and shoulders and her hair. Sam had busied himself getting drinks sorted and I'd tried to think about the cattle. It hadn't worked; I'd been reminded of the trip today. That got me thinking about cattle mating and before long, I was thinking about me mating. Even my daydreams were getting weird.

But unlike before that swim, where Ally seemed to hold back and self-censor what she would say or do when she was with us, she seemed to drop the shield she'd held. It was as if, in that one swim, we'd moved beyond tension to a level of comfort borne of an old friendship. It was exactly what Sam and I had agreed needed to happen between the three of us. We couldn't let our dicks interfere with our job out here, or our friendship. We both knew that if one of us ended up with Ally long-term, the other would be destroyed. But after yesterday's imaginings and last night's dream I couldn't help but be a little disappointed.

If only there was a way that Sam and I could share her.

I huffed out a laugh at that. Ally was far too smart for that. She had far too much self-respect to ever allow herself to be a pawn between the two of us. Not that we'd ever do that to her, but still. There was no way Ally was the kind of girl who'd hook up with both of us either separately or together. There was even less of a chance of it happening more than once and both of us had agreed that once with her would never be enough.

We were in Roma for two nights, the eighteen-hour-round trip too far to do in one day, on top of meeting with the breeder. We happened to be there on the same day as the horse auctions, so it was good timing, but also explained why the caravan park we were staying in was fully booked.

It was so different to what I was used to. Secret paths meandered through tropical gardens, hiding the accommodation among towering trees and lush foliage that would have been suited to a tropical island. It was like night and day to the station.

We each had our own cabin, tucked away in different parts of the park. They weren't much more than a kitchenette, armchair, bed and bathroom, but they were bigger than what I was used to. In fact, I was kind of lost as I padded around the spacious room not having to watch out for Sam's clothes lying on the floor.

I had a few hours before we were meeting for dinner, so I crashed. Last night's interrupted sleep and the long drive had taken its toll. Exhausted, I stripped and climbed between the cool sheets. My head hit the pillow and next thing I knew my phone was ringing, startling me out of a deep sleep. Groggily, I reached for it, but it cut out, and I let my hand fall. It started again a second later and I groaned, fumbling to answer it. I grunted, "What?"

A chuckle. "Morning person I see. Tea's in fifteen. We're meeting at the pub we saw driving in. We'll swing by and grab you in ten."

"Uh ha. Yeah, okay." I hung up without waiting for more and stumbled into the bathroom to splash water on my face. I felt like I'd been through the wringer. The shower suddenly seemed like a much better idea. Cranking up the hot water, I waited until it was steaming and stepped into the spray to wash away the day's grime. As much as I wanted to, I didn't linger. There was no way I'd make the boss wait for me. Even though I moved fast, I was still buttoning up my shirt as I saw them pull up and toot the horn.

The pub was old and comfortable, with a laid-back vibe and the yeasty smell of beer permeating the air. Low padded chairs and big tables meant we could spread out and I found myself sitting opposite Scottie. Menus were already on the table and I could see from a glance that it was typical pub food—schnitties, steak, pies, fish and chips, and spag bol. I'd barely looked over the menu when the waiter sidled up to the table, and I got a whiff of a classic cologne that made me take a second look. His black and white uniform looked like it was tailor-made for him, highlighting every bulge of muscle underneath the fabric. Freshly shaved, olive complexion, with dark hair styled to within an inch of its life, he had an exotic air that was complimented by his almost black eyes. It wasn't like I was checking him out, but I could acknowledge that he owned the room.

"A rose among many thorns." He had a slight accent from somewhere I hadn't heard before. He lifted Ally's hand and kissed her knuckles. "What can I get you…"

"Oh, ah—" Ally hesitated. She was flustered. Blushing, she coughed out a laugh, her free hand going to her chest. "Ally."

"Ally, welcome. What would you like to drink?" He didn't bother taking out the pen and notepad tucked into the small apron tied around his narrow waist. At first blush, he reminded me of Sam, but my best mate was entirely different from this bloke.

"Just a beer, thanks."

"I get off in an hour. Maybe I can give you a private showing of the wine menu then?" I couldn't help my shocked cough at his less than smooth move. What if she was with one of us? It occurred to me that we'd say something if she was. I opened my mouth to tell him to back off—

"I'd love to. I'll be here when you're done." She smiled at him and turned her gaze first to Scottie, who was smart enough to be looking away and conscientiously ignoring what was going on, then to me. I opened my mouth and Ally

narrowed her eyes at me as if to daring me to say something. As much as I wanted to, I wasn't stupid. I held up both
hands and shook my head, clamping my mouth closed.
"Bloody well better not have an opinion."

Food and drinks were served, but I couldn't move past
Ally meeting up with that bloke for a drink. He hadn't even
introduced himself. He could be anyone. Not that I had a leg
to stand on with her. I wasn't stupid enough to tell her she
couldn't or shouldn't speak to him. She was her own
woman and I needed to respect that. Didn't mean I needed
to like it though. So, when Ally eventually stood up to join
whatshisface at the bar and Scottie caught her wrist as she
went to step away, I was relieved. His words told me that
he was just as unimpressed with what was happening as I
was. "Text me when you're back at your cabin and if you
need anything, doesn't matter what time or where you are,
call me."

"Thanks." She smiled at each of us impishly and wiggled
her fingers in a wave. "Night, boys."

I nursed my beer and watched them until I couldn't
stand it any longer. The bloke had snaked his arm around
the back of Ally's stool and he was touching her hair, her
elbow, and her cheek, and getting all up in her personal
space. I gritted my teeth, hating the jealousy churning in my
gut and the jolt of possessiveness that was making my
hands curl into fists on the table.

"Mate, settle down or she'll be spewin'."

"I don't have to like it." I picked at the label on the beer
just to give my fingers something to do.

"No, but you have to respect her." Scottie stared me down, practically daring me to disagree with him. "I dunno what's going on between you three, mate, so I'm only judging based on what I see. You treat her like she's your sister in some ways. But then you get all caveman on her when she lets her hair down. Can't do that."

"We can't very well be hitting on the boss's sister, can we?" I raised an eyebrow at him in challenge, and he and Jono shared a look before both started laughing.

Jono stood from the table and patted my shoulder. "Boy, you have a lot to learn. I'm gonna take a walk back to the caravan park, then hit the sack. See you tomorrow mornin'."

We said our goodbyes and I crossed my arms over my chest, leaning back in the chair. "What's he mean?" I asked, a little too eager to get back onto the topic of Ally.

"If Ally thought for a moment that either you or Sam hadn't made a move on her because you work for our family, she'd castrate all of us. In case you hadn't noticed, my sister is capable of making her own decisions. She's one of the strongest women I know, and one of the best." He looked over to her for a moment. "She deserves every ounce of happiness she can squeeze out of this life. I would never, ever want to be responsible for denying her that. You don't need it, so I won't give you my blessing, but don't let me being your boss stop you from finding your happy too. Hear me?"

Scottie and I were the same age, but he had a maturity I never thought I'd possess. He was wise, and if I hadn't already figured it out, a bloody good bloke too. "I hear you." I sighed and took a swig of my beer. "Any suggestions on what to do if you *and* your best mate—the one that's like a brother to you—likes the same girl?"

He groaned and scrubbed his hands over his face. "Honestly, I'm the wrong bloke to ask about that kinda stuff. Never had a successful relationship in my life and don't really have a best mate." He shrugged. "But I'd sort that shit out fast, or you'll find three relationships are destroyed."

Scottie stood and mimicked Jono's move, clapping me on the shoulder. "My guess is that Ally has no intention of going anywhere with that handsy dickhead over there, but I'm gonna stick around in case she needs me. I'm just gonna do it somewhere where she doesn't feel like we're watching her. Feel free to join me if you like."

I smiled, standing too. "Sounds good."

We'd barely sat down in the beer garden when Scottie's phone pinged. He read the message, immediately looked around and walked towards the bar we'd come from without another word. I didn't hesitate, following him as I spotted Ally with both her hands on the handsy bugger's chest pushing him away. I saw red. Anger and bloody murder coursed through my veins. Storming over to them, I ripped his hand off her shoulder and glared, breathing hard through my nose as I waited for any excuse to pummel him into the ground. Just one thing. The slightest move, and I'd let loose on him. Itching to break that pretty nose of his, I ground my teeth together and fed off the pulse thundering in my veins.

But just as quickly as my anger came on, it subsided. A cool hand on my chest, a calloused finger brushing over my nipple had my attention in an instant. Ally slipped her arm around my waist and leaned into me. "Woah there, mate."

I sucked in a breath and looked down at her, getting lost in those ice-blue eyes. Everything was pulling me towards her. Like a siren, she called me, and the desire to kiss her right there and then was overwhelming. I slid my eyes closed and gritted my teeth, desperate not to become the bloke I'd just pulled off her. I rested my cheek against her hair, breathing her in and trying to calm myself down. "I was worried."

"Lucky you didn't get your head kicked in. Bloody hot-headed bastard." Scottie motioned to Ally, both of them leading me out the door.

Ally held out her hand. "I haven't had another drink. You'll both be over the limit." Scottie tossed her the keys to the Landcruiser and I slid into the front seat next to her. When she was buckled in, she turned to me and added, "I appreciated the caveman act then because he wouldn't take no for an answer, but I don't need you being my Prince Charming every time, okay?"

"Prince Charming?" I asked, every brain cell still focussed on not fusing my mouth to hers and then running my lips over every inch of her body.

"Riding up on your horse and saving me." She looked me square in the eye, not breaking my stare until my brain finally pieced together what she was saying, and I nodded.

When I flicked my gaze to Scottie, he was wearing a far too satisfied smirk.

"Gotcha."

CHAPTER 8

Craig

We had a meeting with the breeder first thing that morning. Their farm was only forty minutes north-east of Roma. The highway became a dusty road that turned into a wide, tree-lined flat driveway. Cattle grates greeted our entry onto the farm, and Scottie drove the short distance to the immaculately cared for house. It was straight out of a magazine—a perfect old Queenslander much like the homestead on Pearce Station, except with all the decorative woodwork added to the veranda. We pulled up, letting the dust settle around the Landcruiser for a moment before we piled out.

I offered the paperwork to Scottie, but he waved me off. He'd been eyeing two bulls from the breeder for months. But given the investment, he'd taken his time making the decision and comparing every option on the market. The vet had been out to the farm to check out the bulls and all their paperwork. From what Scottie had said, the vet read every piece of information he could get his hands on, from full medical records, semen count to reports on feed and artificial insemination results. Scottie had gone through every piece too and now knew it all backwards.

As we stepped away from the four-wheel drive, Scottie nodded towards the pens. "One on the left is Pure Blond. The other is Zeus."

"They're good-lookin' bulls, aren't they?" I mused as Ally came to stand next to me. The two faded gold Charolais were big. They'd dwarf the cows on the station. Happily munching away on hay, they were quiet and calm, but I had a feeling they'd both be spirited.

An older bloke bypassed the three of us, walking straight up to Jono. He reached for his hand, shaking it. "Thanks for making the trip out, Mr Pearce."

Jono smiled serenely, shaking his hand. "Nice to meet you, mate, but I'm Jono. This is the boss." He motioned to Scottie. "Scottie Pearce." Sweeping his hand to us, he added, "And this is Ally Pearce and Craig Williams."

"My apologies, Mr Pearce. Welcome. I'm Jack Stone. Can I get you some refreshments?" The bloke blushed, looking suitably chastised as he shook Scottie's hand.

"I'm good, mate. We stayed in Roma last night. It was only a short trip here."

"All right then. Should we take a look at the bulls?"

We wandered over to the holding yards the bulls were in. They were contained by a thick timber post and rail fence, the wood faded by years of weathering until it was smooth to the touch. Jack stepped up to Zeus's yard and began reeling off statistics. Scottie and Jono grilled him, double-checking all their information, and no doubt comparing it against the data they'd memorized.

Ally wandered off, beckoning to me with a tilt of her head. Hands in her pockets, she walked over to a larger paddock and I followed her, spying more cattle in the distance. There were trees dotted all over the landscape running the length of the fence and green grass grew over the rolling hills.

"Bit different from the station, isn't it?"

She nodded. "It is. Cattle looks good, but. I like what I see." She pointed to the dam in the distance at the bottom of the hill. "Good water supply for them, lots of feed."

"You think Scottie will get both?" I rested my hand on the star picket that had wire running through it to fence off the paddock.

"Depends on the price they can negotiate. He's most interested in Pure Blond. Zeus is a bonus if he can get him."

"What's the process after that?"

"We'll go back into Roma, transfer the funds, then once it goes through, we'll come back and pick them up. While we're waiting for Scottie to do his thing, we can have a wander around the horse auctions."

I nodded with a smile. Driving back and getting the chance to see the stock horses available would make for a great day as far as I was concerned. "Been a while since I've been to a horse auction. Years."

By the time we wandered back over to the others, Scottie was shaking hands with Jack and a lady Jack's age was walking over to us with a smile on her face. "Mrs Pearce?" She held her hand out to shake. "I'm Mandy."

"Nice to meet you. I'm Ally Pearce, Scottie's sister. This is Craig."

I shook the woman's hand and we moved toward the others. "They look happy." Scottie turned to us and grinned and I knew he'd reached a deal. "I haven't been much use here today," I confessed to Ally before we joined them.

"Well, to be honest, we didn't really need you here to help choose the bulls—" Ally put her hand up to silence my interruption "—but I wanted your opinion on the horses. We also wanted to give Sam an opportunity to do his thing at the station."

"Sam would have been more helpful to you here, but I'm glad he's got a chance to show what he's made of."

She nudged me with her elbow. "Don't undersell yourself. You know horses just as well as Sam and if anything, you're more confident with them."

I shook my head. "Nah." I'd suspected the reason for their inviting me, and I was happy for Sam. It was something he deserved. Jono wasn't going anywhere—he and Scottie almost had a father-son relationship—but knowing that Scottie trusted Sam to run the place in his absence warmed me inside. I was also glad that they'd not considered me for the same opportunity. Management wasn't something I was interested in. What did grab my attention though was the thought of getting a horse. I hadn't realized how much I loved the idea until the possibility presented itself.

I was suddenly itching to get a closer look at them. The hour-long chat we had over a cuppa and scones felt like five. The forty-minute drive back to Roma might as well have been a week, but Scottie finally dropped Ally and me off at the saleyards. He said he'd join us after he and Jono went to the bank. I was fine with that.

Each stall had a stock horse in it. This wasn't the Magic Millions, where thoroughbred racehorses sold for millions, but the pedigree on offer was impressive. The horses looked sturdy. Fit and calm, despite so many people being around—something they likely weren't used to. Hay and horsehair filled my senses and memories reminiscent of happy times filled the hole in my chest. I closed my eyes and smiled, at home among the smells and sounds of my favourite animals. Beautiful chestnut browns and dappled greys, mahoganies and the odd black horse had me guessing at their age and how many hands they were. I watched them shift between the pail of water and bucket of hay or pellets and saw the flick of ears or swish of a tail.

My fingers itched to tangle into a mane and feel the wind in my hair as I rode bareback, racing along the open desert plains. I hadn't realized how much I'd missed these majestic beasts until I was around so many. I didn't spend much time in the shed with the horses of Pearce Station. Without one of my own, there wasn't really any reason to go in the shed. Sam's almost aversion to them kept me away too.

"You miss having one, don't you?" Ally squeezed my fingers. I hadn't even realized that I'd reached for her, but her warm hand in mine felt so right that once I'd grabbed a hold, I couldn't let go. She didn't seem to mind it though, as she led me over to a beautiful black-brown mare with white socked feet.

"She's gorgeous." We stepped up onto the metal railing, and I held out a handful of the pellets the lady handling her poured into my palm. "C'mere, girl."

"What's her name?"

"Daisy." The smile in the lady's voice said it all. She was a favourite of hers, and I could see why. Daisy was nibbling the feed from my hand, her soft whiskers and lips brushing against my calloused palm. I petted her nose and neck, scratching between her ears and watching her every move.

"She broken in?" I asked as the lady stepped away to collect a printout on Daisy.

She handed it to Ally. "Absolutely, and she's good with a beginner level rider, but a little more experienced one would be better. Is she for yourself?"

"Maybe."

I turned my attention to Daisy, and Ally continued, "We need another couple of horses for the station. She might be ridden by a few of us, but we're all experienced."

"Daisy would be perfect. She's laid-back, good with other horses and is used to different riders. She's confident among cattle, fast on her feet when it counts but better at longer distance treks."

"Okay, great." Ally smiled, shook the lady's hand, and I gave Daisy a final scratch on her nose.

"She was a beauty."

Ally linked her arm in mine. "She was."

"I think I'd like to put in a bid for her. Maybe."

"You seemed to connect with her."

I smiled. "She had a good disposition. I could see myself riding her."

"Sam doesn't seem to want to do much riding."

I side-eyed Ally. She was looking intently at me and blushed when I quirked a grin at her. She'd tried a few times that day to get me talking about him. His story wasn't mine to tell, but I also wanted her to know that he wasn't scared of them.

"You know Sam's dad bred horses, don't you?"

"Yeah, I do. Did he have a bad experience?" she asked, worry in her voice. A line between her brows marred her forehead. "He wasn't hurt, was he?"

"Not in the way you're thinking. He lost his horse when the bank foreclosed on the Hayes' farm." Eadie may have been a standard stockhorse, but she was one of a kind in Sam's eyes, and he'd loved her.

"Must have been rough. I couldn't imagine losing 'Tella." Her voice was pained. I nodded, remembering all too well the endless days when Sam was walking around like he'd lost part of himself. He had, and knowing I couldn't do a single thing to help him at the time had shredded me inside. Ally wasn't exaggerating when she said he seemed to shy away from the horses. He did. But it was because he'd had his heart broken, and even a decade on, he missed his girl.

"Yeah. We grew up together, but she was his best friend. Don't think that any horse will ever compare to Eadie for him."

We walked and talked and checked out a few more of the horses. I registered as a bidder and confirmed Daisy's lot number before a text came through from Scottie. He was wrapping up at the bank having transferred through the funds. They'd be on their way in a few.

"Any of the horses grab you?" Scottie asked when Ally called.

"Craig's found a horse. Next time we'll bring Sam; see if we can persuade him to get one."

"Great, good luck!"

We kept walking, looking at a few more of the horses, but we didn't get to see as many as I would have liked before the beginning of the auctions were announced. Didn't matter though. I kept coming back to Daisy. I knew she was the one, but I couldn't help the niggling feeling that Sam would be upset if I arrived back at the station with a horse. It was stupid to think of it as a betrayal, but I didn't want to hurt him. Thing was, I wanted this. I was ready and I didn't know whether Sam would ever be.

The auctioneer stood on the walkway suspended above the pens and announced the lots, stepping over to the next horse to auction it. They were still a few sections away from us, so Ally and I got positioned at the front. Before I knew it, Daisy's auction was happening. The auctioneer, dressed in tan pants, a blue check shirt and a brown ten-gallon hat, announced the lot in a warbly voice. Holding a gavel, he started the bidding, speaking so fast that his words ran together. Before I knew it, the bidding was upwards of two grand and I hadn't even put one in yet. My hand shot up, but Ally clamped her hand over mine before the auctioneer saw it. "Not yet. Wait another minute until they finish fighting it out."

Sure enough, two people were going up in two-hundred-and-fifty-dollar increments. Three grand.

"Three-two," the man behind us yelled out, mumbling something I didn't catch under my breath.

"I'm out," the other called.

"Now," Ally said as I called out, "Four."

A curse. "Four-two."

"Five." My voice rang out clearly and I turned to see whether the other bidder would meet the bid.

When he shook his head, I bit my lip, holding back my grin until I heard the magic, "Sold for five gs! Congratulations, sir. See Tom over here for paperwork and payment details."

We signed it up and I was given the bank account details so I could put the transfer through. I couldn't wipe the grin off my face, beyond ecstatic that Daisy was mine. When we'd finished up, I went straight back to her, only to be met by the man I'd outbid.

"She's a beautiful one, mate. Good bidding." He held his hand out and I shook it. "Congratulations." The booklet in his other hand caught my attention. Specifically, the horse on the back cover. My heart lodged in my throat. My belly swooped and the breath I sucked in was harsh.

"Hey, mate, that horse—" I rasped, my voice rough, as I pointed to the auction brochure "—is it here?"

"Yeah, over in the back corner. He's the last lot to be auctioned. About to go up now. Unique colouring, ay?"

"I gotta go," I yelled to Ally, already moving. "That horse. I need to see it." I sprinted, dodging between people. Pushing my way through bodies, tripping and staggering around them. Side-stepping and crashing into a fence or two when the bystanders moved in a way I didn't expect. Pulling oxygen into my lungs, I pumped my legs harder in an open stretch of pens.

My heart beat hard and sweat beaded my brow.

Then I saw the boundary fence. The last lot.

I skidded to a halt.

People were everywhere.

The bids were coming in hard and fast. Five hundred dollar increments at six grand already.

"S'cuse me. Comin' through. Watch out. Sorry." I pushed through everyone to get to the front.

It was her. Eadie.

But it couldn't have been.

The horse was male—a gelding. But his colouring was unmistakable. I'd only seen one other horse with a snow-white coat on most of its body, except for its dark brown neck and head. There was no transition in colour between the patches. It was as if it had been dipped in paint, the colours a stark difference.

I looked up and it was like a punch to the gut. The name on the sign was no longer Hayes Horse Farm, but the logo—

the two horses with flapping manes and rolling hills in the background, the green and brown colouring—was the same. Exactly as it had been a decade earlier when we'd been forced to leave.

This horse was Eadie's offspring. Who knew if Eadie was still alive? It was possible. She'd be nearly thirty, but it wasn't unheard of for horses to live to forty. Still, I didn't have time to find out. On impulse, I yelled, "Eight."

The crowd buzzed and I sucked in a breath waiting for the response. "Eight-five."

"Ten." I only had one more bid left in me, and my bank account would be completely cleared out. I squeezed my eyes closed and for the first time in my life, prayed.

"Move," I heard muttered behind me with grumbling in response. Ally.

The auctioneer was trying to ramp up excitement, droning on in a ramble I barely understood.

She shouldered up next to me and grabbed my elbow. I didn't know what she saw. Whether it was panic, determination, hope, or the inevitable crushing defeat I knew was coming when I was outbid.

"Eleven," the man behind me roared and the crowd cheered. My shoulders sank, the fight gone out of me. I couldn't beat it. I didn't have anything more. I closed my eyes and sucked in a breath, fighting back tears. Damn it. I needed this for Sam. He needed it. Why couldn't I do it for him. Why now? Why not before I'd bid for Daisy.

"Fifteen," Ally called out.

My head shot up and she smiled, just a small tilt of her lips, but it was radiant. And I was screwed. I may have promised Sam that we'd both keep our hands off her, but I'd fallen hard.

"Fifteen-five."

"Eighteen." Ally's eyes didn't leave mine, but I shook my head. I couldn't afford that. The warbly voice of the auctioneer, the hum of the crowd, the shuffling and whinnies of the horses all continued. But it was all white noise. I reached out to Ally and cupped her face, brushing my thumbs over her cheeks.

Then everyone was quiet, and it broke the spell. I looked around at the man bidding, and my lip curled in a sneer. It was dickhead from the night before. Handsy bastard. "Nah, I'm out." He smirked at me, knowing he'd succeeded in making us pay more for the horse than we should have.

"Fuckin' oath. Wanker," Ally spat out under her breath.

"Congratulations, miss," the auctioneer announced. "See Jay for paper and payment details."

"I don't have all of it. I've only got eleven."

"That's okay." Ally squeezed my arm. "Transfer it to us and we'll pay the difference."

"Here you guys are." Scottie's bounced between us. I cleared my throat and stepped back, seeing Ally roll her eyes and sigh.

"We got this one as well as Daisy on the other side of the lot." She turned to Scottie and smiled, but it didn't reach her eyes. She didn't have the same radiance she did when she'd saved me at the auction. I hated myself for upsetting her. But even though Scottie had encouraged me to go for it and make his sister happy, I had Sam to think about too. I couldn't break his trust, especially not when I'd just made the most impulsive decision of my life.

"He's striking." Scottie climbed up on the fence to get a better look at him. "Looks like a good horse. Fit too. Well looked after. What did you pick him up for?"

"Eighteen." Ally crossed her arms and stared at me. I wanted to shrink into myself under the weight of her gaze and then I realized the problem. I hadn't transferred the cash to her yet.

"Let me fix you up—"

"Eighteen! What the hell? You know we're not buying racehorses, right?"

"Let me fix you up with what I have. I'll pay the rest back too. Take it directly out of my wages."

"Craig—" Ally started.

"Ally, what the hell?"

"He's for Sam," I answered urgently, trying to diffuse Scottie's anger. "Sam's horse, Eadie, was the dam, I'm sure of it. I've never seen another horse like her. Until now. The logo's the same too. It's the same breeder."

"Oh." He stared at me for a moment before nodding, his gaze softening as he did. "That's... I get it. I would have done the same. Whatever the difference is that you don't have, don't worry about it. We'll chip it in." I didn't know how to thank him, but Scottie brushed it off.

The bloke with the paperwork waited patiently for us to get it all filled out and give us payment details. It looked like we'd be going back to the bank that afternoon to get all the money paid across. I completed Sam's details, unable to stop my hands from shaking even with the smile I couldn't quite seem to stop. Scottie leaned over my shoulder, collecting the slip with the bank details and the next minute, the horse was ours pending the transfer.

"What's his name?" Ally looking at the papers I was holding.

"Spook." I laughed. "I like it."

CHAPTER 9

Sam

Waru patted me on the back. "You're a stubborn son of a bitch, but you did good today, Sam. Scottie wouldn't have minded if we waited for their help to get all the firewood back though."

I shrugged. "Yeah, but it's nearly all done now. One less thing for him to worry about when he gets home."

Ma smiled at us from the doorway. "He's here now." She waited for Waru to walk out before she spoke again. "You've outdone yourself these last couple of days, Sam. In case Scottie doesn't say it, you handled things better than we could ever have hoped. You cared for those cattle like they're your own."

Her words made my heart swell, pride taking its place in my chest. Craig was a little star-struck by the woman who'd given the middle finger to the haters and run Pearce Station better than her father before her. To me though, she was more like the mum mine had been before everything went down. My ma hadn't been the same after we'd lost the farm—her spark had disappeared. After ten years of hating that my family's place was gone, I suddenly didn't feel so lost at sea anymore. This station was starting to feel like home.

I smiled. Yeah, home. "Thank you. It means a lot to hear you say that."

I looked at the door and grinned when I heard the four-by-four stopping. "Go." She laughed and I was sure I was blushing. Suddenly, there were two people I really wanted to see.

I jogged out of the shed towards the Landcruiser reversing up to the sorting yard. That meant one thing—Scottie had gotten the bulls he was after. He'd been aiming for two. I wondered if he'd managed to get both.

Ally was behind the wheel and she jumped out as soon as she stopped moving the car. "Come round to the back. You have to see this." She grinned and grasped my hand, tugging me to the fence.

Craig stepped between two rails in the fence holding a basketball. Scottie and Jono unlatched the gate on the float and pulled down the ramp. As soon as it was done, Scottie nodded at Craig and he bounced the ball. The dull thud sounded and there was a responding snort. "S'at the bull?" My gaze pinged between Craig and the trailer. My best mate wasn't a bull fighter, so what the hell was he doing?

Footsteps sounded on the metal ramp as the bull backed itself out. His faded gold colouring was striking against the red dirt between the patches of grass growing in the yard. Wide and square, the bull was massive. Easily broader than two men standing shoulder to shoulder, the bull was as tall as Scottie—when he was standing on the first rail of the fence. The bull snorted again, and alarm bells went off. Craig was in the paddock, with nothing between him and the massive beast except a basketball.

"Craig." The panic in my voice was obvious as I gripped the fence with both hands ready to vault over it. Ally laid her hand on my arm and I peeled my gaze away from my best mate to the beautiful woman standing beside me.

"Watch."

I swallowed, forcing my jaw to unclench. I managed it, barely, but I couldn't let go of the fence. I couldn't pull my foot off the bottom rail. Everything in me screamed to go to him and protect him from a bull that could easily charge. What the hell was Scottie thinking? I respected the bloke, but I wasn't comfortable with having Craig act as bait to get the bulls out of the float.

"Relax, Sam. He knows what he's doing."

I huffed, not entirely sure that Scottie did know what he'd set Craig up to do. But what I saw blew my mind. Nan and Ma's surprised laughs from behind me registered in my mind, but I couldn't turn my eyes away from the sight before me.

Craig bounced the ball and the bull's attention was immediate and unwavering. It trotted over to him, lumbering with each step until Craig was face to face with him. He laughed and bounced the ball, spinning it around his back. Bounce. Bounce. Bounce. With every one of Craig's moves, the bull bobbed his head and stepped to the side following it. He was... playing with it.

Dribbling the ball, Craig passed it to the bull and he ducked his head, butting it back before he wiggled his arse end and bounced on thick legs like he was excited.

"What the?" I laughed. Craig was playing basketball with the beast. They met each other move for move—Craig stepped to the left and the bull shadowed, defending the ball. He huffed and bounced, kicking out his back legs. Lumbering forward, the bull stopped directly in front of Craig, looking down at him before he dropped his head. I held my breath. If he charged forward, Craig would be thrown. God only knew what injuries he'd have.

"Oh you big boof." Craig's voice was warm, filled with affection. He dropped the ball and scratched behind the bull's big ears with both hands. With arms outstretched, Craig was practically hugging him and all I could do was stare as the bull shoved him gently out of the way and nudged the ball forward. "You little shit." Craig laughed and charged after him, kicking the ball away before grabbing it and dribbling it along as he jogged back to us.

Ally motioned to them and I couldn't help my disbelieving laugh. "The bull apparently has a favourite toy—the basketball. The owners gave the ball to Scottie to get him in the trailer. Scottie tried for half an hour to get him to move, but he wasn't interested. Jono and I tried and nothing either. As soon as Craig had the ball, Blond couldn't get enough. They were playing together for an hour before Craig walked up the ramp and the bull followed him straight in. Funniest thing you've ever seen. The other bull got a slap to the arse and walked straight up, but Blond wanted to do things his way."

"So you got two bulls?" I shook my head at both the ridiculousness and genius of playing basketball with the bull.

"Yep, Pure Blond—this guy—and Zeus." Ally pointed to the other bull Scottie was easing out of the trailer.

"Out of the paddock, Craig." Scottie nudged the bull and he turned just as Craig jogged over to the rail I was standing on. He clambered over it effortlessly and our gazes caught and held for a long moment. My heart beat hard and my breath caught in my throat as I felt myself step closer. He did too, wavering towards me, our stare never breaking. Tension coiled in my gut and my fingers itched to reach for him. The heat from his body pulled me closer. Need was driving me, everything inside me crying out to wrap him in my arms and reassure myself that he was safe. Someone behind me—Ally—cleared her throat and I blinked, shaking myself out of my stupor. What the hell was I thinking?

He grinned then and clapped me on the shoulder in the ultimate blokeish move and this time my gut churned uncomfortably. His cheeks flushed and he was a little out of breath. "G'day. That gets the adrenaline pumping, hey?"

Scottie walked over to us from where he'd let the bull go and pointed to the full trough and feed buckets. "Thanks for doing that, mate."

"No worries. Welcome back. Looks like you got two real good bulls. They're big bastards."

"Funny fuckers too. Zeus apparently loves clothes hanging on washing lines. He'll pull 'em off and roll in them if he gets near a line, so we need to make sure he's behind the gate."

Scottie checked the gate to the yard, making sure it was secure. "Let's let these two get acquainted with each other for a couple of days before we let 'em loose in the paddock with the others."

"How were things here?" Ally asked.

"Oh, you know. Quiet." They'd be filled in soon enough.

"So ah… can you…" Craig looked to Ally with a furrowed brow. Why was he fumbling his words? "Ally?"

"I need to move the fourbie. Why don't you guys stay here while I turn it around?" She smiled at Craig and squeezed his arm. It was as if she couldn't get away from him quick enough, but Craig's reaction to her had me on edge. He sucked in a deep breath and fidgeted, shifting from foot to foot. Scottie bumped his shoulder and nodded, holding his gaze for a moment. Craig settled and nodded back. What had him on edge? Was he scared? Nervous? Why would he be anxious around me? Unless…

Oh shit.

My gut sank and that hollow feeling returned. Shame sent my head spinning. No. I closed my eyes and wished for my suspicions not to be true. Were Craig and Ally together now? But then I realized that I'd just effectively wished for them not to be happy, and I hated that I went there. I rubbed a hand over my heart, trying to ease the piercing ache. The breath I sucked in was painful. A vice-like weight sat on my chest, crushing my heart. I opened my mouth to speak but nothing came out. I had to tell Craig that he had nothing to worry about. I wouldn't stand in his way. I wouldn't hold it against him. How could I? I loved the bloke. And Ally.

If getting two bulls wasn't the only thing that came out of their trip, I would be happy for Craig and Ally. It'd kill me to watch them together. To see them falling in love. But I'd do it. I'd step away. I'd never come between them. All I wanted was for them to be happy. If they had that together, I couldn't ask for more.

My two favourite people could be happy together. Craig and Ally were perfect for one another too. I should be happy for them. No, I *was* happy.

I was hurt.

No.

I was crushed.

But Craig deserved happiness. He'd put his life on hold, standing beside me through thick and thin while I tried to hold my shit together. I'd never begrudge him love. And Ally... it was hard to believe that someone as amazing as her could be real. But she was right there in front of us.

"It's okay, Craig," I said softly, my voice rough from unshed tears. "I'm happy for you."

He shook his head, his brow furrowed as if he was confused. "What? Never mind, don't answer."

Ally pulled the Landcruiser up in front of us and Scottie was in the back of the float as soon as it stopped moving. When I heard clanking and Scottie's voice, calm and soothing, from inside the float, my curiosity got the better of me.

The mare Scottie eased out was beautiful. The deepest of browns—so dark she was almost black with white socks, her tail swished as she stepped backwards. She held her head up, looking around, relaxed but interested.

Craig petted her long nose fondly. "This is Daisy. You're a beautiful girl, aren't you?" The horse nudged him, and I knew he was already head over heels in love with her.

I choked out a laugh, thrilled that he'd found a horse. Had I jumped to conclusions too soon? Was I completely wrong about Craig and Ally possibly being together? A tiny beam of hope pierced the darkness that had cloaked my shattered heart in shadow. God, I hoped that I'd gotten my assumption completely wrong.

Even though I shouldn't.

"Hiya, darlin'." I stroked her neck gently. She nickered and Ma stepped forward, reaching for her.

"You already know who has treats, don't you, Daisy?" Ma chuckled and pulled a few slices of apple from her apron. I smiled as the horse deftly plucked them from Ma's hand and went searching for more.

"Oh, Scottie," Nan breathed, awe in her voice. "He's spectacular."

I turned to where Nan was looking to see a second horse, and déjà vu hit me with the force of a Mack truck. I was fifteen again and standing in Eadie's stall, saying goodbye to my best friend. I gasped and tears sprung to my eyes, the shock of the vision before me making me lightheaded. I reached out, my fingertips touching the horse before me. Coarse hair met my hands, the warmth and strength of the animal before me so clear even with just a whisper-soft touch.

Words fled me, and my heart beat as fast as a racehorse galloping into the sunset. My hands shook and my breath shuddered as it left my lungs in a whoosh.

I was overwhelmed. I'd gone from mourning the loss of a relationship I could never have, to seeing Scottie's new horse. The seesaw of emotions nearly brought me to my knees. But now I understood. No wonder Craig was nervous. He would have known my reaction. He would know just how desperate I would have been for this horse to be mine.

I may not be able to call him that, but seeing him gave me something I never thought I'd have back—a connection to Eadie.

The similarities between them were uncanny. She was an anomaly in the animal world. An Australian stock horse that looked like a patchwork quilt. And this horse was a spitting image of her. It wasn't impossible that they shared a bloodline, but my dad had never wanted to breed her in case her unique colouring was a symptom of something not so innocent. But she wasn't mine anymore. Who knew what the new owners had done.

Captivated with every move the horse made, I reached out again and touched his face. His long mahogany mane lay over his eyes, and I gently scratched him there. Our eyes met and he regarded me as I silently petted him. I couldn't get any words beyond the lump in my throat. He had the same eyes as Eadie and as mine filled with tears, I sniffed and shook my head. He had almost the same markings as her too—closer than any other horse I'd ever seen. They were probably more pronounced than Eadie's were, with larger patches of dark brown contrasting wildly against the snow white of his coat.

He stood so much taller than me but lowered his head to mine, nuzzling my hair. I huffed out a laugh, that was as much of a cry, and reached for his neck. Resting my temple against his cheek, I closed my eyes and petted wherever I could reach with shaking hands. He wasn't Eadie, but this magnificent creature had her genes and somehow, I was privileged enough to see him. I was awestruck. Absolutely blown away by him.

"Sam." Craig gently pressed his hand to my lower back. "This is Spook."

"He's Eadie's, isn't he?" The wonder in my voice was unmistakeable.

Craig nodded. "He is. You okay?"

I sucked in another breath and let it out slowly, trying to calm my breathing. I was shaking, more than I had been when I'd first seen him. I shook my head, then nodded and settled on a weird combination of both. I had no idea if I was okay. It was as if I'd been lost in a fog and it was finally clearing. But the scenery being revealed was beyond what I could process. It was unreal.

"How?" I paused, clearing my throat so I could get the words out. "How did you find him?" My voice cracked and I blinked before wiping my cheeks from the runaway tears.

"Pure dumb luck."

"Scottie's lucky. He's beautiful." Jealousy borne of a dream to have my horse back twisted in my gut as I spoke.

"No, Sam." Craig moved and grasped my shoulder in his big hands. They were warm and solid. Familiar. "He's yours."

Craig eyed me as if expecting a reaction, but nothing came. The words entered my brain, but I couldn't comprehend them. I couldn't make sense of them. When he squeezed my shoulder, I turned, looking at his hand, before staring at him trying to process the words he'd just spoken. It was as if I was having an out-of-body experience. Like my mind had detached itself from my physical being. "Sam," he repeated. "You okay? You still with me?" The furrow in his brow deepened and his lips pursed.

I opened my mouth to speak and all that came out was a sob.

"Hey, it's okay. It's okay." He wrapped me in his arms. I went willingly, holding him close with my free hand, my other still on Spook.

I cried then, hot tears spilling on his shirt. I grieved for all the years I'd buried the pain of losing everything. For the loss of my identity as much as my home. For my best friend and his grief. For my horse and my family and how nothing had ever been the same again. I cried tears of hope, of moving on and finding a new home. For finding myself again. And receiving the best gift I could have ever been given— my own horse.

I hiccupped. "I... I can't believe...."

"He's yours." Craig cupped my face in his hands and looked me in the eye. "He's yours. He'll never be taken from you. Ever."

"You promise?"

"I signed the paperwork in your name. Forged your signature and all." One side of his lips tilted up in a ghost of a smile. "I promise."

"I love you, man. You did this for me. You do so much." My arms went around his waist and I pulled him close again.

"It wasn't only me. Ally and Scottie chipped in too. We wanted this for you. We love you too, Sam."

I sucked in a shuddery breath and grinned, my eyes welling again. "I have a horse."

"You do." Craig laughed, warmth blazing in his eyes. "Wanna ride him?"

I nodded, suddenly eager and finally looked around. Ally stood with Scottie, his arm around her as they watched us. Ma and Nan had retreated to the veranda and Waru, Yindi, and Jono were watching over the bulls, all of them conspicuously looking away. I loved these people for the family they gave me and for their attempt at giving us space. "You guys wanna ride with us?"

"I'd love to," Ally said, and Scottie nodded with a smile.

Craig clicked his tongue and petted Daisy's neck, encouraging her to walk with him to the shed where we stored all the gear. She followed without hesitation and soon, so did Spook. Scottie and Ally went a different way to us, heading towards the paddock where their horses were milling about. We heard a whistle and the thud of hooved feet galloping on hard ground. Daisy was calm and collected. She waited patiently as Craig slipped the halter on and adjusted it to fit comfortably before brushing her down, ready to be saddled.

I watched them, brushing Spook the whole time. My horse. Damn, it felt good saying that. I couldn't believe he was mine. The high from knowing it made my head spin and gave me so many butterflies that I was floating. "Hey, Spook, you gonna be a good boy too?" Craig passed me the halter he'd retrieved, and I slipped it onto my gelding. He tossed his head, his mane tussling in the move. He was a feisty one, and I grinned, loving how I could do this and come back the very next day and the one after that and do it all over again with him. I took my time, letting him get used to me and learning his moves too. Getting to know each other was important, especially because I didn't know how he'd been broken in. If it was with a rough hand, then I'd have to show him how different it was to have a rider that respected him.

My moves were gentle as I tried to communicate that he could trust me. I spoke calming nonsense to him until he relaxed, praising him every time he was patient and let me strap on another piece of tack.

Craig and Ally were already outside with their horses saddled and ready to go, but I was reluctant to go faster. I didn't want to rush things with Spook. His comfort was the most important thing to me.

"Here." Scottie startled me as he tapped me on the shoulder and passed me a quartered apple. I took it gratefully and held a piece out to Spook, adding how well he was doing.

"Thanks." I nodded to him. Once again, words weren't enough, but they were all I had. Scottie had done more for me than I ever dreamed, and now he'd given me something so incredible that I got choked up and my eyes welled every time I looked to the beautiful animal I'd been given. I'd shied away from horses for so long that more than one station owner had said if I was scared of horses, I'd never make it as a career stockman. It wasn't fear holding me back; it was heartbreak. But Craig had known. He'd fixed it. He'd somehow persuaded Scottie to part with his hard-earned cash to make Spook mine. I cleared my throat before my eyes brimmed with tears again and looked to Scottie. "For everything, you know. You've given us a home and a job. But getting this guy—" I ran a hand down his long neck and breathed through the wobble in my voice. "—means more than anything. Chipping in to pay for him... I appreciate it. Truly."

Scottie smiled gently and clapped me on the shoulder fondly. I think he understood exactly what I couldn't quite put into words. "Ally wouldn't let the other bastard get him. He was a right dickhead." He shrugged then, and added, "I just handed over the cheque. But I'm glad you've got a mate like Craig. He's good people. When he saw Spook's photo in the catalogue, he didn't hesitate. Shot through like bloody Wile E Coyote to get to his auction."

"He's the best mate anyone could ask for."

"I envy what you blokes have. It's rare." I suspected from the haunted look in his eyes that there was a deeper meaning there that I couldn't decipher, but he turned his focus onto tightening his horse's saddle before I could ask.

"That's a good darlin'," I purred, earning me a nudge from Spook when we were ready to go. We wouldn't be taking them out far that afternoon, instead just letting them get a feel for us riding them in the smaller paddock with the rest of the horses. Scottie and Ally were there as our leads, showing our new horses what to do if their training wasn't up to scratch.

We entered the yard and I walked Spook around with the reins, letting him get comfortable and used to the sandy dirt underfoot. In some places it was hard packed, and in others, where the horses didn't walk as much, it shifted as if we were walking on dunes by the beach. I notched the saddle one hole tighter and mounted him in one smooth move, petting his neck as he sidestepped and tossed his head, before kicking his legs out and taking off.

"It's okay, Spook." I held on as he cantered wildly around the paddock, trying to keep my voice soothing. I held the reins gently, but I was out of practice. I knew nudging him forward would give him room and get him to stop bucking, but doing that and staying on was a challenge. "Shh, boy." My voice jarred each time his galloping hooves connected with the ground. I struggled to run my hand down his neck, but I tried, keeping my touch gentle. "S'all right. I won't hurt you."

Scottie and Ally brought their horses in close on either side of me, and Craig had Daisy trotting in front of us in an instant, all three of them slowing down together. Spook followed. I didn't know whether he was reassured by the other horses or me, but he fell back to a walk, until all four horses were taking a stroll around the small paddock with us on their backs. "That's it, buddy, calm down. Testing me, hey, Spook?" As he slowed to a stop, I rubbed his wither and grinned at my companions. "He's a feisty one. How broken in is he?"

"Looks pretty green to me." Scottie eyed him, checking his stance as Spook shifted underfoot.

Craig looked away, embarrassment colouring his cheeks. "The bloke said that he was well broke but performed best with an experienced rider."

I laughed. "I'm a little out of practice. Looks like we both might need to up our skills, hey, bud." I petted his neck again. "Let's see if we can do that a little better this time, hey?" The others pulled their horses away, and I nudged him gently with my feet, letting him read my body language. Sure enough, when he got a feel for me, he rode smoother, not bucking or carrying on like a pork chop anymore.

I couldn't help the whoop that left me as my heart soared and the wind ruffled my hair. If flying was pure freedom, riding a horse came a close second. As the sun began to drop low on the western horizon, lighting the sky in a harmony of pinks, oranges, and yellow and casting lengthening shadows on the deep red dirt, I laughed and nudged Spook to go faster. Elation. Joy and warmth and happiness all mixed together in one rainbow-fuelled flock of birds filled my belly. What I could have sworn was only a moment later, except that the sky was now dark, I was slowing Spook down and turning him around to re-join the others. Craig was putting Daisy through her paces, commanding her in tight circles, side steps and stop and go movements. She was a good horse. Clearly more advanced in her training, she would be a good influence on Spook if we could keep them together.

Ally high-fived me as I pulled up next to her. "You looked good out there with him. Comfortable."

"We just had to get to know each other a little, didn't we, bud?" I petted Spook's wither and dismounted him, nowhere near as gracefully as I would have liked. I was already stiffening up, unused to riding a horse after so long on motorbikes and four-wheelers.

It was good to be eating dinner with a table full of people again. Those few days without Craig, Ally, Scottie, and Jono there were strange. Not because it was uncomfortable, but because it was as if the family had been split in two.

Our family.

Ma had everyone in stitches as she mimicked Nan panicking over the risk of her veggie patch getting eaten. Cows getting through the fence would have meant that it was destroyed.

Waru motioned in the direction of the paddock. "Stray eucalypt just came down. Landed on the fence and punched a hole in it. Sam here had Yindi and me rounding up the cattle with the dogs and putting them into the right paddock again while he worked on the fence and getting the tree cut up."

I could practically see the wheels turning in Scottie's mind, planning out the next few days' work. "We can bring it back tomorrow. Chuck it in the shed and use it for firewood."

Before he got too far into his mental planning, I clarified. "Most of it's done. Still need to clean up the branches but nearly all the trunk is cut. There's still some on the back of the ute, but what I did in the first load is stacked for you."

"What? How'd you manage that with only three of you?" Scottie's gaze bounced between the three of us.

"He worked his arse off, boss. We'll only have an hour or two work out there tomorrow to clean up going by how much he brought back." Waru's praise, between mouthfuls of food, warmed me.

Yindi threw me under the bus, raising an eyebrow at me. "We brought the horses and dogs in so we could get the other ute and go back. We'd just started out when Sam drove past us on his way in."

"You didn't have to do that, Sam. If we all pitched in tomorrow, you wouldn't have had to kill yourself getting it done. You could have just jury-rigged the fence."

Nan placed her hands on the table as if to push up and leaned forward, giving me the stink-eye. She wanted me to feel guilty. I wasn't. "I tried to tell you that, didn't I?"

"You did, Nan," I conceded with a nod, trying to placate her. I needed her to understand—for all of them to under-stand—that I took Scottie's trust seriously. He'd given me a job to do, and I wanted to see it through. It was important that he knew he wouldn't be walking home to a disaster every time he stepped foot off the station on the odd occa-sion that Jono couldn't look after things. "But I didn't want Scottie to come home to a mess. I thought I'd give it a crack and see what I could get done while Waru and Yindi looked after the animals. They worked just as hard. Bloody cows were spread out everywhere."

Dinner had barely wrapped up and I was yawning al-ready. Even though I said I'd just given it a crack, I hadn't. I'd killed myself trying to get the tree cut and loaded as well as the fence mended before Scottie got back. Giving him a reason to trust me was important, but now all I wanted to do was to crash.

"Go on. You look exhausted." Ma patted my shoulder as I rubbed my eyes and tried to stifle my yawn. Every blink was like running my eyelids over sandpaper.

I yawned and took the opportunity to get up from the table. "I am wrecked. Night."

Craig opened the door to our cabin a few minutes after I'd climbed into bed. I barely heard the snick of the door as he shut it. He missed the creaky board outside our bed-room, and he closed the door to the bathroom before turning on the light. "S'all right, mate. You don't need to be tiptoeing around. I'm still awake." I yawned again and pulled the blanket up higher, letting the soft squeak of the fan turning in slow circles lull me into exhausted relaxation.

Craig slipped into his bed a few minutes later and I turned to look at him, tucking my hands under my face. "Thank you. I don't know that I can ever say it enough."

"Your reaction was thanks enough. I know how much you loved Eadie. I couldn't replace her, but when I saw Spook, I needed you to have him." I wanted to reach out to him and hug him for thinking of me. No, for doing more than thinking. Anyone else would have taken a pic and shown me. Craig bought the damn horse so I could have him.

"Scottie said something about Ally not wanting the other bastard to have him. Said he was a dickhead. What was that about?" Craig's lip curled as if he was disgusted, and I propped myself up on my elbow so I wouldn't fall asleep mid-conversation. "Spill."

"First night we were there we went out to the pub for tea. There was this slimy bloke who was flirtin' with Ally when he took our order. Asked her to have a drink with him when his shift was up." I raised an eyebrow at him, a little taken aback at the anger in his voice. "Anyway, turns out this bloke is a handsy son of a bitch. Ally had to push him off her. Me 'n Scottie were already walking over to them when she did it. I nearly put the bloke on his arse. Then we see him at the auction the next day bidding on your horse." He shook his head, ridding himself of the sneer on his lips.

I had no idea how much Spook had cost, but if Craig was bidding against someone he had a grudge against, it would have been high. Ridiculous most likely. I had no doubt that the bloke deserved it, but Craig shouldn't have to pay for it. He was my horse, my responsibility, and I would make sure Craig wasn't out of pocket. "I'll pay you for him. How much was he?"

Craig shook his head, a soft smile playing on his lips. "Nah, mate Just enjoy him. That's enough for me."

I nodded, all sorts of guilty that Craig had used his money to buy Spook. But I knew him well enough not to bother arguing. His loyalty was absolute. The only thing that outmatched it was his stubborn streak. It ran a mile wide. I rubbed my eyes, exhaustion dragging them down. "You were nervous to give him to me."

Craig looked away, and in the dim light I couldn't see it, but I had a feeling he was blushing. His voice was quiet when he huffed out a laugh and agreed, "I was."

"I thought you were gonna tell me something different." I couldn't look him in the eye when I confessed my fear that he'd broken the promise we'd made to each other, and I hated myself for it. But I'd also been gutted thinking I'd lost any chance with Ally. It was stupid—we'd promised each other never to make a move, so I never had a chance with her anyway. Never mind that I thought I'd lost him too. "I thought you and Ally had gotten together. When she went off to get the Landcruiser and Scottie was being all encouraging, I thought he'd set it up and that we'd all be celebrating you two being an item." I shook my head unhappily. "I kinda hated you a little. Then I wanted to kick my own arse because of it. Instead you go buy me a horse and make me feel like an even bigger POS."

Craig didn't say anything for a time. He was fiddling with his doona when I looked up. "I saw red when that bloke was touching her. I wanted to protect her. I'm fallin' for her, man. I know you are too, and I know that we said we wouldn't do anything…"

"But?"

"There is no but." He sighed. "We said we wouldn't make a move and I won't. I can't guarantee I won't wanna kill any bloke who does put his hands on her… But I've got to look at the positives. We'll always be mates even if she does move on. If one of us were with her, it'd leave the other alone, and I dunno that I could handle that. I sure as shit don't want it to be you getting left behind either. So, unless she'll have both of us, it ain't gonna happen."

I huffed out a humourless laugh. "Yeah, nah. As if. She's not that kind of girl."

"She wouldn't want either of us two deros anyway." Craig grinned at me and I laughed.

"Speak for yourself. I'm 100 percent grade-A man here."

Craig laughed again and shook his head. "Yeah, mate, you're as virile as a bull and just as randy."

I chucked my pillow at him and collapsed back onto my bed before getting a face full of it thrown back at me. "You're right though. We don't exactly have much to offer her." Stuffing the pillow under my head again, I watched the fan spin lazily, barely circulating the thick heat hanging in the air. "Should we ask her? I mean, that's stupid isn't it?"

Craig huffed. "That's like asking if you like your balls attached to your body. She seemed to relax with us the other day at the billabong—"

"It's like she's finally feeling comfortable, hey?" I mused, adjusting my semi thinking of her in the water with us, naked. I'd wanted nothing more than to pull her close and kiss her, then pass her to Craig to do the same. My balls tingled as I imagined Craig and I looking after her. But this time when I closed my eyes, it wasn't only her in my arms; Craig was too. The memory sucked the breath out of my lungs. Fifteen-year-old me had wondered what it'd be like to make out with a girl. I'd been worried that I'd screw it up, and I thought asking Craig to practice would be a better idea than fumbling around clueless. But now, lying in this bed, my best friend almost within reaching distance and the woman we'd both been fantasizing about in the main house, I was having an epiphany—did I want both of them? We'd never spoken about our kiss; sometimes I wondered whether I'd dreamed it, but I hadn't imagined the touch of his lips against mine. And I hadn't imagined the desire licking up my spine when I'd caught is gaze and he'd held it—back then and earlier that day.

Craig's words snapped me back into the present. "Yeah. She knows she's safe with us. I don't want her to think for a second that she's not."

I cleared my throat. My voice was rough when I responded. "Me neither."

"Night, mate. Don't want to keep you up."

He was expecting me to fall asleep, but a bomb had just dropped on me. My world had shifted.

I wanted my best friend too.

But there was no way it'd ever happen. Not only was Ally not that kind of girl, Craig sure as hell wasn't that kinda bloke. Was I? I had no idea. But the thought of kissing him again certainly didn't turn me off.

CHAPTER 10

Ally – Five years later

The station was a bit of a bubble. Time marched on and our isolation meant that we largely did our own thing. The freedom was great, but at the same time, the seclusion meant I was kind of stuck too. We went on a ride a few weeks ago, doing exactly the same sort of thing we'd done a million times before, and it occurred to me that I was living in a loop. I was twenty-nine years old and I'd never had a real boyfriend. Hook-ups, sure, but never a relationship. It was kind of pathetic. I knew *who* I wanted, but I also knew it was never going to happen. I wasn't stupid.

Unless I changed, nothing else would. I hadn't exactly intended to go out and find a replacement, but maybe that's exactly what I needed.

Then I'd happened on Phil.

It wasn't love at first sight; I wasn't even sure whether that was a thing. But he was nice enough. That was the problem though. He was... nice. On paper, he was everything a woman would want—he had a steady job, a house, he was settled and looking for a relationship. All those things were great, but there was no spark between us. I thought I could probably grow to feel more for him as things progressed, but we'd caught up a few times and I was still on the fence. I liked him well enough I supposed, but we were probably better off being friends.

It'd all happened pretty quickly. He'd asked me out a few weeks ago, inviting me to join him for drinks. We were at the pub, so I'd literally just shifted tables to sit with him. Was that dating? I hadn't thought it was a big deal, but he'd reacted like he'd won the lotto. It was flattering the way he showed me off to his mates. He'd puffed up his chest, acting like I was the most beautiful woman around. Since then we'd caught up a few more times. They were dates, I supposed, so maybe we were dating. Maybe?

There wasn't much to do in Longreach at night except eat some grub at the pub or in a few of the restaurants the locals knew were decent, or go for a walk along the main street. Even still, Phil had made it as romantic as he could. He'd bought me flowers and had held my hand, pulled my chair out and opened doors for me.

After drinks that first night, we'd taken a walk and he'd kissed me. That was nice too. He was trying, and I was grateful for that. He made me feel special. Appreciated. Desired too. I couldn't say I'd ever really felt that with anyone I'd been with. The hook-ups I'd had were a matter of need and want. There had been plenty of want those times, but the small things he did made me appreciate him. But I still couldn't say that much more than friendship had developed on my end.

He'd been like an eager puppy. Sweet and attentive. Full of energy to show me that he was keen. I could tell he was disappointed when I'd politely refused to go home with him, but he said he understood taking things slow. He still wanted to see me again, so that was nice too. He'd called me the next day asking when I was coming into town again.

That next weekend we'd decided on the movies. I was standing in front of the motel with Craig and Sam while they decided what they were doing when Phil showed up and flashed the tickets he'd bought. Craig and Sam had been talking up going to see the same movie, so I'd invited them along. Going on a double date was fun. At least I thought it was until Phil got a little snippy. Craig hoarded the popcorn as per usual, and Sam and I had ended up in hysterics as we fought him for each handful. Phil didn't join in. He sat there, hoarding his own popcorn with his arms either crossed over his chest glaring at the screen, or awkwardly wrapped around my shoulders.

I felt bad for him; I knew he was trying to make a good impression, so when he asked me to go home with him again, I didn't want to reject him. Letting him down gently seemed like a nicer thing to do, so I suggested that he and I find somewhere we should share an ice cream together instead. The only place open in Longreach at eleven at night are the servos, so we'd ended up in a booth eating Golden Gaytimes before he drove me back to the motel. Sam and Craig were sitting outside their room having a beer when we arrived and patted the third chair they had with them when we'd walked up. Phil didn't bother asking to come

inside, and I didn't invite him either. I think he finally understood that I wasn't ready to do anything more than hold
hands and make out a little.

That night he was coming out to the station to have tea
with us. I thought it was a bit premature, but he insisted
that meeting Nan and Ma was the gentlemanly thing to do.
I was nervous as hell so when Nan snapped at me for pacing
and told me to set the table, I did it just to get my mind off
things. Decades of us sitting in the same spots meant that I
placed the cutlery and mats down without even thinking. It
was automatic now. I should have put more thought into it.

I smoothed down my one and only dress and headed
outside to meet Phil on the veranda when I saw the dust
trail coming down the drive. He stepped out of the car and
I noticed he'd gotten dressed up too. He looked good wearing pressed pants and polished shoes as well as a button-up
shirt. He filled them out nicely.

He came up the stairs and looked me up and down, smiling his approval. "You look lovely. Hi." He kissed me then, a
soft, lingering kiss. I could feel eyes on me, and that had the
blood rushing to my cheeks, making them hot. Self-conscious and awkward, I stepped away and led him inside. I
didn't even realize I hadn't spoken to him until I saw Jono
looking at us. He smiled and nodded when we walked past.

Phil went to open the door, but I put a hand to his chest
stopping him and smiled. "Hi. Thank you for coming."

"It's a hell of a drive. I'm glad you warned me that there
were dirt roads. I wouldn't have thought I was on the right
track otherwise." I didn't like the tone he'd used. I couldn't

figure out if it was annoyed or just unimpressed, but I shook it off. Maybe he was as nervous as me.

"We love it here."

He nodded and opened the door, shifting so I could go inside first. When the door slammed behind him, I flinched. Everyone knew that you didn't let the door slam, didn't they? Conversation ceased and I blanched. Every pair of eyes in the room shifted to us instantly, and I tripped over my words. "Um, ah…" I cleared my throat and watched as gazes skittered around the room, clashing. The silence was deafening.

Scottie rounded the corner from the kitchen with a platter in hand, and he made quick work of setting it down and holding his hand out to Phil. "G'day, mate. I'm Scottie. Nice of you to come out. Ma and Nan have cooked up a feast, so pull up a chair. Make yourself at home."

"Thanks. Nice to meet you."

Still holding Phil's hand, I led him over to Ma who was placing the last tray of freshly baked bread rolls into a basket. Waru was there waiting for her and took the wicker bowl as soon as she'd dropped the final one into it. She looked up and smiled, and I wanted to hide. "Ma, this is Phil."

"Evenin', Phil. Thanks for joining us." She held out her hand and he took it, shaking firmly.

"Nice to meet you, Mrs Pearce. Thanks for having me over." He handed her a bottle of wine that I didn't even realize he'd been carrying, and Ma smiled politely at him. It was the fakest smile I'd ever seen on her. She took the bottle and placed it gently on the bench, making no move to open it.

"Lovely, thank you."

He wrapped an arm around me, puffing up his chest like a proud peacock and the desire to hide flared again. Everything about this felt wrong. His hands on me were possessive, not affectionate. It was as if he was staking his claim. With my mum. That combined with the door slamming and giving us a bottle of grog wasn't a good start to the night.

I could forgive him for the wine. I should forgive him. Phil lived just outside of Goondiwindi. He wasn't city by any means, but it was obvious that he'd never stepped foot on a station. Anyone that had, knew that stations in these parts were almost always dry. We couldn't risk alcohol fuelled violence or the dangers of drunks going walkabout in the middle of the desert or fucking around on machinery, so it was easier to remove the temptation altogether. He either didn't know it or didn't care. I hoped it was the former.

Phil's introduction to Nan was a little smoother. She seemed charmed by his easy smile and he was the consummate gentleman to her. When Ma called everyone to sit down, he led Nan to the head of the table and pulled out her chair. Scottie hiked up an eyebrow and I gave him a backhanded slap to his arm and hissed, "He's trying."

He lowered his head to mine, speaking so only I could hear him. "You actually like this bloke?"

I shrugged. "I s'pose."

Scottie nodded and pursed his lips together. "Okay."

Craig and Sam had already piled their plates up high and were sitting in their usual spots. Nearly everyone was seated too by the time Phil made his way back to me after pouring Nan a glass of chilled water. He wouldn't know it, but Nan never drank it chilled. It hurt her teeth too much, so she always went for the pitcher with the room temperature water in it. Another thing he wasn't to know, but the effort he was putting in with Nan was heartening.

It didn't make me feel any more comfortable though. If anything, I didn't want to be there, and that was squarely my problem. I just couldn't picture this becoming a regular thing. I wondered for half a second whether it would be as uncomfortable with his parents and I dismissed the idea. There was no way in hell I was doing that. No chance I was going to meet his parents. I definitely wasn't at that point. When would I be? I had no idea. I smoothed down my dress again, hating how wearing it made me feel—like an insecure, uncertain teenager.

That therein was the issue. I was uncertain. I had no idea what I was supposed to do. What was the protocol for a date visiting the station? Did I fill up his plate? Did I tell him to sit and wait on him? He was perfectly capable of doing it himself. So, I did nothing. I waited for him to return to me and then passed him a plate and the tongs. He could dish it up himself while I did mine.

I froze mid-step when I saw his eyes dart around the table and his lips purse, his gaze hardening at the back corner. It was where I normally sat. Between Sam and Craig. *Oh shit.* I'd set the table like normal, meaning the only empty seats weren't next to each other. One was between Craig and Sam and the other was directly across from it. I should have shifted my setting over to the other side so I could sit next to him, but nerves and pure force of habit had made me set the places in the same way I always did. We always put visitors across from Sam, Craig and me. But he wasn't supposed to be an ordinary visitor. He was supposed to be my date.

This time it wasn't a desire to hide, but nerves that were clawing in my belly. I hesitated again and Phil nudged me forward with a hand to my lower back. His gaze hadn't left Sam's, who was staring him down with an amused quirk on his lip. Craig wasn't even fazed. He had his free arm resting on the chair I normally sat on while he swapped his glass with Nan's, giving her the tap water.

"So…," Phil asked expectantly with an unimpressed purse to his lips. "Where do you want me?"

"I'll move the setting." I picked up my cutlery and place-mat one-handed and reset it next to his as he sat down. The grin on Phil's lips was more of a sneer. A baring of teeth that was as much about Craig and Sam as it was about me. I didn't like the dick-measuring competition he had going on with them. I didn't like being on edge or constantly second guessing myself, and in the five minutes we'd all been together, I'd managed to do all of it.

Nan passed over my glass and smiled encouragingly at me, but I was already counting down the minutes until it was over. It was going to be a hell of a long night.

And it was.

Nan tried to include Phil in the discussions, but Phil got quieter as the night wore on. Then Craig told him about what we'd done the day before, going to check on a bore that didn't seem to be working properly. We'd stopped by the billabong to see whether there was any water left in it, but it was a puddle. He'd told Phil about going swimming there but warned him about the crocs.

Scottie laughed and between breaking bites off the bread roll he was eating told Phil about our childhood trips to the billabong. "I used to scare Ally when she was little with stories about monster crocs in the billabong. There aren't any for kays, but a five-year-old doesn't know that."

"A bloke in his twenties doesn't know that either when they're not from around here." Craig pointed his fork at me and with a twinkle in his eyes added, "You got us good that day, but the swim afterwards was fun."

I laughed, more of a huff of self-consciousness than anything else, and tried not to flush thinking about that swim. Sam and Craig naked.

"Going for a swim sounds like fun." Phil turned to me, resting his cutlery on his empty plate. "Maybe you could teach me how to ride tomorrow. We could go visit the billabong."

I shook my head and smiled sympathetically at him, thankful for the out. "Ah, no. It's a fair ride—too long for a beginner. You won't be able to move if I made you ride for that long." I motioned around the table. "We've been riding all our lives so it's no big deal for us to spend the day in the saddle, but you won't be able to walk after a few hours. I'd offer to take the ute out there, but the billabong is almost dry. We haven't had any rain here to replenish it for ages."

"Oh. Yeah, I suppose you have smaller water sources than we do in town. Makes sense."

Conversation after that kind of died out as we finished up dinner and Ma dished up baked apples and homemade ice cream for dessert. The sounds of cutlery clinking against bowls were soon over and Sam and Craig got up to clear the table.

Phil was staying the night in the guesthouse, and I took the opportunity to show him to it. With his overnight bag on the floor by the bed, he eyed it and looked at me. It was an open invitation, one that I wasn't sure if I wanted to take up. I knew that once I'd slept with him, he would want to make things more serious. He'd made it clear that he had his future mapped out and was now looking for a woman to slot in beside him. At least I could stall my decision.

"Scottie will be setting up the bonfire. We should join them."

He smiled, but it didn't reach his eyes, and he followed me out. It was awkward between us now, but the night wasn't beyond saving. I just didn't know whether whatever relationship we had was. At least Phil had seemed keen on the bonfire when Scottie suggested it. It was as good a chance as any to distract Phil from Sam and Craig.

Phil immediately went to Scottie over at the woodpile when we walked outside. They had few things in common, but Scottie had at least made an effort to ask Phil about his job and what things he enjoyed doing. Phil seemed to be gravitating to him now, which was good. It left me with a little breathing space. There were things about Phil that I genuinely liked, and I needed to remind myself of that. He was considerate and made an effort. He was romantic too. Small gestures that I had never even considered were important to him. Things like tasting the wine before accepting the bottle and asking for a table in a more private area. He'd said that he wanted to show me that I deserved the best, and he was trying to be that. But he didn't slot in here in my space, and I knew that if we were to take it further, I'd be the one going to him. I doubted he'd make the trip out to the station again, and I wasn't sure if I was relieved or disappointed.

Scottie's awkward attempts at being sociable got a little easier while he and Craig were building the fire. Scottie had chopped up a few logs and tossed them into the pit, getting halfway inside before calling out and offering Phil a drink. While Craig made a mound of smaller twigs and bark, Scottie dashed inside and returned with a bottle of ginger beer for Phil and the lighter. This time, I didn't even feel bad that it wasn't me asking whether Phil wanted a drink.

Sam wrapped his arm around me, and I leaned into him, watching their interactions. Phil said something to Scottie and Craig shook his head, rolling his eyes. Scottie pointed to the stumps on the ground and Phil's eyes widened before he chuckled. Even I could tell it was forced. "Wow. He really doesn't do the outdoors, does he?" Sam looked down to me and met my glare with a quirk of his lips. "Sorry, not my place to say anything about him." His gaze travelled over my face and down my body, lighting me up inside. When his tongue darted out to wet his bottom lip and he tilted my chin up to meet his gaze again, my breath caught. The searing heat, the naked desire in his stare stole my breath. It didn't matter to my body though. It was as if he'd flicked a switch inside me, leaving me a quivering pile of wanton need with just a heated look from those soulful browns. I involuntarily pressed closer to him, even though I knew it was so very wrong. His long-term secret partner was only a few metres away from us. Oh, and my date too.

I shook myself out of it. That right there was the very definition of stupidity. I'd repeated the same mantra to myself for years. *Don't fall for the gay guys.* I'd failed. But now I was deluding myself into thinking that his... annoyance maybe, derision perhaps, was desire.

Sam cleared his throat and my gaze was drawn to those pouty lips that I would do almost anything to kiss. *No!* To watch Craig kiss. "Can I tell you that you look beautiful?"

Struck dumb, I nodded.

"Well then, you look beautiful. He's a lucky guy."

An hour later and Scottie had retired, leaving Phil and me, Craig and Sam around the fire. They'd wrapped me in a blanket to ward off the cold of the autumn night and ducked inside to make me a Milo when I was still shivering. Phil awkwardly wrapped an arm around me but hadn't made any further moves. It surprised me, but at the same time I was glad he was getting the idea that I just wasn't feeling it. I supposed my backing away from the bed earlier had given him enough of a hint. I wasn't averse to sex—it'd been a damn long time since I'd had any—but it was hard to get excited about the prospect of getting naked with him when I was struggling to get past the notion of him being well… nice.

That was the issue.

I couldn't think of an adjective other than nice to describe him.

When I yawned, Phil rubbed his hand along my back and surprised me again. "Why don't you head off to bed? You've had a long day."

"Oh. You sure?" He must have seen the surprise in my gaze because he smiled and stood, nodding a goodnight to Craig and Sam. "Um…"

"Ally, I don't think we're meant for each other. You're nice and all, and I could see myself having a future with you, but I don't like competing, or being a third wheel. I'll head off first thing tomorrow." He turned and walked away, not even giving me a chance to respond. He didn't pause in his journey up the guesthouse steps and in the door. I opened my mouth, thinking I should say something to him, but then I realized I didn't care enough to stop him.

So instead of calling out to him, I tugged my blanket tighter around my shoulders and walked around the fire. I didn't even need to say a word. Sam and Craig shifted, opening more space between them and I sat down. "I just got dumped."

"He didn't deserve you anyway." Craig wrapped an arm around me, pulling me close. Sam leaned in too, rubbing his hand down my back. I wasn't an idiot. I knew Phil had meant that he didn't want to be in competition with Sam and Craig. If only he was. If only they showed more than brotherly love for me. It was ironic that Phil had just broken up with me because of them. In reality, they weren't even playing on the same cricket pitch as me. Hell, we weren't even playing the same sport.

At least being single meant that I didn't need to worry about blokes getting their nose out of joint because of my friendship with them.

Now all I needed to do was remember that they were out of reach.

CHAPTER 11

Ally – Seven years later

I was in a rut. No, I was in the bottom of one of those opal mine shafts that delve straight down into the ground with sheer, unscalable walls. I was in so deep that it was perpetually dark. I needed a break. I needed a change. Life wasn't what I thought it would be. I hadn't gotten laid in forever, but I hadn't really wanted to either. Every time I went into Longreach, I met the same people. I was chatted up by the same blokes who used the same lines on me. I'd hang with the same friends and do the same thing. Every weekend. Week in, week out. Just for a change I'd started going to church with Ma and Nan, staying home on Saturday nights and driving in just for Sunday morning. I just kept on digging that damn hole even deeper.

I was bored.

I was unhappy.

Dad had invited me to stay with him in Sydney for a while, and even though the city wasn't for me, I'd been thinking about moving there just for a change of pace.

I always thought that life would have... more. More smiling. More affection. More love. It wasn't that I wasn't happy with my family. I knew they loved me, and we laughed together all the time. But it wasn't what I really wanted. I was lonely. I was a thirty-five-year-old woman who'd never had a boyfriend—unless you counted the disastrous stint dating Phil—and I lived like a bloody nun.

I was frustrated and angry. I wanted to blame fate for dealing me a shitty hand of cards, but I couldn't even do that. It was my fault and because of that, I was sad. More than anything else, it was melancholy that hovered over me.

I wanted to be swept off my feet. Romanced and wined and dined. I wanted to curl up on the couch with my man and cuddle. Naked. I wanted kissing and sex, but I wanted more too. And I was never going to get it here. I'd been half in love with two men for a decade, but they just weren't into me, and that was okay. I wasn't self-centred enough to think that the world revolved around me, or that Sam and Craig would suddenly become bisexual after a couple of decades together. They were gay. Not that anyone knew it—not even me for sure. They'd never confided in me. Still. They were hesitant to advertise their relationship to the world, and I understood that. But we'd been mates for so long that their failure to tell me hurt more than them not being into me. I wouldn't rock the boat—I could guess how uncomfortable a working environment that would make for—so I respected their choice not to tell me. What else could I do? Their friendship meant too much to me to risk it by outing them, even if I could wait until it was just the three of us around to ask.

Seeing them together though broke my heart. They had the kind of relationship I'd always wanted. It was rock solid, unwavering for so long that sometimes I took for granted that relationships weren't always as picture perfect as theirs. And yet, there was never more than a secretive look between them. A knowing glance. Their touches didn't linger. They never stood too close or showed any kind of affection to each other than the blokey kind between mates.

Even if I couldn't have what they had, I still wanted Craig and Sam to be themselves around me. We spent enough time together that they should know I'd never judge them for loving each other. I thought they would have figured that out by now, but they never wavered. Never even hinted it. Then I realized that maybe they just didn't know how to bring it up after so long. Or maybe they just didn't trust me. I couldn't help but pull away. For every night I spent with them, it was one less that they could curl up together on the couch or while away the hours in bed together. It was precious time that was passing us all by and I wouldn't be responsible for them not having any alone time anymore.

So, my options were to keep doing what I was doing and stay stuck in my rut or shake things up a little. I'd tried dating in Longreach and that had failed spectacularly. Maybe I needed to look further afield.

But first, we had a visitor arriving at the station, and then a muster to run. It was going to be a few hectic weeks.

I loved being out there though, and if I did take up Dad's offer to move, this muster would be my last time out in the desert. I wanted to enjoy every moment. Days on horseback and nights sleeping out there in the open, lying on the sandy red dirt and looking at a sky full of stars while the warmth of the fire seeped into my bones. It was one of my favourite things.

The couple of days of mending fences that we'd just returned from had been hard work and I'd been dusty and sore. Last night was almost worth it though. A perfectly clear sky. A campfire. Billy tea, damper cooked in coals, and a stew that we'd warmed in a pot hanging above the fire. Then afterwards, Waru and Yindi told us about Yindingie and the Catfish. It was a story of the rainbow god turning a man into a fish when he'd boasted about his swimming abilities, despite never having tried to swim.

But then everything had come crashing down. I wasn't sure whether they gravitated to each other in their sleep and needed me between them to keep some distance, or whether Craig and Sam believed they needed to protect me like they would their baby sister. Whatever their reason, I slept between them, just like I did every time we were out in the open. It was both infuriating and achingly sweet. It made me want to run in the opposite direction; reaching out to them wasn't an option.

No, being loved by them was an impossible dream, and the pain of wishing for it for over a decade was made even worse by the rumours that had resurfaced at the pub. Rumours that both Craig and Sam had hooked up with different ladies. I knew that they needed to keep their relationship under wraps and crafting stories of their exploits with women was the best way to do it. But their need to even start the rumours broke my heart. The thought of them having to go through with it to quell any doubts, killed me. I'd blinked away the tears of betrayal, angry tears borne of frustration and injustice for two men who loved each other and couldn't say "bugger it" to the world and simply be true to themselves.

They were tears I had no right to cry. But cry I did when I thought of how Sam's heart would break as he imagined Craig giving himself to a woman, or how Craig would have had to fight every protective instinct in him as Sam got intimate with a lady he had no interest in. They'd slept soundly beside me while I'd cried, and when my tears had dried, I'd watched the twinkle of the stars overhead, praying to the universe to lay out the path I should take.

Should I stay, or should I go?

But unlike The Clash's classic song, it wasn't someone else who needed to tell me. It was my own heart. My own future that needed to be decided. Waru and Yindi's story had come back to me then: the catfish forever trying to shift back into human form so he could take his place in his tribe, lost because of a lie. He'd built a Bora Ring in the creek and swum endlessly in circles trying to undo Yindingie's magic. Would that be me? Swimming in circles forever, wanting and wishing for two men I couldn't have? That's what staying would mean. Or I could leave, strike out to Dad's. Maybe try uni.

Weary, I dried my hair with the towel in my hands and watched the dust being kicked up by the vehicle coming down the long drive. When the black ute pulled up at the station, its tray filled as high as its roof and covered with a tarp, I knew our visitor was serious about staying as long as he'd planned. I grinned, excitement at meeting the new guy zinging through me. Throwing on a pair of jeans and a tee, I jogged down the wide timber stairs and stuck my head through the door. Scottie sat at our long table looking more uncomfortable than I'd ever seen him. Fidgeting and tense, his jaw was clenched, and his ears were as red as the flush that had crept up his neck. I bit my lip and grinned, trying not to laugh at my poor brother. He was a good bloke, the best in fact, but he used staying at home and hiding as a coping mechanism for anything outside his comfort zone. I figured that our guest—Peter, I thought his name was—had just unwittingly shattered my brother's delusion that by marooning himself like an island, nothing unfamiliar would ever intrude.

"Hey, new guy," I greeted, still smiling, and not even feeling remotely sorry for my brother's discomfort. "Scottie here has no manners, and Nan and Ma will keep you chatting all day. Want me to show you round before tea?"

Peter looked at Scottie, then smiled at me and I had to bite back a laugh at Scottie's scowl. I liked this guy already, purely for being able to ruffle Scottie's perpetual calm. "Sure."

He was cute in a nerdy kind of way. Really young too. He couldn't have been much more than twenty, but maybe it was his pale skin dotted with freckles and his fiery red hair that gave him a babyface. "I'm Ally." I shook his hand and smiled.

"Pete or Macca. I'll answer to both. Nice to be here. Thanks for having me."

"You're welcome. We're pleased to have you. Come on, I'll show you round." I pointed out the comfortable couch that took up most of the lounge room. "You've got a tele in the guesthouse, but this one here is bigger and we all tend to gather together one or two nights a week. You're welcome over anytime."

We wandered outside and I helped him unload his duffel and a smaller satchel stuffed full of books and a laptop before taking him to the guesthouse. "This here is where you'll be staying. You've got three meals daily included in your rates, so don't hesitate to join us for brekkie, lunch, and tea. When we're on the muster, it'll just be you, Ma, and Nan. Jono will be there for a bit in the mornings too. But don't worry, you're still welcome at the table even though most of us will be gone."

We entered the guesthouse and the history practically spoke to me. Memories of generations of Pearces were within these walls. Ma had crawled on the floorboards as a babe in arms, and Pop before her had done the same. It'd been the station's gathering place for four generations. Only Scottie and I had grown up in the main house, thanks to Dad insisting that we needed more space when he'd moved here. Since Pops passed and Nan had shifted into the main house, it had languished, deteriorating as it lay vacant. We'd asked Jono if he wanted to move in, but he was happy in his little cabin. Waru and Yindi had said the same. Now, since its restoration we'd been able to rent it out and keep the house in a state Pops would have been proud of. Making a few bucks from it had been a bonus; I hadn't thought it'd actually be popular, but we often had people stay.

Macca quickly dropped everything on the kitchen table and looked to me. "Righteo, where to now?"

We walked to the springer paddock, then across to the big shed, worker's cottages, and back towards the main house via the veggie patch, before heading over to the paddock abutting the stables where the horses were. "So, you ridden before?" I opened the gate and whistled for 'Tella so I could say hello. Our horses were gathered around feeding on the hay bale we'd dropped fresh in there that morning, but she cantered over when I called her, kicking up the fine red dust as she moved. She was pissed with me for having gone away overnight and not taken her. It was obvious in the way she kept coming, moving closer without slowing, only to stop short a few feet from me. Shaking her mane and stamping her foot, my horse huffed and nudged me, playfully pushing me back a step.

"Hey, girl," I soothed. Macca barked out a laugh when my ungrateful shit of a horse nudged me again. "Yeah, yeah. I know I haven't been to see you in a coupla days. Feels like we haven't been riding in ages. But I bought a peace offering. Here." I held out the apple I'd snagged from the fruit bowl in the guest house and explained to Macca, "This is 'Tella, short for Nutella."

"She's beautiful. Big too. The others aren't as big as she is, are they?" His tone was uncertain, and I could see him edging back behind me, clearly not wanting to get closer.

Side-eyeing him, I sighed. "You aren't confident with 'em, are you?" My tone was harsher than I meant it to be.

"I've ridden before, but it was a long time ago. I just didn't want to overstep boundaries. What are the rules about petting a lady's horse?"

I couldn't help my reply. He'd walked straight into it. "It's not the same as petting a lady, so feel free to give her a rub." His reaction—absolute shock and embarrassment— had me biting down on my lip as I stifled a laugh.

"Ah…" He hesitated, blushing a fiery red. He was a shy one, and so very young and innocent-looking. He reached forward, tentatively petting her. The wonder in his eyes made me smile; she was undoubtedly beautiful.

Macca's gaze scanned our surrounds and I watched him, imagining seeing our property through his eyes. Appreciating how truly special this land was. The never-ending blue of the sky was a shade unlike anywhere else I'd ever seen. It was as if it took the red of the dirt as a challenge to see which of them could glow brighter, the saturation of the colours reaching a level that was unique to the outback. The only thing that was faded was the vegetation. Soft blue-greys and muted greens that spoke of the struggle to survive. It was a surprise that there was even anything left standing. We were in the grips of the longest, harshest drought we'd ever seen. Years without rain.

My decision on whether or not to leave teetered on the edge of my consciousness. I'd walked away once before and returned, unable to shake the pull of the land calling me back to her. Could I do it again? Would it stick this time? Was it really an option? I wasn't sure, but I couldn't ignore it anymore. The thought had been niggling away in the corner of my mind longer than I'd cared to admit.

Macca had walked away, and I wondered if he'd spoken to me. I hoped not. I didn't want to seem rude to our new intrepid traveller. Jogging to catch up to him, I explained, "Scottie's horse is Tilly. She's a buckskin."

I listened with one ear to their interaction, the quiet hum of conversation between them as they bonded over Tilly. Scottie was obviously comfortable around our family, but he rarely interacted with others away from the station. He did a road trip twice a year, insisting that he go by himself. Once to Brissie and the other to Sydney, each time for the agricultural shows. No doubt when he was away, he'd spend all his time with the cattle. He was a loner most of the time. But it made me smile listening to the quiet appreciation in Scottie's voice as he explained that his horse was usually as standoffish as he was. Macca focussed all his wide-eyed concentration on my brother and Scottie relaxed, opening up to him. It was good to see. He needed it. But then Macca's attention shifted to me and he was smiling, and Scottie was gone with a huff. I wasn't sure what had happened, but Scottie's mercuriality was a shock. He was so even-tempered, so calm all the time that it drove me batshit crazy sometimes.

I looked at the setting sun and my stomach rumbled as if it were on a timer. "Dinner's up. Freshen up and come straight back to the house. I'll see you in there."

We'd booked the trucks weeks in advance so that they arrived to collect the cattle the day after the muster. When the booking for the accommodation came in over the same timeframe, we knew it'd be a juggle. Ma and Nan would stay at the homestead, and Jono returned there every evening after being in the air all day with the chopper, so Macca wouldn't be alone. But we usually liked to have a few more hands on deck with a visitor, just in case they decided they wanted to go on a trail ride or try learning the myriad skills that city-folk had no opportunity to try out.

Scottie had thought about rearranging the muster, but Ma and Nan insisted they'd be fine. Turned out, they were. As soon as Macca learned more about the muster, he'd been raring to go. The way he'd carried on that first morning riding his four-wheeler was ridiculous. Whooping and laughing, he was in his element. Who would have thought that the city boy would fit in so well? He was a good bloke. Fun to be around too. But the more I watched him, especially the way he interacted with Scottie, the more I suspected he was carrying a secret—one that gave him a fair amount in common with Sam and Craig. It wasn't anything specific which gave it away, but he seemed to hang off Scottie's every word. The blushes and the shy glances when he thought no one was looking had only confirmed my suspicion.

Escaping the circle of our group, I sought out some space. God, what I would do to have a man look at me like that. The loneliness bubbling under the surface of my skin flared. I was a mess, my emotions swinging like a pendulum from one extreme to another in a matter of seconds.

I went to 'Tella. She was my getaway. My loyal, beautiful friend. Leaving the station meant leaving her too. That knowledge had kept me up more nights than I could count. But I was here now, and I'd cherish every moment I had with her. I ran my hands over her, soothing myself with her warmth. I got lost in the motion, trying to get a hold of my wayward heart and head.

"Can I help?" a soft voice asked. Macca

"Just checking her over. Making sure she's right for another go."

He joined me, petting Nutella and running his hands down her neck and legs. He reached down, plucking something out of the short hairs on her cannon, the lower part of her leg. 'Tella shook her head and nudged him. "Got something?" I asked.

"Just a husk or something. Didn't want it sticking into her."

"Thanks," I said brightly, forcing a smile. I looked around and motioned in a wide arc with my hand. "You're loving it, aren't you?"

He grinned, his smile lighting up his face. "Totally. Best day of my life."

"It's good you're settling in. You're good for him." I kept my voice low so that no one else would hear us, but he stiffened, looking around in a panic. I was right.

"Scottie and I have become friends."

"Unless I'm reading you completely wrong, you're crushing on him. The looks, the smiles, spending your day glued to his hip." I hadn't meant to confront him. Forcing him to come out to me hadn't been my intention. I wasn't trying to scare him either, but Scottie wasn't gay, and I hated the possibility of a misunderstanding arising between them because of a crush. He paled, and I instantly regretted saying anything, but I needed to explain myself. "I dunno how he'd handle it if he found out that you're sweet for him, but he's kinda clueless anyway, so you should be safe." He visibly swallowed and failed to school the panic in his expression. I rested a hand on his forearm. "Hey, I'm not gonna tell anyone. Your secret's safe with me."

He looked like he had no idea what to say. "Yeah, um... Have I been that obvious?"

"Only to someone who's not used to seeing new people round."

"Oh great, so everyone." He threw up his hands and huffed.

"Don't worry about the rest of them. It'd never even cross their minds that you're gay or bi or whatever." Well, some of them maybe; I had a feeling at least Craig knew. "Hero-worshipping Scottie maybe, but they'll never think you're attracted to him." I smiled, trying to ease his concerns. "For the record, it makes no difference to me. You're a youngin', but you fit in here; that's what's important."

"Thanks, Ally. I appreciate you saying that."

"All good here?" Craig asked, his big arms crossed over his chest and a scowl on his face as he stared Macca down.

"Yeah, mate." I breezed by him, unable to be in his proximity at that moment. My emotions were too close to the surface and seeing Craig protective and snarky at our newcomer had me wanting to climb him—ironic when he was acting like an overbearing big brother. I plucked my water bottle from the saddlebag and took a swig, hiding from conversation with the others.

We continued on, moving the cattle towards home in a steady drive. Nutella's hoof beats and her steady sway underneath me rocked me gently. The wind in my hair and the winter sun on my face had me smiling, then choking on the dust thrown up by the cattle. A fine, fiery-red haze floated around us, coating our skin and getting into everything. Our wet season was in summer, so our winters were always drier, but this drought had persisted for years. The endless stretch of blue skies was beautiful, but desperation had set in too. I wished rain would fall. I'd give anything for it to happen.

Making camp that night, we all ended up in our normal positions. Except for Scottie. Scottie had pushed his swag out further than he normally would have and told Macca to get in closest to the campfire. Macca looked at Scottie like he'd hung the moon and Scottie's lips quirked up in a smile. It was gone quickly, but the ghost of it remained in his eyes. He was happy and I was grateful for the friendship developing between them. It seemed to be pulling Scottie out of his self-imposed exile.

I looked at the two men who insisted I sleep between them and sighed. I was sick of being the buffer between them after so many years.

We laid down and the sounds of the night filtered through the quiet. The lowing of the cattle, the crackle of the fire. A howl cut through the air, the mob shifting and mooing, a frisson of disquiet passing through them. Then a bark. Scottie and Macca were talking quietly, Scottie explaining that the howl had come from dingoes and the bark was from a feral dog. He'd seen tracks earlier in the day. It was a big dog and by the looks of it, was crossbreeding with the dingo. The family pack had more pups than a full-blooded dingo pair would produce and feeding them in this landscape—the dry desolation caused by the drought—would be difficult.

More calls. From different places. They were surrounding the mob, looking for weaknesses. A sliver of unease passed through me this time. If they attacked, the mob could stampede. We'd have no hope of getting out of the way in time if they headed in this direction.

"If they attack, will they avoid us?" Macca asked. "I'm guessing they're going for the cattle, but will they keep away from the fire or do they need the light?"

There was a pause before Scottie answered. "They're avoiding us—usually use the cover of darkness for sneak attacks. Maybe if we made some fires round the mob, we could buy a few hours' sleep."

Macca rolled onto his side to face Scottie "Or we could split up and build a perimeter of campfires? Rather than moving around all night stoking fires, we could just stay out there with each one."

"Everyone's had a long enough day. To have to do more tonight'd—"

"You two gonna put a lid on it? Some of us wanna get some shut-eye," Dennis, the new guy who wasn't really new—he'd been here for going on eight years—grumbled from next to us, our heads not too far away from each other. Rather than whack him with my makeshift pillow, I opened my mouth to respond, but Macca beat me to it.

"Mate, can you not hear the howls? I'd rather keep the mob safe, wouldn't you?"

Waru spoke from across the campfire. "The dingo are hungry. Fires around the cattle might work to ward off a hunt."

"So, we do that then." I sat up, put my jacket on and shook out my boots. Craig and Sam were moving too, and Den sighed and began shuffling around. I paid no attention to him.

Scottie sat up, surveying each of us. "If we're gonna do this, everyone's got to take a gun. Keep it loaded and next to you. You hear anything, see anything, you fire. Anyone hears a shot, get there, quick smart. Our safety is our number-one priority, right?"

We all agreed, and Scottie continued, "Right, Waru, Yindi, and Den you stay here." In a move so typically Den, he made a happy sigh and I rolled my eyes. Den was a great help around the station and a good enough bloke, but he loved his sleep above all else—even more than the bottle of Bundy that accompanied him everywhere he went off the station. "Craig, Sam, and Ally, you three go to the northern edge of the mob. Take the ute. Radios on and keep an ear out." Then to Macca, he added, "We'll go to the southwestern corner on the four-wheelers. Let me grab a couple of logs off the back of the ute so we don't run out of fuel for the fire, and we can go."

It only took a few minutes, and we were off, slowly circling the mob to our position in the north. The ute lurched to the right as Sam navigated over ruts in the ground and super soft patches of sandy dirt. Sitting between the two of them, I slid, pressing into Sam before he righted the vehicle and I straightened. Craig wrapped his arm around me, holding me to him until we pulled to a stop a ways away from the cattle.

"I'll get a few twigs to get the fire going if you can make a clearing and get the logs into place." Craig pulled the torch out of the glovebox and clicked it on, shining it into the distance before bringing it closer in. There were no reflections from eyes, and the relief that coursed through me was like a weight being lifted off my shoulders. Sam and I worked from the light cast by the ute's headlights, clearing away dried grass and piling it up before striking a match and beginning the campfire. Craig was back a moment later, snapping sticks to use as kindling until the fire was hot enough to burn the logs. They'd burn through the night, giving us warmth for hours.

Before I had the chance to get my swag, Sam was laying them out, putting me between them again. Something in me snapped. In my mind's eye, I could see the highlight reel from my life and the picture wasn't anything like I had imagined it would be. I'd grown up with women who took no shit. They were strong and independent. They didn't need a man to be happy. Both had achieved far more than any man thought them capable of, and I loved them for it. I loved that I'd learnt I could do the same. I knew I didn't need to map out my life according to some arbitrary timeline of getting married, having kids and watching my husband go out and achieve his dreams. I think it was one of the reasons why Phil and I could never have worked out. But I'd let staying strong and independent come at the expense of building the life I'd really wanted. I'd coasted along, being satisfied with mediocrity rather than chasing what I really wanted. I hadn't wanted to rock the boat—the risk of having to leave my family and friends and my home had pushed me to a standstill. I'd acted out of a fear for far too long.

Did I keep going how I had been? I couldn't do it. Not now that I'd finally woken up to see just what I was giving up. But I had no idea what to do about my future. What would it hold? I wanted to share my life, fall in love. Start a family. I wanted to grow old with someone.

Or more than one someones.

But that was never going to happen.

If I wanted to chase happiness, it meant leaving. It meant giving up everything important to me to find the path I was meant to take. The city hadn't been the place for me years ago, and now I knew that the outback wasn't my place either. I didn't want to leave. I didn't want to walk away from my job, my family, my home. I knew that once that happened, the ties were invariably cut. Nothing would be the same between us again. Dad had shown me that. Same with my aunts who lived in Brisbane—Ma rarely spoke with them.

But what other choice did I have? Waste another decade? Two? Nan had told me once when Craig and Sam had first moved here that I'd know when to act when the time was right, and I'd found the bloke for me. I'd lived in hope for so long, but at the same time, I knew that being with the men I wanted was an impossible dream. Turning my back on Craig and Sam would break my heart, but continuing to live in the shadow of their love would bleed me dry.

The irony of what had shoved me the rest of the way to my realization wasn't lost on me. A gay man pining over a straight one, while I was a straight woman pining over two gay men. It was the makings of a 90s sitcom. But the way

Macca looked at Scottie, like he was meeting his childhood hero in the flesh—pure adoration, awe and wonder all in one look—made me wish for that too. Desperately.

It was kind of pathetic how unlike the strong, independent women who'd raised me I was. They never would have let themselves fall so deep into the rut I was currently in. I'd settled. I'd coasted along in life, waiting for things to change but knowing they wouldn't. Repeating the same thing over and over and wishing for a different outcome.

But I couldn't do it anymore. I couldn't keep pretending to be happy. I needed to stop letting life pass me by and grasp the bull by the horns so I could ride that bastard. It was time for me to chase what I wanted. I just didn't have any clue how to do it.

I needed to be honest with Sam and Craig—not about the way I felt for them, that wouldn't do any good. But letting them in on what I wanted my future to look like would be a start. I owed them that after our years of friendship, even if they didn't trust me with their secrets. More than a decade's worth of friendship was between us. Maybe me coming forward to them would be the push they needed to unburden themselves too.

All I knew was that I couldn't sleep between them. Not that night, not any other one. "Guys, you don't need to do this. I don't need to be between you."

"Yeah you do." Craig's response was simple, and it showed just how much he thought it was perfectly normal for us to sleep that way. It may have been that way in the past, but starting now, I was changing things.

"Seriously, I don't." I picked up my swag and moved it, before shifting theirs closer together. "We've been friends for a decade. You don't have to hide with me anymore."

"What?" Sam asked, his brow furrowed, his gaze snapping to Craig before settling on me again. I couldn't see their expressions, but I knew in that silent moment a hundred unspoken words would have been said.

I wished I could communicate with them as easily.

I rubbed my forehead, frustration and exhaustion setting in with a headache that was starting to pound behind my eyes. It was late. Maybe I needed to let it go for the night. "It doesn't matter." I sighed. "But I'm not sleeping between you. The two of you can sleep next to each other."

Craig shrugged and picked up his swag, moving it to the other side of the fire so that the three of us were surrounding it, rather than in our usual formation.

"Ally, what were you talking about?" Sam asked when we were lying down, the quiet crackle of the fire and the lowing of the cattle the only noises in the quiet of the night.

I puffed up my bag, shifting the contents so it was more comfortable to use as a pillow. "Let's not talk about it now, Sam. I need some sleep." My words were clipped, frustration more at myself rather than with them colouring my tone. He didn't deserve any attitude, but I was broken, unable to censor my emotions anymore.

I closed my eyes, blocking out their questioning gazes and refused to deal with the discomfort that was now hovering between us like a bad smell. Sleep didn't come easily, but I must have drifted off at some point, because when I blinked my eyes open, the sun was cresting the horizon, lighting the grey sky and turning it into a pale blue. It would increase in its brilliance throughout the day. Another perfect one no doubt.

I looked around only to see that Sam and Craig had moved their swags, bracketing mine so we lay in the shape of a boomerang curled around the fire. I shook my head and sadness overwhelmed me. Frustration too. Shaking out my boots, I slipped out of my swag and pulled them on before doing the same to my Drizabone jacket.

Dew had beaded on the suede, but it had done its job keeping me warm all night in the near zero temperatures out in the desert. I tipped the remainder of my water bottle over the fire before mixing the ashes and embers and taking Sam's water bottle from his outstretched hand. Once I was satisfied the logs were cool to touch and wouldn't reignite from the heat, I handed it back to him and rolled up my swag. The sun was higher in the sky now, and I heard the thwap, thwap, thwap of the chopper in the distance. Jono was on his way with our brekkie and fresh water supplies. We'd agreed to meet back at the original campsite to eat and begin the trek home. I made to move, ready to drop my rolled-up swag into the ute, but Craig grasped my wrist, standing close to me to stop me from walking away. Sam bracketed my other side, running a hand down my back to rest at my waist. "You okay, Ally?"

I shook my head and blew out a breath. "We need to talk. The three of us. I have something I need to tell you and I need you to know that you can tell me things too. I understand if you don't want to tell me, but I need you to know you can. And that it's okay."

"What is it you need to tell us?" Sam asked.

Jono circled in the chopper overhead and I indicated to it. "Now isn't the time. Maybe when we get back."

"Okay," Craig agreed. "Maybe we can talk tonight after tea."

CHAPTER 12

Craig

I'd looked nervously over Ally's head at Sam. What the hell did she want to tell us? Whatever it was, she wasn't happy. We'd noticed it for weeks—she was pulling away, turning us down whenever we invited her over. But she'd never shut us down like she'd done last night and now she wanted to talk? My gut churned, anxiety swirling around. Sam looked just as ill as me, worry lines pinching around his eyes and his lips pressed into a thin line.

Her shoulders slumped and head down, Ally made her way over to the ute and slid into the middle seat. Sam tossed me the keys and I jogged over to the driver side. The short trip was quiet, not a single word spoken between us, which just served to ratchet up the tension. As soon as I'd pulled up, she nudged Sam to get out and she was gone, striding over to the fire, and reaching for the cup of billy tea Yindi was holding out to her. Disquiet settled in my bones and I shivered.

"Any idea what's going on?" I shook my head at Sam's question, and he blew out a breath. "This doesn't feel like good news."

"Yeah. Nah."

We were within cooee of the homestead. Another half-day trip and we'd be home. Sam and I were in the ute, while the others were on horseback, the four wheelers, or in the chopper. We were driving back and forth, working with Jono to push the mob forward and keep the strays in line.

My body was weary, my mind running in circles all day. Pulling up at the gate nearest to the sheds was a relief, but our day wasn't even close to being over. I jumped out to open the gates to the smaller springer paddocks so we could sort the mob ready for the trucks to arrive in the next couple of days. We'd be herding the bulls—both Blond and Zeus included—and the weaned bull calves into one paddock. In the other, we'd sort the cattle being sold for beef production, with the rest of the mob being let into the smaller paddock so we could keep a closer eye on them during calving.

The homestead right across from the yard was beckoning me to sneak off and have a decent wash, albeit one that I'd be having with a sponge and a bucket of water. A sleep in a soft bed would be welcome too. Until then though, I had work to do.

Ma and Nan watched from the veranda as we pulled in. I waved, smiling, and noticed Sam doing the same from the ute. I could imagine the sight from their perch. A cloud of dust in the distance, coming closer. The thwap thwap thwap of the chopper as it circled and swooped, and the rumble of the four-wheeler engines drowned out with the mooing of the cattle as they neared the end of their journey on Pearce Station. The family returning home, coming back safe and sound after days away. They'd be proud of seeing how hard their children had worked. We cared as much for the beasts in our charge as they did. It was more than Pearce Station's livelihood; they were good, honest people who wanted to create harmony so everything could thrive.

I could imagine what it was like for Nan to have waited for her husband to return home too, when Ma was a kid watching her dad gallop in on horseback like a hero of the wild west. I knew from speaking with Ally that her dad had never once gone on a muster—it was always Ma riding in on high. I wondered if he'd ever experienced the swell of pride at seeing the stock so carefully nurtured from calves on wobbly legs to fully grown with calves of their own—the circle of life being played out before his eyes, and the relief in seeing his family come home safe after making such an arduous journey. Of being there to welcome them home. It was as if history was replaying itself. A pattern that had repeated generation after generation on this land, season after season. The simple act one that had happened countless times, but with every occurrence, it left those involved with a sense of both relief and wonder. The tradition and the history gave it a certain romance, and when I closed my eyes, I wondered whether anyone would ever be waiting for me.

We made quick work of getting the already saddled Daisy and Spook out of their stalls in the shed, momentarily leaving the mob in the others' capable hands. We were in the midst of the cattle within moments.

Sam was a hell of a picture riding Spook. The horse moved elegantly, his movements fluid as Sam directed him with a nudge of his heel or a shift in his weight on the saddle. Holding the reins loosely, giving Spook the freedom he needed to respond, Sam exuded confidence and skill that was… sexy. The more I thought of it, yeah, sexy was a bloody good description. Long and lean, tanned skin, and work-roughened hands. Dusty and tired and yet still loving every minute on his beloved horse.

The dogs twisted and turned, like they'd been doing the whole muster at Ally's command until I saw her dismount and sprint towards the fence. Vaulting it in one go, Ally barely slowed down, running towards the homestead. My heart instantly in my throat, I looked around trying to figure out what was happening. Then I saw it. Scottie was standing over Macca, the other man on his arse in the dirt. Scottie looked thunderous, anger radiating off him in waves. "Sam," I called, and motioned to the goings on over the fence with a tilt of my head.

"Shiiit," he breathed. "Man, what the fuck's the newbie done?"

"Whatever it is, he's about to get his arse whooped for it."

We were off our mounts running to the fence in a heartbeat, climbing it and jumping down as Scottie stormed off. Ally looked up at us and the devastation she wore stopped me in my tracks. She shook her head and her shoulders fell, before I watched her pull herself together again. Taking a deep breath in, she squared her shoulders, raised her jaw and hardened her glare. She nodded to us and even though I wanted to help, I knew she had it under control.

Our dismissal came with her words "You heard my brother. You've got ten minutes to pack your shit up and leave."

We stood there, shoulder to shoulder wanting to help, but knowing that it wouldn't be welcomed. I didn't know how, but I knew it was something that Ally needed to do. Maybe not for her, but for Scottie. I'd never seen his feathers ruffled. He was always so calm and collected. He never flinched at hard work; he was always the first to get stuck in and the last to finish. We were all mates, but he held himself apart from us too. He was a loner, and yet in the week that Macca had been here, the two of them had clicked. Whatever Macca had done to get himself kicked off the station, it was bad. Scottie came galloping out of the shed on Tilly, barking orders, and staring daggers at us as he rode by. I sighed and followed Sam, back to the fence and over it to get to our mounts waiting patiently for us.

Adrenaline was wearing thin and exhaustion was setting in. I was only half watching what I was doing, my eye over my shoulder waiting for Ally to emerge from the guesthouse. But Scottie's harsh words made me snap to attention. "Allyra," he yelled, full naming her for the first time in the decade plus that I'd known him. "Get it done. We need you out here."

"You wanna watch how you speak to Ally," Sam all but growled from atop his horse as I opened my mouth to object.

The look Scottie shot him was murderous and he ground out, "Shut it, Sam."

"Mate," I warned, white-knuckling the reins in my hands. I forced myself to loosen the grip and unclench my legs. "I don't give a shit about what's going on over there. You'd better bloody watch your mouth and your tone."

"Or what?"

"Or I'll tell Nan." My threat sounded childish. Dobbing on him to his nan probably was, but it had the desired effect. Scottie paled and nodded. He respected that woman more than anyone else in the world, and he'd never knowingly disappoint or disrespect her. I'd been star-struck by Ma when we'd first arrived, but it was nothing compared to the way Scottie looked up to his nan. He was in awe of her.

Scottie dismissed us all an hour later, looking like someone had kicked his puppy. He'd watched the dust cloud kicked up by Macca's ute as he pulled away until it disappeared in the distance. Then he'd sent Waru off after him. I had half a feeling that I'd see Waru coming back with Macca following, but when he rode back in and nodded at Scottie, I knew he was seeing him to the boundary.

I'd wanted to stick around and play ball with Blond. It sounded ridiculous, but the big old bull had never stopped loving it, and I was the only person around who would play. I had the basketball pumped up, sitting in the shed waiting for me to grab it when I put Daisy away, but Scottie needed the space, and frankly I needed a wash.

It wasn't until I was clean, all the dust that'd permeated every crease and crevice of my body gone that I felt almost human again. My stomach growled loudly, practically curling in on itself as it protested the hunger that'd built from a full day of relentlessly hard yakka. Sam was waiting for me on the couch, dressed in clean jeans that hugged every inch of his long legs and a soft-looking hoodie that I could picture myself burrowing into. His still-wet hair flopped on his forehead, and my hand twitched with the desire to brush it back just to touch the silky strands. I didn't know what was wrong with me, and I couldn't help but remember the last time I'd been awkward around him—the one thing we'd never spoken about again. The time we kissed. My cheeks heated and I looked away, suddenly shy. I wished that my towel hid the movement I had happening in my dick. But I couldn't help it; he looked damn good.

"Ah, I um… I'll give you some privacy," he stuttered as I opened the cupboard with all my clothes in it.

"S'all good, I'll get dressed in the bedroom." My voice was too high and my smile too bright to be genuine.

"Sure, okay."

He turned away and I slipped out of the room, my grey sweats and a tight white thermal top in my hand. When I looked at what I'd grabbed, there was one important thing missing—my jocks. Fuck. There I was wearing loose grey sweatpants with nothing holding the package in place and my uncooperative dick deciding it was suddenly taking an interest in a person I had no right to be looking at.

What had happened to me since that morning? It was as if a switch had flipped. I needed to get my head back in the game. And that game was tea. I shook off my thoughts, pressed down on my filling dick and pulled on my trackies and a pair of old sneakers.

"You ri…" Sam choked as I emerged from the room. He coughed and looked away, adjusting the legs of his jeans as he stood. He already had a pair of boots on, their laces loose so they'd be easy to slip off when we got to the homestead.

We walked together, shoulder to shoulder over to the homestead. Scottie was still hard at work with the cattle, Nan standing watch at the fence as he wheeled and turned Tilly on a five-cent piece.

Finding our usual spots at the table, on either side of Ally, I leaned in and asked, "Everything okay?"

"No, not really. We'll let everyone know when Den gets here." He walked in the door only a moment later.

"Help yourselves." Ma dished up two plates and set them aside, keeping them warm in the oven. "Scottie and your nan will be a while, I think."

After we'd served ourselves and we were all seated again, Ally cleared her throat, calling our attention to her. "So, you all saw what went down this afternoon. Turns out that Macca wasn't exactly who he said he was. He was here under false pretences. Scottie's angry. He feels like he's let all of us down because he let him onto the station. He hasn't, but he needs to realize that himself. So, give him some space and understanding please."

"Is it something we need to worry about?" Sam asked and my heart lurched painfully at the uncertainty in his tone.

"We aren't sure. We've got a call into the lawyer to check what rights we have."

"Why was he here?" Den asked.

Ally smiled sadly. "It's not something Scottie would want me to talk about. But we'll take care of it."

"Is there anything we can do to help?" Yindi asked.

Ma smiled her thanks. "We'll ask the lawyer. We're sorry to be vague. We don't want to be, but at this stage we don't know enough to tell you more."

"He would've gone to Longreach. We can head there. Have a chat to him about not coming back."

Ally smiled and squeezed my forearm. "I appreciate the offer, but no. It's not worth risking you two landing in jail."

"I won't lay a finger on him." I smiled, taking her hand in mine.

"I don't believe you." She laughed, patting my hand with her free one.

The creak of the screen door sounded and conversation ceased, all eyes on Scottie as he stepped over the threshold and paused. He looked at the table and I followed his gaze to the empty spot next to where he usually sat.

Swallowing hard, I looked away, wishing we'd thought to have Den, Waru, and Yindi spread out more. No words were spoken. He squared his shoulders and strode straight past us, his socked feet not making a sound on the hard-wood floor. He made for his bedroom, the quiet snick barely sounding as he closed it.

Nan sighed and slipped into her seat. We looked to her, waiting for her comment. When she did, she was confident; there was no room for argument in her tone. "We'll sort this mess out. We've been through worse and come out okay." She paused and shared a look with Ma who'd just placed her plate in front of her. "Let's eat before it gets cold."

There wasn't much talking after that. We ate, clearing everything off the plates and going in for seconds. When Ma dished up dessert, Sam asked Ally if she wanted to join us for a cuppa on our veranda. "I know you wanted to talk."

"I did. But I think… Scottie needs me."

"Go," he assured her. "We aren't going anywhere."

The last two months had been hell. There were some pretty big dramas between Scottie and Macca. They'd kept it all hushed up, and even Ally had refused to fill us in, but the tension in the air could have been cut with a knife. It was frustrating, but Sam had kept at me, saying I needed to back off—he didn't think it was any of our business if Ally didn't want to tell us. She said that it was a personal issue between Scottie and Macca, but the mention of lawyers had both me and Sam worried we'd be turfed out again on our arses. Some old wounds were too easily torn open again.

Ally had begged us to trust her and Scottie. She'd promised that the station wasn't at risk, but that they needed to protect the land itself. It sounded like semantics to us—we didn't see what the difference was. Then when we saw Scottie up and head into Longreach and come back with Macca in tow, we were even more confused. Ally wouldn't talk and we'd been pissed off. Ma and Nan had assured us that we shouldn't beat Macca into the ground and Scottie had told us how much he appreciated our loyalty. But he still wouldn't budge on telling us what happened. In the end, I'd thrown my hands up and told 'em all I needed to be fed more horseshit if I was gonna be a mushroom and kept in the dark. They'd fucking laughed.

But then things got serious.

The Ekka had come and gone, and Scottie did his lone pilgrimage to the agricultural show in Brissie. Except this time he took Macca. It was the first time he'd gone with another person and there were more than a few raised eyebrows and pissed off mutterings at the dinner table when we'd found out he'd picked the new bloke instead of us. When they came back, Scottie was sick as a dog. A few nights in hospital and he was with us again, but so damn weak it wasn't funny. The man who'd never missed a day's work since Sam and me had arrived on the station had been barely able to get out of bed. We were worried, and when Nan got sick and we were fucking terrified. She was the glue that held the station together and if she hadn't pulled through, I didn't know what we'd do. It would happen one day—we all knew that—but thankfully not yet.

Ally and Ma hadn't left her bedside in weeks, caring for her round the clock and we were all pulling extra shifts to keep everything running smoothly. With two people down, it'd been endless amounts of hard yakka, but we'd pulled through. We were all a little worse for wear though. By the time tea rolled around at night, we were all falling into our chairs, stuffing our faces and staggering back to our cabins to crash. We were all working on empty and even though Scottie was almost back to normal and Ally was getting back into it too, things were only getting busier. Now we were in the middle of calving season and we were scrambling, taking shifts to patrol at night keeping predators at bay, rescuing abandoned calves and getting them feeding on the bottle. Poddy calves meant round the clock feeds and keeping an extra close eye on them. Even though we'd brought them right up between the homestead and cabins, the feral dogs would still attack. They had no choice—the drought was taking its toll and they were starving.

Scottie and Macca were taking the night shift and Ally, Sam, and I would see in the dawn. Lying half-awake on the couch, I was contemplating heading off to bed. It'd be a bloody long day without getting some decent shut-eye, but I was comfortable and cool and I didn't want to move.

The knock at the door had me cracking open an eye, and by the time I managed to sit up so I could stand, Sam was on his feet, the tele muted.

"Can I come in?" Ally called as I rubbed sleep from my eyes, still groggy.

"Yeah, course." Sam pulled the door open and motioned for her to enter.

"Hey." Ally smiled tiredly. She seemed happy, which was good; she wasn't coming with bad news.

"Come 'ere." I lifted up my arm so she could snuggle into my side. If I fell asleep like that, I'd be a happy man.

"I'd rather..." Ally motioned to the footstool I'd just had my feet up on. She sat down, elbows resting on her knees and clasped her hands. "I, ah..." She furrowed her brow and pursed her lips together. "I know we'll see each other in a few hours, but I wanted to pop by." She hesitated, not continuing.

"You're always welcome here," Sam said. "You wanna hang with us for a bit? Maybe have a cuppa?"

"I've just had a Milo with Nan. I wanted to talk to you guys, if that's okay?" I nodded my encouragement and Sam did the same, while she sucked in a deep breath and blurted out, "I'm not really happy here. At the station. I haven't been for quite a while. Before all this happened..." She waved towards the homestead. "I was thinking about leaving. Maybe not for forever, but for a while at least. I dunno if that'll happen now, but with everything that's gone down it's made me realize that I'm settling. I'm not happy and I deserve better. I deserve more. I'm lonely. I want love in my life. I want... I dunno. More. Maybe that sounds selfish, but—"

"It's not selfish, Ally." I had to force the words out past the lump in my throat, not because I didn't believe them, but because what she'd said both broke my heart and terrified me. I watched her take another deep breath, and I reached forward with shaking hands to clasp hers in mine. They were cool to the touch, a contrast to my clammy ones. My heart thundered in my chest, panic enveloping me with her confession. I'd always known it was a possibility—Ally meeting someone or leaving altogether so she could try something new. I'd just never expected it to render me a freaked-out mess. But every word she'd said was true. She did deserve more. "You deserve to be happy."

"Yeah, I do." She nodded, her gaze shifting from mine to Sam's. "It's taken a bit for me to figure out what I wanted, so..." Ally dropped her gaze and withdrew her hands from mine. "I'm just gonna lay it all out there."

"Okay?" Sam hedged.

She blew out a breath and tucked a piece of hair behind her ear before shifting on her seat, moving so she sat cross-legged on the small stool. When she wiped her hands on her jean shorts and shifted again, it took everything in me not to soothe her nerves. "Tell us anything, Ally. We're here for you."

She looked down, playing with a loose thread on her shorts. "I know about you guys. I have since almost the beginning." She wrung her hands together, never looking up at us. Ally continued speaking, her words coming faster again. "You've got this epic love story. You've been best mates since you were kids and then, what? High school sweethearts? You fell in love. You've travelled half the east coast together, working with one another and living the life. You've got decades under your belt as a couple and it's obvious you're happy." Her voice dropped to almost a whisper. "I want that. I want you..." She pressed her fingers to the bridge of her nose and still looking away, sucked in an uneven breath.

I sat there stunned. I opened my mouth to speak but nothing came out. I looked to Sam who had paled and swallowed heavily. That's what she thought about us? That Sam and I were a couple? It was... I had no idea. I wanted to say it was so out of left field that I was shocked stupid, but at the same time, it kind of wasn't. I'd thought the same but dismissed it before the idea could take root. It wasn't right. We weren't like that. But hearing her perception made something warm unfurl in me. Something that had been kept under lock and key. Hidden to everyone, even myself. Or maybe not myself. Maybe it was the giant pink elephant in the room. I'd conveniently ignored it for a couple of decades, but that big bastard was sick of waiting in the closet.

"Ally—" I started.

"Who do you want?" Sam asked urgently before he waved his hand and scrunched up his face. "I mean... don't answer that. That's not what I meant. You said, 'I want you.' What does that mean?"

"I didn't mean... Never mind."

"Didn't mean it or didn't mean to say it?" I asked quietly.

"I..." She sighed heavily. "It means that I wish the two of you would look at me like more than your sister. I've been half in love with you both for a decade and you don't even see me, but that's okay. You're together—" I tried to interrupt, but she held up her hand, stopping me in my tracks. "The world doesn't revolve around me. It's not like you have to want me or whatever, but I hear rumours and if they're true, I wish you didn't have to do it. If you needed a beard, I wished you'd just come to me." She huffed out a humourless laugh. "I want that for real."

"Ally, we aren't…" I said at the same time as Sam blurted, "We didn't think you'd go for it."

"We aren't together," I finished. "We're mates. That's it."

"Sam?" Ally peered at him, waiting, her face serious.

"It's true." He looked away when he spoke, with a tone that I hadn't heard in a long time. It was as if he was sad. But that couldn't be right.

"Not what I meant." She narrowed her eyes at him. "I wouldn't go for what?"

"Oh." He looked to me wide-eyed.

"Spit it out," she ordered, looking imposing even as she sat there staring at us in a tiny pair of denim shorts and a black singlet with spaghetti straps.

"We both liked you and we didn't want any of our friendships to fall apart, or to hurt each other, so—"

"So, you friend-zoned me." Ally stood slowly, moving over to the window. We had a clear view of the southern paddocks from it, but at night, the only thing visible from inside our cabin was the dark. "How long?" she asked quietly.

"Ally—" Sam began.

"No, you listen here." She whirled around and pointed at us both. "You decided how this was going down without even talking to me. Without even letting me be involved in a decision that directly affected me. How long ago did you decide that for me?"

"Within a few weeks of us getting here." I didn't hesitate to give her my answer. My confession would change our dynamic. I'd quite possibly lose her friendship forever, but if I owned up to it, maybe Sam would be protected from the brunt of her anger. It was time to finally have this conversation. "It was my idea, Ally."

"Stop protecting him," she shouted at me. But it wasn't rage in her eyes. It was betrayal. And her tone was like a slap to the face. "Stop bloody protecting him! I trusted you. Both of you." She rubbed her forehead and fought back a sob. "Twelve years, damn it. Bloody hell, nearly thirteen. I trusted you to tell me the truth. You promised me you would." Angrily dashing at the tears leaking from her eyes with short swipes of her hands, she squared her shoulders and stared down at us still sitting on the couch.

"I thought the two of you were together. I've wanted you both for over a decade. I was young and stupid, and I spent all that time trying to be strong and independent and yet wanting you both. I tried dating and that clearly didn't work. All I wanted was for you to see something in me. But I understood that I wasn't what you wanted."

She waved her hand in the general direction of town four hours away and her voice fell to a pained whisper, tears

trickling down her cheeks as she spoke. "I heard the rumours, but I dismissed them. How could you sleep around
on each other when you were committed? But then I kept
hearing them. I cried for you. Do you have any idea how
much I hated hearing people talk?" She shook her head and
looked away, wiping her chin with the heel of her hand. "I
kept thinking how hard it must be hearing the lies. Then I
thought maybe you were doing it to protect each other.
Knowing you were getting intimate with women just so you
could keep your secret broke my heart." Her shoulders
sagged and she seemed to fold in on herself. "Thinking
you'd have to go through that when you were committed
to each other… the despair you must have felt flayed me."

My heart cracked in my chest at the same time as her
voice broke and she let out a sob. "The whole time I wished
you'd just tell me. I wanted to be there to protect you. I
would have made up a bloody relationship with you just so
you didn't have to share yourselves with anyone else." She
covered her mouth with her hand, as if she was physically
trying to hold back another sob. "It would have destroyed
me. But I would have done it. For you. I would have sacri-
ficed what I wanted for you. Written myself out of the dating pool—not that there's much of one—but I would have
done it for you. The joke was on me though, wasn't it?" She
huffed out a laugh that held no humour and shook her
head. Then she whispered, "You ruled me out of conten-
tion. I never even had a chance." Her lashes were wet with
tears, her lips turned down and shoulders slumped. "I was
never enough, was I? Not even worth the risk."

Sam and I were on our feet and standing before her in a split second. "Ally." Sam touched his thumb to her chin. "We never meant to hurt you. We wanted to protect what we had with you. It's not that you weren't worth the risk; it's that we were too scared to chance losing you. We thought loving you from afar was the best thing we could do."

"So if I found a bloke—if Phil and I had worked out—you would have been okay with that? You would have just stood by and never even made a move?"

"He would have had to have proven himself." My tone was defiant. Even to my own ears I sounded petulant.

She shook her head. "I saw you, Craig. I saw the dick measuring you two were doing with him. You go all caveman and scare everyone away." Disappointment and disbelief and a healthy dose of anger coloured her words. All I felt was shame. "How many times have you been content to love me from afar while sticking your nose in and chasing away any man who shows one iota of interest in me? No one was ever intimated by my gruff brother. No, they were always worried about my two pit bulls growling every time a bloke got close."

"We've never done that." My protest, while vehement, was an untruth. I'd done exactly that on more than one occasion. She didn't respond, just looked at me with a raised eyebrow. "Yeah, okay," I admitted. "I wasn't doing it to keep you for myself though, or for us. Or even for you to stay single. I wanted you to end up with a bloke who'd treat you right. One who'd treat you like we wanted to."

"Yet you didn't show me the courtesy of something as basic as being honest with me after I made it clear that was the one thing I expected." Her words had the force of a kick to the chest from a horse. The crushing pain in my ribs was a physical ache, not just an emotional one.

"No, we didn't," Sam agreed slowly. Quietly. "For what it's worth, I'm sorry. I know I can speak for Craig and say he's sorry too. What we did was fucked up. It was immature and stupid, and we have no excuse for letting it continue as long as it did. We should have explained how we felt, how we feel. We didn't though and that's unforgivable no matter what our reasons were."

"Why didn't you tell me?"

"Remember your birthday that first year we were here? The first time we went to the billabong?" He smiled sadly. "You were finally comfortable with us. It was as if you realized we wouldn't take advantage of you."

She pushed past us and sat on the footstool again. "That was the day I started thinking you were together. The way you looked at each other then. It was so full of love. I thought you were gay." I didn't have any idea what look she was talking about, but she'd clearly seen something that wasn't there. I sat back down on the couch, leaving the seat between Sam and I free. She looked at me and added, "You dragged him out of the water, pushing him up the bank and getting him as far away from danger as possible without any care for yourself—"

"Your croc joke." The memory came back to me, and I realized she was right. There was something between us in that moment. Terror had curled its bony claws around my throat and squeezed, stealing my breath. I'd been robbed of coherent thought. I reacted on instinct, trying to get Sam to safety. To protect him. The relief that had surged through me when Ally reassured us there were no crocs in the water had nearly brought me to my knees.

"You remember, don't you? You know exactly the moment." Her question was directed to me, and all I could do was nod. It was true. I did love him. I wanted to protect him and keep him safe. But it didn't mean I wanted to fuck him. That's not what blokes like us did. We were mates. We shared an unbreakable bond. But it wasn't sexual, no matter what my traitorous dick had thought more than once over the last few months. It'd just wanted some action.

She continued. "What about the rumours? They're true, aren't they?"

"We've both been with a few of the women in town, but I haven't slept with anyone in…" I paused to think back, unable to remember the last time. "At least a year."

"Three for me," Sam added, and my gaze shot to his. He shrugged like it was no big deal and he turned to look at Ally. "Didn't feel right when I knew who I wanted."

"Purely physical for me," I added, agreeing with his sentiment. "I never wanted anything more than a one-night stand. Felt like I was cheating on both you and them."

Ally nodded and scrubbed her hands over her face. "I… I have a lot to think about. I didn't expect this and I dunno what to do now."

"The ball's in your court, Ally." Sam reached for her hand and threaded his fingers with hers. "I wish I could undo the hurt we've caused. If I'd thought—if either one of us had thought—for a second that you wouldn't castrate us for making a suggestion like the one I'm just about to make, we would have fessed up a decade ago." He looked to me and I nodded, encouraging him. "We want you. Both of us. We want to date you; we don't just want to fuck. I dunno how we'll work out the logistics, but whatever you decide, I'm willing to go with it."

"I am too," I added. "If you're prepared to share any part of you, I'll take it and we'll cherish it." I leaned forward and tucked a lock of her hair behind her ear and brushed her soft cheek gently with the pad of my thumb. "We aren't pressuring you. If you decide that you can't forgive us, we'll understand, and nothing has to change." I paused. "Or maybe it will—whatever you want to happen, we'll go with it."

"Thanks," she whispered, shaking her head and looking infinitely sad. "It's a lot. I'm just not sure where to go from here. I know you've said you want something with me, and I know how I would have reacted to that news a half-hour ago, but it's more complicated than that now. I feel like I've been betrayed by my best friends and I need to work out how to move past that. Whether I even can."

I wanted to hold her, to never let her go. To tell her that we'd done it because we were genuine. We were trying to keep her in our lives in whatever way we thought we could, without hurting the other. We clearly didn't put two and two together and were doing the one thing we'd tried to avoid—hurting her. We had a lot to make up for. I hoped one day she'd give us the chance. But it was up to her now.

Maybe now was a good time to start prayin'.

CHAPTER 13

Sam

I closed the door and rested my head against it. When Craig came up behind me and squeezed my shoulders, I couldn't resist anymore. I turned and wrapped my arms around his shoulders, pulling him to me. I needed the contact. I needed the comfort. We'd ballsed it up. Big time. By trying to protect each other, we'd broken her heart. We hadn't even considered that as a possibility, convinced that she'd never even look at us.

Irony was such a bitch.

Now I was questioning whether we were ever serious enough about Ally to deserve her. Maybe we should have encouraged her to date more. To meet someone. There were good blokes who'd been interested in her and all we did was run them off. One of them might have done better by her than we had. We'd treated her like shit and all they did was show their interest—tell her she was pretty. Ask her for a drink. A hook-up. Even the ones we thought of as low lives were unlikely to have hurt her as much as we'd managed to.

But when I thought about another man touching her, my blood boiled. I wanted to tear him limb from limb. Was it just jealousy or something a hell of a lot deeper? It seemed like a stupid question. I loved her; I knew I did.

But could I love her completely if I'd also fallen for Craig?

Could a person love two people at the same time equally? Was it even possible?

It was real to me. Was that the answer?

Every time I thought about either one of them, the butterflies in my belly took flight and I couldn't help but smile. My heart went all light and fuzzy and they were the only people who I could imagine coming home to. I wanted to grow old with them. I wanted to get naked with them. Both of them.

Maybe that made me a deviant.

Or maybe it was supposed to be like that between the three of us.

Craig tentatively wrapped his arms around my waist and when I held him tighter, he pulled me against him, holding me close. Thick muscles surrounded me, and I was enveloped in his warmth. I sank into him, melting against him. Resting my forehead on his shoulder, I breathed him in. Not for the first time in my life, I had to bite back a groan and will my dick to play nice—actually, not to come out and play at all—when I was near him. The last thing I wanted was for him to jump back disgusted when I needed him, and I couldn't let him go. Not yet. I breathed in the scent of citrus and cardamom like a drug. I'd been addicted from the first moment I'd smelt it and with the emotional turmoil I had going on, I just wanted to get drunk on him. If only Ally was here too.

I was confused and my heart hurt, but standing there in the protection of his arms, my world was at least partly righted.

"You okay?" The rumble of his murmured voice passed through my chest and settled there as he ran one hand up and down my back and kept me anchored to him with the other.

"Honestly? I dunno," I confessed with a huff. "I'm a little all over the shop."

"Ally's comments throw you for a loop too?"

"Yeah." I didn't add why. I knew him well enough to know that I couldn't be completely honest with him.

"You'll be right." Craig pulled back, gripped my biceps and laughed awkwardly. "Bloody hell, 'ay. Look at us. Ally thinks we're poofters and we're standing here snuggling together. No wonder."

"Yeah." His words knocked the wind out of me, while he stomped on my heart with his size ten boots. "Just look at us." I understood then why Ally had been pulling away from us. My silence, Craig's unconsidered words, and both our actions must have flayed her. He'd certainly managed to wreck me. "I'm going to bed."

Without even turning the light on, I stripped and pulled the sheet over me as I crawled into bed in just a pair of undies. Facing away from Craig's bed, I hiked up the sheet to my ears and closed my eyes. There was no way I could face him when he said shit that cut me to the quick. I didn't know why he did it. Why he suddenly turned into this… loud-mouthed bogan. When his defences went up his words were as sharp as a knife.

I heard the tap run for a moment, then Craig brushing his teeth, the switch of lights being turned off, and finally the bed next to mine creak. He sighed. "You awake, mate?" I ignored him, squeezing my eyes closed and willing myself not to cry. At least before Ally knew, I could live in denial. I could let myself believe that both were unobtainable, but with Ally's confession had come a tsunami of emotion and I was struggling to contain it. When Craig sighed again, I bit down on my knuckle and waited out his silence. "I'm sorry if I fucked up your chances with Ally. I don't deserve either one of you. But I'll make it right if I can. I'll walk away if that's what it comes down to."

"Don't," I croaked, rolling over to face him. "You don't get it do you? I don't want to choose between the two of you. I love you, you damn mug."

He huffed out a laugh and smiled at me. "I love you too, mate." He slid into bed and pulled the sheet over himself. "Night, Sam."

"Night."

The grey-brown smoke in the distance made the hairs on the back of my neck prickle. Craig and I were on horse-back, checking the fence line between the springer paddock where the cows and calves were, and the strip of bush bordering the larger paddock where the bulls and weaned bull calves were. The wind blew hot and the acrid smell washed over us. "Mate, I'm not liking the look of that fire, and Spook's getting antsy."

"Yeah, me neither." He paused, his hand shielding his eyes as he looked towards the bulls and bull calves gathered in the shade of the trees. "That sensor's gotta be wrong. Blond's never wandered off like this before."

I followed the line of his gaze, looking into the glare of the sun at the small mob of animals. He was our prize bull, and by far the biggest of the cattle at the station. But he wasn't with the others. Pulling the binoculars out of my saddle bag, I scanned the length of the paddock, trying to spot him in the distance. "Nothing. No sight of him."

"Shit," Craig muttered. "You're right, we need to get back. I don't wanna be away from the homestead while this fire's hanging around. Let's go."

We circled around looking again at the smoke. Even though I kept one eye on it, I was distracted. By Craig. In the saddle he was a drink of cool water, and I was thirsty as hell. Dressed in faded jeans that looked soft to the touch, with a rip at the knee and an old Metallica tee, he was hardly the epitome of style, but those jeans hugged his thick thighs and muscular arse and the tee pulled tight across his shoulders, his pecs and biceps bulging under the fabric. His white straw hat was ridiculous, but so classically Craig's "I don't give a fuck" attitude that it suited him perfectly. Every part of him was fit and firm and like I wanted Ally, I wanted him too. The picture he cast up there in the saddle was irresistible. His natural ability as a horseman was on show, and I drank in his easy gait. Holding the reins loosely in his right hand, he used subtle shifts in his weight and movements of his feet to guide Daisy, and she responded immediately.

With a click of his tongue, he set off, then looked over his shoulder, grinning at me. "You comin' or you gonna sit there staring?"

"Calm your tits." I grinned right back at him and nudged Spook to catch up.

We returned to the homestead at a trot and went straight to the stable to get the gear off the horses and let them into the paddock. I looked out, watching the smoke, and seeing the change in direction of the wind.

Then there were car tyres spinning. Dirt and gravel being kicked up. Ally screamed for Scottie, panic in her voice.

My heart stopped. Then it thudded, strong and fast. Craig was already running towards them as my legs unlocked and I sprinted. I cleared the fence in two bounds, and caught Craig as he stumbled, hauling him with me. I expected to see an accident that would have Scottie fighting for his life, or worse. But all I could see in the distance was a dust cloud.

I still didn't stop running, skidding to a halt only when I was beside her. Craig was close behind me.

Ally was shaking. Sobs wracked her body.

"Ally?" I grasped her arms and hauled her to me. She came willingly, burying her face in my chest. "What's going on?"

"Macca's out there." Her voice wobbled and she held onto me tighter. "He's not with Waru, and Waru's not answering. The wind shifted and now he's out there alone and directly in the path of the fire."

"Christ." I dared not utter what I feared. Scottie would be lucky to make it in time. Unless he was driving like a bat outta hell, we'd be recovering Macca's body. But I had a feeling Scottie wouldn't be giving up easily. He'd risk his neck for every one of us, but there was something that told me he'd go the extra mile for Macca. Usually he was buttoned up tight, but there'd been a spring in his step and a tiny smile on his face ever since Macca had retuned. I suspected that Scottie's feelings went far deeper than them being just mates. Macca too though—he looked at Scottie like he'd created the blue of the sky and the red of the dirt just for him. The kid was filled with wide-eyed wonder for every detail of the station, but he practically worshipped the ground Scottie walked on. Some of the looks they shared when they didn't think anyone was watching had me half believing that every ounce of sweetness and adoration they harboured for each other translated into fire between the sheets.

Now it was a waiting game to see if Scottie would reach him in time. I prayed he would, because the alternative—Scottie losing him, this station losing him—was unfathomable.

An hour had passed. Each second seemed interminable, every tick going slower than the last.

"Jesus Christ, I hope he's got him." Ally paced, her boots thudding against the timber floors of the homestead. Ordinarily Ma would have clipped her across the back of the head for wearing boots inside. This time it was the least of our concerns.

She dialled the satellite phone again. No answer.

Hanging up, she slammed her fist on the kitchen bench and wiped tears away again. Yindi was beside herself, huddled between Ma and Nan, rocking as she sat waiting for Waru to come home safe. Den and Jono were pouring over old maps, spread out on the table, calculating distances, wind direction and measuring water supplies. If the wind turned again and the fire headed towards the homestead, we likely wouldn't have anything to save it with. Water was already scarce. Fighting a fire—any fire—would make it run out quick smart.

Ally dialled again and she laugh-cried. "Oh my God, Waru, it's good to hear your voice. Where are you? Are you safe?"

I couldn't hear what was being said on the line, but Ally was nodding at Yindi. The older women comforted each other, Yindi covering her mouth and silently sobbing. Ally wiped the tears streaking down her cheeks with the heel of her hand and whispered, "Get to them. Please."

She hung up and, with shaking hands, dialled the satellite phone we'd given Pete. Again. There was still no answer. Nothing. Scottie had left without one, so we had no way of contacting him, and we were all still on edge. Dialling again and again, swearing under her breath every time there was no answer, Craig gently prised it from her hand as she was about to slam the phone against the bench. "Where the fuck is he?" she shouted. "He can't be dead!"

Craig hit redial and closed his eyes, as if begging our guest to pick up. I didn't know how he did it, but the ringing stopped and a muffled voice came over the line, so quiet we could barely hear him. Ally screeched, "We need to find him."

"I got to him, Ally. I got him." Scottie sounded shaken to the core, his voice unsteady, and full of emotion.

"Oh, thank God." She went lax against Craig. "We've been trying to call, but he didn't answer."

"What about Waru?" Scottie asked.

"He's okay. He should be there any second."

"All right. I'm bringing him home. I'll speak to you soon." The line clicked off and I stepped forward, running my fingers through her hair. Craig looked like he'd aged a decade in ninety minutes. I didn't blame him; I was feeling it too. There could have been a very different outcome to that call, one that I didn't want to contemplate. Craig hugged Ally tight and I squeezed his shoulder before leaning down to kiss Ally's head. Craig's smile was relieved, and I noticed the shake in his hands as he ran one through his hair.

"That was far too bloody close for comfort. You young ones will be the death of me." Nan's comment broke the tension and was exactly what we needed to get smiles on all our faces. This should be a celebration—one to match the relief we were all filled with.

Ma got up and went outside, arm in arm with Yindi. Nan followed and we took the cue too, going to wait for the trio outside. We didn't spot them coming, unable to make out the two columns of dust being kicked up by the vehicles against the haze of grassfire smoke. The acrid stench in the grey-brown air would hang around for days unless the desert winds blew it away—but that was the last thing we wanted. Wind would only fan the flames and even though the fire had passed us, we weren't out of the woods yet. The cattle were close by so we could get to them, but even if we were there for them, we wouldn't be able to do much. The lack of water meant we were little more than sitting ducks, completely at Mother Nature's mercy.

Waru pulled up to the homestead first and Yindi sprinted to him, jumping into his arms and touching every inch of his face and chest. They stood there, wrapped in each other for long moments. When Scottie parked a few feet away, all eyes shifted to him and Macca. Scottie got out and dashed around to the passenger side and my gut clenched. Was Macca okay? Surely Scottie would have said something if he wasn't. Jono could have had the chopper ready to go so we could get him to help quicker. Instead, Scottie helped him out and pulled him in his arms, kissing him gently. Forehead to forehead, they whispered and both men smiled, never letting go. My heart beat hard, expanding and spreading a warmth through my chest. Happiness for my boss—my friend—filled me to overflowing, and I pulled Ally close, hugging her as she wiped her face from her still-falling tears.

Craig had stepped forward, his spine ramrod straight, a scowl on his face. Scottie saw him and subtly shifted Macca, stepping in front of him to bodily shield him from the others. Disgust radiated off Craig, his lip curled up and his eyes a cold, hard brown. Scottie didn't back down, raising his chin and straightening his shoulders in defiance. It was as if two roosters were facing off against each other right before a cock fight. Sizing each other up. The air crackled with tension, a dangerous electrical current sparking between them.

"Seriously? We're not gonna say anything?" Craig spat out. I closed my eyes. I knew what he was going to say, and all the fight deserted me. My body shut down, curling in on itself to protect my heart from his eviscerating words. "Look, I'm as glad as anyone that you're back, but mate, you're a fuckin' poofter?"

I was exhausted. Years of yearning and it had come down to this. His words broke something inside me, grief overtaking me. The tiny spark of hope that maybe one day he'd finally see me in the same way that I saw him was extinguished. The loss of that tiny flame left me in darkness, stealing my breath and sapping my energy until I couldn't even hold myself up anymore. I slumped, but Ally was there to catch me.

She reached up, her hand cupping my face. "I'm still here. Never forget that." Her whispered words reassured me. I nodded and closed my eyes, soaking up her strength.

"Anyone else here have a problem with Scottie and Pete, and you can fuck right off. Sorry, Ma, Lynn." Jono spoke with an authority brooking no argument. His reaction gave me another zap, like a defibrillator to the chest.

Craig stood still. Rigid. But when he turned to me, I knew. "C'mon, Sam, we're leaving."

Ally dropped her arms from around me, and I squeezed her hand before stepping up to Craig. I loved him. I always would, but I couldn't keep torturing myself. He didn't want me. He didn't want us. Hell, it was probably a good thing that the three of us had never progressed past hugging. I could only imagine what he would have been like had I accidentally touched him. "No, Craig. I'm staying. I'm done running."

"I'm not comin' back for you, Sam," he warned, stepping closer so we were chest to chest. "It's been you and me against the world since we were kids. You're giving that up?"

"No." I shook my head. "You are. This is our home, Craig. This is where we belong, and you know it. But if you need to leave, I won't hold you back. I've done far too much of that over the years to force you to stay. Especially when you feel like this."

His jaw ticked; his teeth clenched tight. He narrowed his eyes and scowled. "It's not right, Sam."

I shook my head gently, disagreeing with him. My heart was shredded, lying bleeding with scrape marks and gashes from the wounds he'd unknowingly inflicted with his words. I had nothing left to lose by being honest. "It's as natural as anyone else in love."

He reared back like he'd been slapped and backed away from me. His eyes were wide as if he was seeing me for the first time. Maybe he was. His gaze hardened and he gritted his teeth again before his lip curled up in disgust with me. "Goodbye, Sam."

I couldn't say the words. My throat, thick with emotion, closed over, and I had to bite back a sob. I didn't want this to be the end of us. Thirty-eight years of being together day in and day out. I'd loved him for more than half my life. Probably my whole life if I were being honest. Blinking away the tears threatening to fall, I whispered, "I'll miss you."

Jono clapped his hand on my shoulder. "Go to your girl, mate. She needs you." I sucked in a shaky breath and held my head up, carefully hiding the emotions swirling inside me like the destructive winds of a hurricane as I turned to her. Ally met my gaze and she held it, stepping slowly towards me as I did the same to her. We sank into each other's arms, and I took the comfort she was offering. The love. God knew I'd need every ounce of it when the shock of what had just transpired wore off and the knowledge that I'd never likely see him again sank in.

I couldn't look. Couldn't watch Craig make that last journey to our cabin to collect his things. I couldn't be there to see Jono taking him to Longreach, knowing he chose prejudice and bigotry over me. Over his family. Over his home.

Ally nudged me towards the house, pushing me down into my seat. "I really hate that this station is dry sometimes. I need a fucking whiskey."

Ma pulled the step out and Den eased her out of the way. "Where is it?" he asked.

"Top shelf. Back right. There's only one bottle."

He reached up, feeling around and lifted it out. His face fell when he saw that it was indeed whiskey, not Bundy Rum like he drank. He shrugged and took it to Ally where Ma had already placed the small glasses. There was only enough in the bottle for one shot each, but it would have to be enough. The closest bottle-o was a four-hour drive and even though Jono would be passing it, he wouldn't bring any back with him even if we asked. He respected Ma's decision to make the station dry far too much to give into the temptation to have a drink, even if these were extraordinary circumstances.

Ally passed around the glasses—one for me, Den, Ma, and Nan. Neither Waru nor Yindi drank, so they stuck with the ginger beer Den had pulled from the fridge for them. Finally pouring one for herself, Ally raised her glass. "Cheers," she mumbled, before tossing back the shot. She cleared her throat, and I did the same, tears springing to my eyes as the aged whiskey left a trail of fire when it slid down my throat.

I coughed and gasped. "Smooth."

Nan hummed. That woman was double my age and twice as strong as a damn bull.

We sat quietly and Waru finally spoke. "I didn't realize the fire was so close. Blond tangled himself in the fence. I had to cut it away and get him checked over before I fixed the fence again. When I looked up, the fire was right there.

The wind had shifted while I'd been sheltered by the trees."
He sucked in a breath, his voice wobbling again as he spoke.
"I dropped everything and sped to the ravine, but Scottie
was already there. The fire had passed through. If Scottie
hadn't rescued Macca, he'd be dead." He choked back a sob
and turned in Yindi's arms. "It would have been my fault.
The boss asked me to keep him safe and I didn't."

"Scottie won't blame you." Nan laid a hand on his shoulder in comfort. "If he had a go at you before, it was because
of the adrenaline. Macca's safe. That's what's important."

The screen door banged shut and all eyes were on Scottie and Macca, holding hands there in the kitchen. He
looked... radiant, his smile wide. It was as if all the weight
on his shoulders from years of being alone and keeping that
part of himself a secret had lifted. Now, he held his head
high, his shoulders back. His eyes were filled with a spark
that I didn't think I'd ever seen in him before. It made the
shittastic clusterfuck that had just happened seem kind of
worth it.

He scanned the room and his expression faltered, the
joy there a moment earlier dropping in an instant. "Where
are they?" His voice wavered as he pointed first to Craig's
chair then Jono's.

"Craig wanted out, so Jono's driving him to Longreach.
The rest of us...." I shook my head, unable to fathom why
Craig would do it. "Scottie, it makes no bit of difference to
any of us who you love. And Macca, you're a good bloke." I
shrugged, trying to convey my support without coming out
myself. It made no difference now, I supposed. Craig was

gone. "We're happy for you." Ally nodded, tucking in closer to my side.

"Thanks, mate. I appreciate you sayin' that. But if you'll excuse us, Pete's just agreed to move in with me."

Nan rose and wrapped him in her arms, squeezing him tight. Despite losing a lot of weight this last winter, she was still strong and full of life. The season hadn't been kind to any of us, but especially not her, the bout of influenza nearly stealing her from us. "I'm proud as hell of you, Scottie." She reached out for Macca, pulling him close too. "Make sure you treat each other right."

"We will, Nan." Macca smiled at her before they swept off towards Scottie's room, each of them carrying bags, probably filled with Macca's clothes.

Tea was a strange mix of sombre and light-hearted. Jono was notably absent. The days he missed Ma's cooking were few and far between. Craig's absence was like a giant gaping hole in my chest, and I was dreading going back to the cabin knowing I'd be alone there. I was tempted to crash with Den, but he was a grumpy bastard who snored like a chainsaw most nights, so got his own cabin.

Everyone except Scottie and Macca moved to the loungeroom, the two of them retreating to their new bedroom. It was sweet seeing how Scottie doted over Macca, constantly keeping a hand on him. I didn't blame him. After coming so close to losing a person I loved, I would have needed the reassurance that he was still safe in my arms too. When the snick of the lock on their door sounded, Nan turned on the stereo, playing some good old Lee Kernigan to muffle any sounds. Ally had laughed, shaking her head at Nan, and it took my breath away. She was a sight for sore eyes, the most beautiful woman I'd ever seen.

"They're young and in love." Nan waved Ally off. "Better to give them their privacy."

"Think Jono will be back tonight?" I settled in next to Ally on the comfortable old couch with a cuppa, hoping that I could spend all night there with her.

"Ma got a text from him to say he's on his way, but he'd be back late. He had tea with Craig before coming back." She yawned and moved to stand. "I'm wrecked. I'm gonna head upstairs."

"Oh, okay. Sure. I'll, ah... head off then. Night." I extracted myself off the couch and managed a small smile, my insides crawling with dread. It'd been a bloody long time that I'd been completely alone. Sure, I would do jobs on the station, spend a few hours by myself, but it was rare that it would be any longer than an hour or two. We tended to work in pairs or, in our case, the three of us. But now I'd been cast adrift and was floating around unmoored, unsure of the direction the tide would take me.

I stepped out onto the veranda and looked over to the sorting yard and the open driveway abutting it. I'd stood and watched the basketball matches Craig had played with Blond more times than I could count. It always went the same way. The bull would be in a defensive position, while Craig bounced the ball, taking shots against the ring we'd fashioned from a discarded piece of metal. Every part of this station held memories of Craig's time here. Every day he'd been here indelibly etched into the dirt. Now I had to go on without him, and I wasn't sure how.

I trudged outside and along the darkened drive until the sensor lights on each of the cabins lit up as I passed. My hands in my pockets and my head hung low, I stopped at the door to the cabin. I couldn't bring myself to open it. The darkened interior of the cottage wasn't where I wanted to be.

The two people I wanted were now spread apart. Hours of distance separating us. Would I ever see him again? I supposed it didn't matter anymore. He chose prejudice over love—Scottie and Macca disgusted him. If he ever found out about me, I'd disgust him too. I couldn't bear to see that look on his face directed at me. It was better this way.

If I told myself that enough, maybe I'd start to believe it too.

CHAPTER 14

Ally

How could he?

He left us.

My mind was spinning. My heart was shattered. I was numb, yet every inch of my body ached, the pain of losing him lancing through me, ripping my heart out and shredding my soul.

He hadn't said goodbye. He'd walked away without a backwards glance. Gathered his things and left.

I'd watched from my spot at the table as Jono drove the ute away, taking Craig onto his new life. A life where we weren't with him. I'd never contemplated losing him like that. I'd never imagined there would be a day I'd wake up and he wouldn't be right there with Sam. That he'd choose to walk away.

I'd been dead wrong about the kind of man Craig was.

CHAPTER 15

Craig

W hat had I done?

I'd been uttering the same question over and over since I'd said goodbye to Sam. I'd left them. I'd walked away from the two people who meant the most to me. I'd acted like any sane bloke would. Or I'd thrown a temper tantrum fit for a five-year-old. I couldn't decide which. Either way, going around in circles wasn't helping convince me that my reaction had been proportionate to what had gone down.

I'd had forty-eight hours to simmer down. Jono's taillights hadn't even disappeared down the road when I was hot-footing it to Bob at the co-op. I'd walked in there in a huff and told him I was after a new job. He knew everyone; if there was any employment available, he'd know about it.

I hadn't expected his ire when he asked me why I'd left. I hadn't even thought about what it'd mean for Scottie if I revealed the secret he'd managed to keep for decades. But thinking before I acted wasn't my style, was it? I'd just opened my big mouth and blurted it all out, then walked away, leaving everyone else to deal with the consequences of my actions. I was destined for the dole now and I hadn't even given Scottie notice before nicking off. He was short-handed. Served him right. Why did he have to be gay? It was a shitty thing for him to throw at us.

But was it? Had he really done anything wrong? All I could think of was the look of disappointment on Ma's and Nan's faces when I'd spoken. It wasn't directed at Scottie, but at me. They'd supported him. So had Ally and Sam, Den, Jono, Waru, and Yindi. Not one of them had reacted like me. They probably all thought it though. I was the only one brave enough to say anything.

I had to keep thinking like that. I couldn't think about the emotions that crossed Sam's face when he'd said good-bye. I couldn't think about Ally's shock. The horror and betrayal that had flitted over her features.

I'd destroyed the trust that the two most important people in my life had placed in me. I'd fractured friendships, probably beyond repair, all because Scottie was a fairy.

No. It was because of me. My prejudice. My small-mindedness. My lack of respect and understanding.

What had I done?

I tipped the schooner back and drained the rest of the beer I'd been nursing. I was alone now. I had to get used to that. Maybe it was for the best—at least Sam would now make a move on Ally without feeling guilty about leaving me out. The two of them could move on with their lives. And I'd still be alone.

Self-loathing was the order of the day apparently. And I had enough to feed an army. I turned the glass on its base, rolling it around and around, barely resisting the temptation to bash my head against the darkened wood of the bar top. I was a fucking moron.

Scottie was a poo—no. He was gay. I had to stop thinking like that—but so what? I still didn't understand why it infuriated me so much. I thought back. I reached into my earliest memories looking for something that planted the seed of hatred. But there was nothing specific. Not until I turned fifteen.

Not until that summer.

That day when the dust motes floated aimlessly in the late afternoon haze, and I had my first kiss.

The empty glass landed with a thud on the counter, slipping from my fingers as everything became crystal clear.

Fuck me.

We'd been practicing. That was it. It was no big deal, but I'd taken all the vitriol, all the words of revulsion, the dirty looks and the hatred against *those* people to heart. Why? Just because I'd practiced with my mate. I hadn't even enjoyed it. It was just a means to an end—the training we'd both needed.

I had nothing to be worried about, and now I knew why I'd been bent out of shape about it, I could let it go. Yeah, it was fine.

I needed to find some way to tell Scottie that I didn't hold a grudge against him. It was no big deal that he liked blokes. I didn't care.

At least I wasn't like that. I liked women. I loved them. I loved Ally.

Oh fuck, what had I done? I'd left her.

I'd left Sam.

I sucked in a breath, fighting the pain of the vice crushing my chest. I might never see them again. I motioned to the bartender, asking for another beer. I was going to get maggoted. Drown every emotion bombarding me. It wasn't like I had anywhere to be, or anyone to go home to.

The laugh cut through the noise in the bar and I stiffened. I knew instantly who it was. I'd heard it more often these last few weeks, but some over the twelve plus years I'd lived and worked at Pearce Station. It was Scottie.

My courage fled, but my limbs seemed to work on autopilot, taking me to their table. They sat with only the corner of the table separating them, drinks in hand. With smiles on their faces, they looked happy together, relaxing on a Thursday afternoon with a beer. Scottie looked younger than his years. The frown lines he wore had disappeared, replaced with crinkles around his eyes when he smiled. Macca met my gaze first and I saw him whisper something out of the corner of his mouth as I stepped closer to the table.

"Craig," Scottie greeted me with a nod when I stood before him, his voice devoid of any emotion. The poker face he wore was world class—I had no idea whether he was getting ready to deck me or walk away.

"Mate, I need to apologize." I cleared my throat when my nerves got the better of me. "Can I interrupt you?"

Scottie raised an eyebrow, and all my fight seemed to disappear, draining out to leave me a husk of a man. Every inch of bravado I thought I possessed fled. Finally, Scottie motioned to one of the empty chairs and I slumped into it, barely able to hold myself up anymore.

"What brings on the change of heart?" He placed his beer bottle down on the coaster, lining it up so it was dead centre. If I didn't know better, I'd say Scottie was nervous. But what would he possibly have been nervous about? It wasn't as if he even needed to give me the time of day.

I opened my mouth to tell him I was fine with him being gay. That it was his decision and it didn't matter to me. Instead, the words I thought I was too fucking chicken to admit spilled out. "I walked away from Ally and Sam. They're my best friends, and I walked away because I was stupid. I broke us apart. It was a knee-jerk reaction. I was shocked and I didn't think. When Sam chose to stay with Ally over leaving with me, I realized I'd made a mistake. My pride got in the way and—" I shrugged, trying to play off the overwhelming sense of loss I'd thrust on myself. My loneliness over these last couple of days had swamped me in a darkness that I wasn't sure how to find my way out of. "—I had to follow through. Jono drove me here and for four hours didn't say a single word. We had tea and he tried to talk some sense into me, but I wouldn't listen." I sucked in a breath and folded my hands together, stopping the shake in them. "When I said bye, he told me he was disappointed in me. I went to the co-op to let Bob know I needed work if anyone was looking. He asked me why I was leavin', and I told him it's because you're gay."

My heart thudded in my chest, shame drowning me. I was disappointed in myself too, but the thought of letting down Scottie and his family—the same ones who'd opened their hearts and their homes to Sam and me half a lifetime ago—weighed more on me than I cared to admit. Tears sprung to my eyes and I rubbed them, with the heel of my hands, stymieing their flow. But my verbal diarrhoea continued. "Saying it now sounds as ridiculous as it did when I told Bob, but the way he reacted... I don't think I've seen anyone so disgusted, and I was ashamed of myself for acting exactly the same way. I didn't ask if you were okay—you'd just been in a bloody fire for God's sake. You're good to us, Scottie. You're a good bloke. You didn't deserve the way I treated you. Nor you, Macca. So, I'm sorry. I'm sorry for outing you too. I should have thought about it, but I didn't."

Scottie sighed and closed his eyes. "I won't stand for any disrespect, Craig. One snide comment, one smart-arse remark and you're out. But I appreciate your apology. If you wanna come home, we'd be happy to have you back."

I must have looked like one of those circus clowns, my mouth hanging open and my eyes wide. "Seriously? Because yeah, that'd be bonza."

CHAPTER 16

Sam

It was the third time since Craig had left that I'd walked away from Ally when all I wanted to do was curl into her. She had pushed me away the night of the fire. Last night she'd done the same. Tonight, she hadn't even sat with me after dinner—not that it mattered anyway. She headed up to bed within five minutes of the kitchen being cleaned.

I wanted to tell her she meant everything to me. That I'd stayed because I loved her. As much as it hurt to admit, I'd known right from the beginning that I'd never have a chance with Craig. It was a pipe dream. Something that I'd been misguided at best—a fucking idiot at worst—to even think of. But Ally was real. And instead of staying with her, I was leaving the homestead and heading to my empty cabin.

It wasn't only that I didn't want to be alone. I didn't want to be apart from her and with the stilted conversations we'd had and the fact that she was actively avoiding me, it was as if a gulf had opened between us. The chasm that had formed when Craig's departure detonated the fragile connection we were building after finally being honest with each other had destroyed any hope of bridging the gap. I could have been on another planet to her.

Dejected, I shoved my hands in my pockets and trudged away. My heart grew heavier and the little light of hope that had flickered on when Ally had told us that she'd wanted us for as long as we'd wanted her was snuffed out. I ached, every part of my being ripped raw.

My boots thudded on the hard-packed dirt drive, each pained step taking me away from the one person I needed. She was in the house behind me. Why was I walking away?

I stopped. Paused. Closed my eyes and breathed through the agony. It was a painful reminder that there were no longer two people on the station who mattered. Craig had left. I hated him a little in that moment, then hated myself for being disloyal. But it wasn't me who had packed up and walked away from us.

I opened my eyes and looked up to the sky, taking in the serenity of the moment. Wishing I felt that same inner peace that the outback had. It usually calmed my soul. Before we'd arrived, I didn't know it would bring me as much solace as it had. The wide-open spaces and ruggedness of the desert were inextricably part of me now, and I a part of it. The stars were familiar, even though I'd never be able to name the constellations they formed in. The sounds, the smells, the place. I was part of something important here. My life was meaningful. I made a difference in some small way. But meaningful and contributing weren't enough any-more, not after what I'd lost. What we'd lost. I wanted to make my home here. I wanted love and a family. I wanted to watch my kids grow up right here on this land of red dirt and blue skies.

My resolve strengthened and I straightened. I needed to get my shit into gear and I would do whatever it took to make it happen.

Shaking out my hands, I breathed in a lungful of the crisp night air and blew it out slowly, my breath creating a fog in front of me. I nodded and spun on the heel of my boot to go back into the house. I crossed the threshold, looking around the room. Ally wasn't down there, so I called up the stairs for her. Had she watched me walking away from her window? Had she seen me return?

Conversation ceased. Jono wore a small smile and Den looked between Ally and me as she walked down the stairs wearing a fluffy robe. "Mind if we have a word?"

She nodded, moving closer as she descended the stairs, carefully placing the mug she was holding down on the table before following me outside. We didn't go far. I led her around the veranda to the front of the house, away from prying ears. This was something I didn't want overheard by the others, but it needed to be said.

"Ally, look—"

"I didn't want to choose—" She closed her eyes and her shoulders slumped. I took her hands slowly in mine. They were rough and calloused like every one of us who worked here. They were beautiful.

"I never would have asked that of you." She was so close. I could lean down and kiss her. I closed my eyes, wishing I could. Wishing I had the right to. "Never." I smiled, but it was a sad one at best. "I need to tell you something. Can I do that?"

"Course."

"I'm sorry. I'm sorry that I let you down." I shook my head, the pain of what I'd done like a sword stabbing me through the heart. "I'm sorry that I didn't have the courage to tell you how I felt." I rubbed my thumb over the soft skin on the back of her hand and wished that she'd tell me I could touch her anytime. That I could love her and hold her. "I'm sorry we interfered and didn't let you experience relationships and love like you deserved. I'm sorry I stole a decade from you that I can't give back. You deserved everything and all I've done is taken from you. Your happiness, your..." I paused. "Fuck," I muttered as it dawned on me.

"What?"

"I've always wanted a family. Pictured myself with a couple of lil' tackers running around my ankles. I've stolen that from you too."

She huffed out a surprised laugh. "I'm not that fucking old!"

"No, but what if you don't meet someone now?"

"Are you saying that you don't want this? Us?" She enunciated her words slowly. Precisely.

"No." I shook my head. "I want it. I want us. But you've pulled back. I didn't think...."

"I don't know what I want. I feel like you did take all those things from me, but I know you didn't mean it maliciously." Her words struck like a physical blow, knocking the wind out of me. I rubbed my chest, trying to ease the ache. This time it was Ally who squeezed my hand and stepped closer, placing the palm of her free hand over my heart. "And I got something in return. I got years of friendship from two of the best men I know. Even though I haven't had many relationships, I've had one with you. I've had one with Craig. It was friendships, not what I dreamed of, but now the three of us are over. He's gone and I don't know how to deal with that. I don't know who we are without him. I need to find somewhere for just the two of us."

"Yeah." My voice sounded strained, the vice in my chest tightening. I nodded. "I don't know who I am either." I looked away, blinking back tears. Ally wasn't the only one of us struggling.

"You really do know, don't you? We all did the one thing none of us wanted, didn't we? We hurt each other." When I nodded, she continued. "How do you see us together in the future without him?"

I shook my head, not really knowing how to be without Craig. We'd spent time apart, sure, but we always knew we'd be together within a few days or weeks. But this time, I was realizing that I might never see him again. And that broke something inside me. Half of my heart had cracked and dropped like an anvil, shattering when it landed, sending shards of the finest slivers cascading along the ground and spreading like the concentric circles of a pond.

I was lost, and I didn't know how to piece myself back together. But I did know that Ally was still here with me and if anyone had the power to mend what Craig had destroyed, it was her. I wanted to give her the world, and I would fight until my last breath to be there for her and repair the hurt Craig had inflicted on her too. "I want us to be a family." I cupped her cheek, brushing my thumb over the soft skin there. "I want to wake up next to you and make love to you. I want to hold your hands and grow old together. I want to be sitting on those rocking chairs right there with you when we're Nan's age, watching our kids and grandkids run this station."

"What about Craig?"

"I wish he were here. I wish he'd never left. I wish that it was the three of us watching our kids run around. Laughing and living and loving each other."

"Did you ever tell him?" She cocked her head to the side.

"I don't…" I shook my head, not having the energy or the will to deny my feelings anymore. "No, I never told him."

"How long have you loved him?" she asked, lowering her voice even more.

"Years."

"Oh, honey." She wrapped her hand around my nape and pulled me to her, pressing her lips to my cheek. I melted into her comfort, wrapping my arms around her waist and holding her tight. "Do you think we can get there?"

"I really want to. I want everything with you. I know Craig does too."

"Why isn't he here then? Why isn't he fighting like you are?"

"Because I was an idiot. A self-centred blind arsehole who just didn't get that leaving this station meant that I would be leaving the two of you too."

I tensed. That voice was as familiar as my own. Craig. My heart thudded in my chest. Was I hearing things? Was it ghosts of his memory speaking to me?

Ally's eyes widened and she shifted, moving so she could see around me.

"Craig?" she whispered, a mixture of joy and anger in her tone.

I still couldn't turn around. What had he heard? It was one thing to admit to Ally how I felt, but I couldn't tell him. Not after his reaction to Scottie and Macca. No, if I wanted our friendship to have any hope of getting past this, I needed to keep my trap shut.

"I might have lost my head there for a few days. I'm sorry." He stepped close and, standing shoulder to shoulder, he wrapped an arm around Ally's waist, his hand touching my own. "But even though I wasn't here, but out there"—he motioned over his shoulder in the vague direction of Longreach—"don't think I wasn't thinking of being here with you." He tipped Ally's face up and pressed a soft kiss to her forehead, his lips lingering. It was chaste by all accounts, but watching him kiss her so gently and affectionately made my heart skip a beat. I leaned and ran my nose up her cheek, pressing my lips against her temple.

Ally jumped backwards, instantly putting enough distance between us that it might as well have been an ocean. She bit her knuckle and shook her head, tears springing to her eyes. "No. I can't. I won't. You can't just fuck off then come back here and act like it's all okay. You left, Craig. You walked away from us. You destroyed all my trust in you. All my faith." She turned to me and glared. "And you? What, you're just going to stand there? You tell me you want this, us, and you're just going to let me be the one who pulls us up? Are you not going to stand up for yourself? Fight for what you want?"

I closed my eyes and hung my head in shame. She was right. I was a coward, but my throat had closed, the words getting stuck. When I opened them again, Craig was looking at her intently. I could see the sorrow in his eyes, the sheer force of will he was using to hold himself back from reaching out to her to beg for her forgiveness. But he respected her space, just like I'd always known he would.

"I'm sorry. You're right. I had no right to come back here. To interrupt you. I had no right to think you'd even want to hear me out." His quiet words were filled with anguish. "I know I've broken us, and that you don't trust me anymore. I don't deserve your trust either. But I've learnt my lesson. I understand now. I'm not asking for forgiveness, just time. I wanna make this right. Explain what I learnt by walking away, but should have known all along."

"I don't know that I can." Her tears fell in earnest now. She looked at me and I knew. It was partially because of my confession. Because even after we'd worked our way through Craig leaving then coming back, we'd still have a final secret hanging between us. One that could never come out. She wanted me to come clean. But how could I do that when I'd seen his reaction to our boss?

In the grand scheme of things, Craig spent little time with him, whereas we'd slept in the same bedroom for decades. For God's sake, how could Craig possibly be okay with my feelings when he'd hightailed it outta here after seeing Scottie kiss Macca? I shook my head, silently begging her not to say anything, but also not to leave things between us like this. But there was no point.

"I'm sorry." She turned and dashed inside, leaving Craig and me alone, my heart beating out of my chest and at the same time shattering into a million pieces.

Craig's pained groan from next to me had me closing my eyes and clenching my jaw, concentrating all my effort on not reaching for him. Because if I did, I honestly wasn't sure whether I'd knock him for six or show him how the other half of my heart—the part Ally didn't own—beat for him.

CHAPTER 17

Ally

I didn't make it two steps inside before Jono was grasping my arms and halting my progress, his body blocking the path past the table and up the stairs. "What did he do?" I shook my head, unable to answer him. "Did he hurt you?"

"Not the way you think. It's screwed six ways from Sunday."

"You let me know if you want me to give him a talking to, okay." Scottie looked up to Jono like a father. I hadn't ever really done that. Dad and I were closer. We kept in touch, unlike he and Scottie. Not that that's what Dad wanted. He wanted to have a relationship with his son, but Scottie had cut him off completely, turning instead to Jono, who'd accepted the role wholeheartedly. I'd always adored Jono—in many ways I wished that he and Ma had gotten together years ago. They would have been a better match than Ma and Dad. I also understood why Scottie had done it. Jono was the kind of man who would have been a great father. His solid presence and reassurances had solved many a problem on the station. He was kind and caring and with his attention turned on me, I felt his unquestioning love for me as the daughter I knew he'd wanted.

"Could you check on them?" I asked. "To make sure they're okay?"

"They?" He furrowed his brow in question.

"Craig's back." I looked to Scottie and Macca who were standing close, chatting to Nan and Ma. "He didn't tell you?"

Scottie shrugged like it was no big deal. "We were getting to that. Got distracted."

"Whatever," I mumbled, uninterested in whatever excuse they had. Three days ago, life had been good. Then a fire roared through the station and my world had imploded. It'd ripped apart so much of what I'd held dear that I didn't even know where to start trying to fit the pieces of the mangled wreck back together.

"I'll check up on them, love." He patted my shoulder awkwardly and stepped aside, letting me pass. I heard the back door close on my way to my bedroom where I curled up on the bed, my mind spinning in circles with everything that had happened in the last few days.

If it wasn't bad enough, now that Craig was back, we'd had to break the news to him.

Blond lay dead before us. For all Waru's efforts to free him, the bull had wandered straight into the path of the flames. It was a wide front and the wind had whipped it up, spot fires skipping ahead of the front, leapfrogging so it travelled faster and faster along the tinder dry ground. Even patches of dirt with no remnant vegetation—and there were lots that were simply bare—had been singed. The smoke lay thick, lingering in the air the day after the front had passed through. During the thick of it, Blond could easily have been disoriented, his brain starved of much-needed oxygen.

The loss of the big stud bull was a major blow to the station. The mob had increased production and the quality of calf had improved significantly since we'd brought him on. As sire to the majority of calves, Blond was essential. Thankfully, we were insured, so the financial loss wasn't going to cripple us, but his death was another setback that we had to bounce back from. Emotionally, it was taking a lot higher toll than simply making a claim for reimbursement.

It was especially tough on Sam. He'd known how much Craig had loved the damn bull. The first rule of any livestock production was to never get emotionally tied to the cattle. But we'd all broken that rule when it came to Blond. Seeing him interact with Craig had given us all a soft spot for the big beast, and the double whammy of Blond's loss and Craig leaving had hit Sam hard.

When we hadn't been able to get a read on Blond's tracker on the monitoring app, I'd forced myself to accept the worst. Before we'd even set out, I'd known. I'd steeled myself for the sight of him. But it didn't help. It hadn't taken much to find Blond. Waru's directions were spot on. The bull had only moved a hundred metres or so away from the mended—now burned—fence.

The sight of his blackened hair and burned body lying motionless had shattered me. The wildlife had already started devouring him, a murder of crows feasting on his carcass. We hadn't needed to get close to know he was gone. Even still, Sam had, sliding off Spook and trudging over, spine bent as if he was curling in on himself. He shooed away the crows and then ripped off his hat and threw it. As if finding Blond's carcass had been the last straw for Sam, he'd run his hands through his hair, tugging on the ends. The pained roar that had escaped his parted lips had broken something in me. I'd resisted going to him, trying to respect his need for privacy, but I hadn't ventured far away. I couldn't. I'd never heard him so desolate, battling a loss so deep that he was breaking to pieces.

I didn't know how long he'd stood there, breathing hard, anger radiating off him. But when he returned, he strode straight past me going to Spook when I'd reached for him. I stood there, waiting for him, waiting for a sign that he would turn to me rather than his horse. It was as if Spook could read him, dropping his head low so Sam could take the much-needed comfort he offered. But Spook didn't stay still for long, nudging Sam away after a moment. I went to him then, running my hand down his back, but he'd stiffened at my touch, and I'd backed off.

*****

Craig's face paled and he muttered a curse, his skin looking ashen in the light of dawn. "When? The fire?" His voice cracked with pain and even after a sleepless night when I learned just how deep the secrets between us went, and the hopelessness of our predicament had weighed heavily on me, my heart broke for him. The tears I hadn't managed to keep at bay the night before threatened to fall again.

"Yeah, mate." Sam squeezed Craig's shoulder and cleared his throat while Craig had looked away. He sucked in a breath and pulled free, walking away from us. His boots crunched on the dirt and he kicked at a stray rock, sending it soaring in a high arc.

We could barely hear him when he spoke. "I want to see him." It was a six-hour round trip on horseback, one that 'Tella and Spook had already done. Craig could do with the bonding time with Daisy again. She'd fretted so much the day that we'd taken the other horses out that Scottie ended up working with her just to keep her occupied. We saddled up and began the trek out to Blond's grave.

Craig had a special bond with the bull. From the moment they'd seen one another, there was a spark. A tether that kept bringing them back to one another. Playing basketball with a bull may have seemed a little out there, but it was their thing. Even though it only happened a few times a year, after every muster Blond was rearing to go. He'd let himself be guided into the sorting yards and patiently wait there until the herd had been moved around. Then he'd scan the landscape non-stop until he spotted Craig. If he wasn't there holding the basketball, Blond would snort and huff and bellow until he got his game on. Craig had never once missed it, and now I wasn't sure what he'd do. Post-muster basketball games had become a kind of crazy tradition that'd developed at the station.

Now that Blond was gone, Craig needed time to say his goodbyes.

The red dirt was still freshly turned, the small mound that marked Blond's grave already starting to settle. Craig moved stiffly, looking over his shoulder at us as he walked towards it, while Daisy waited patiently for him to water her. I was still angry with Craig. Betrayal sang through my veins, fresh from his departure and raw from his return. But as angry and upset as I was with him, I couldn't let him do it alone. I dismounted 'Tella and went to stand beside him. I heard Sam do the same, while our horses joined Daisy under the only tree in the vicinity not touched by fire. It was an old eucalypt, tall with its branches splaying wide. We'd wanted to bury Blond under it, but its roots spread almost as broad as its canopy, and the last thing we needed was to topple the old tree. Instead, we buried Blond where he'd fallen, beside a smaller copse of trees scorched black with the inferno. The grass fire had run hot and fast, the strong winds having pushed the front along before it could lick through the trunks of the trees that followed the meandering of the dried riverbeds. This line of vegetation linked up with the ravine Macca had been in when the wind turned, changing the direction of the fire.

We stood together, Sam and me flanking Craig as he stared at the mound we'd packed down as hard as we could with the excavator. Shoulders hunched, he looked weary, like he was carrying the weight of the world on his shoulders. I reached out and linked my arm with his and Sam stepped closer too, not quite touching Craig, but letting him feel Sam's solid presence. "It's stupid for me to be cut, but I feel sad, you know?" He shook his head and continued, not waiting for an answer. "I can't help but think about why he abandoned the other bulls and came so far away from them. He's nowhere near water. What if he suffered?"

"Waru said he was calm." Sam turned to him as he spoke, his gaze soft. "I like to think that Blond came out here to have some alone time. He always did want to do things on his own terms, even die."

Craig shook his head, his voice wobbling as he spoke. "I should have been here instead of Waru. Scottie wanted him with Macca, but I should have insisted. Maybe I could have saved him."

"You can't beat yourself up, Craig." I leaned into him, resting my head on his shoulder. "It's just one of the shitty things that happens on a station sometimes. Blond was a good bull. He gave a lot of himself and helped get us through some tough breeding seasons. His legacy won't be forgotten."

"Yeah." He cleared his throat and nodded. "Yeah, he did." Craig pulled away from me, squatting at the base of the grave. "See ya, old mate. Ask for deposable thumbs in the next life, yeah. We'll tear up the court again one day." He patted the red dirt a couple of times and returned to Sam and me.

We walked to the big old tree, Sam with his hand on Craig's shoulder as we trudged over. We fed and watered the horses, letting them rest while we ate an early lunch of sangas and tea. The silence between us was awkward and I hated it. I wanted to go back to how we were, but I didn't even know if that "us" really existed, or if we were a figment created by deception. I didn't think we'd find out either. Until we could hash it all out—come clean and own up to where the hurt was festering the worst—I didn't see a way forward. And Sam just wasn't ready.

I didn't know if he would ever be.

He'd seen Craig's reaction to Scottie and Macca, and now that Sam had him back, I doubted he'd ever do anything to rock the boat again. It wasn't fair though—this love triangle we found ourselves in was sure to implode if we didn't talk it out soon enough.

It'd all go to shit. Just like it had a few days earlier.

"I feel like there's a lot of things that might've turned out differently if I hadn't pissed off," Craig said out of the blue. "I'm sorry I ballsed it up so badly."

"You told us why you came back." I played with the cotton on my cut-off shorts, unable to look at either of them when I raised the proverbial elephant in the room. "But you didn't explain why you reacted the way you did to Scottie and Macca."

Sam looked away, the set of his shoulders tense. Apprehension radiated off him. I knew he both wanted to know and didn't. He feared Craig's answer, and what it would mean for them. For him. Maybe I shouldn't push. Maybe I should keep my mouth shut for Sam's sake, but Scottie was my brother and I needed to know too.

"I don't really know, to be honest." He spoke slowly, and I could tell he was choosing his words carefully, concentration lines marring his forehead. "I wish I had a better answer, but honestly, I just don't know." He shook his head. "All I know is that I should have thought about things before I spouted off. It wasn't fair to anyone and I hurt both of you."

Sam stood up abruptly, wiping his hands on his jeans. He adjusted his hat and gathered up the containers of food. It was busy work, completely unnecessary but it clearly gave him an excuse to walk away. To get some distance between himself and Craig. This was Sam running. "Should we start heading back? Don't want to be out too late." Even if it took us twice as long to get back as it did to arrive, we'd still return well before sundown. But I didn't argue, and I didn't want to push things any further. Not when we were teetering on the edge.

Beginning the long journey back, we rode in silence, each one of us lost in our thoughts. Once upon a time, I'd hoped for an outing like this so I could spend a few hours alone with them. I'd wanted to know what it was like to be with them. Dreamed about them wanting me. Things were much simpler when I'd thought they were together. Having them had been a pipe dream, one that was never to be fulfilled. Back then, running away to Sydney had seemed like a good idea. Not anymore though. Everything had changed. But at the same time, nothing had.

Instead of being stuck in a rut, I was stuck not knowing how to move us forward. Could we ever push through the mistrust between us? Could we ever hope to work things out? The only way I could see it is if we were honest with each other. Except that we were falling into old habits again and telling partial truths.

I wasn't sure if I could ever trust them again, especially when I knew Sam wasn't being entirely honest—if he was lying about his feelings for Craig, what else could he lie about? And what if Craig just upped and left again? He hadn't given us a reason why he'd walked away, never mind a good one. I'd been quick to forgive in the past, but this time those things were adding up and the warning bells were sounding. Klaxons wailing so loudly my ears were ringing. Fear crawled up my throat, paralysing me from moving forward. From forgiving them.

But mostly my reluctance was because I couldn't help but think Sam would wake up one day and hate himself for never telling Craig. Or would Craig find out and piss off out of here? Sam didn't ever plan on telling him. He was prepared to live the rest of his life loving Craig from afar. How was that possibly the way to live? I wanted him to come out, to be honest about his feelings. But I'd seen with my own eyes what Craig thought of Scottie, a man he'd respected for over a decade. I completely understood Sam's reluctance, but surely hiding wasn't the answer either. He was still living a lie. It wasn't fair to either of them.

It was either one or the other though—tell him or don't. There was no in-between. No medium ground that would make all of us happy, and after a decade of waiting for them, where did that leave me? We were so close to making a relationship work, but at the same time, we were teetering on the edge. I didn't want to choose between them, and Sam shouldn't have to either. But Craig's choice was important too, and the chances of him wanting to go there were Buckleys and none.

It was late afternoon by the time we'd finished with the horses, and my mind was spinning in circles. I walked through the door and Ma called out, "Did you get the sheets on?"

"What sheets?" I asked.

"Sorry, love. Thought you were your nan." She stuck her head out of the kitchen, a tea towel in her hands

"What's Nan doing changing sheets? Why is she changing sheets?"

"Pete's friend is coming to stay. He called in a flap and Pete was worried. Apparently, it's unlike him. By the sounds of it, something drastic happened at his work. Scottie invited him to come up and stay. Don't know how long he'll be here for, but looks like he'll arrive tomorrow arvo. So, we're getting the guesthouse ready."

"Lemme freshen up and I'll go takeover for Nan." I dashed upstairs, cleaned up and jogged over to the guesthouse, where Nan was still struggling to get the sheets on the bed. Looking at her since she'd fallen sick over the winter still scared me. She'd lost so much weight and hadn't yet fully recovered. Even a couple of months on, she often needed a nap during the day.

"Hey, Nan." I went straight to the bed, taking over from her.

"Ta, love. I wasn't sure I'd be able to make it, but your ma's got enough on her plate with me not being able to do much these days."

"She doesn't mind, and neither do I." I took the cleaning cloth off her that she'd picked up and motioned for the chair. "I can do the rest. Take a load off."

Nan eased herself into the small armchair in the bedroom and sighed. "This old body...."

"You've had a rough year. Look how long it took for Scottie to feel like himself again after he got sick."

"Yeah, I'll happily put this year behind us." She huffed and shook her head. I knew exactly what she meant.

"Me too." I sighed and sprayed the dresser down, wiping its surface with disinfectant. Straightening the antique silver hairbrush and mirror set, I lined them up on the white doily. It was my great grandmother's. Maybe even her mother's.

"Want to talk about it?" Nan held out her hand, motioning for the brush I'd just been holding. After passing it to her, I sat on the floor, my back to her front.

"I don't really know." She began brushing my hair, moving slowly as she gently untangled the knots from it.

"I remember doing this when you were a little girl. I asked you once what you wanted to be when you grew up. Do you remember what you told me?"

I huffed. "Yeah. Between astronaut and princess, I think I wanted to be a station owner like you and Ma."

"And look at you." The pride in Nan's voice was obvious. I looked over my shoulder, facing her.

"Are you proud of me, Nan? I wonder whether I've done... enough." I shrugged, unsure of myself. I'd been doing a lot of second guessing of myself lately.

"I was proud of you from the moment you were born, Allyra, and I will be proud of you until the day I die and beyond. You could never do anything that would change that."

Could I tell her? Did I dare risk my family turning away from me because of what I'd done? But no, they weren't like that. Scottie had the same fear, and Ma and Nan were nothing but supportive of him when he came out. Would Nan be there for me too if I confided my secret to her? I needed someone to talk to—the two people who'd always been there for me were, as much as myself, the cause of all this mess. "What about if I've fallen in love with two men?" I hung my head, uncertain but hoping her reaction wouldn't be too negative.

"Oh, love. Are you just realizing this?" Nan rested her free hand on my shoulder.

"No." I shook my head, biting down on my lip.

"Good, because anyone with eyes can see that the three of you are meant for each other." She patted my shoulder and continued, "They love you and it's obvious you love them too." My breath hitched and I clasped my hand over my mouth, willing myself not to shatter and turn into a sobbing mess. Nan didn't push me, and she didn't stop brushing my hair either. "You know, the thing I'm most proud of your mother for is her resilience. She is tough." She sighed.

"I wish she didn't have to be all the time, but that's not our life.

"When your pops warned her about marrying your dad, she stood up to him. She said it was her life. I can remember it like it was yesterday." I could hear the smile in her voice at the memory. "She stood up to him. Told him that he may be a more experienced stockman than her and she'd always respect his decisions on station matters, but he didn't know her heart. She had no compunction in telling him that his, or anyone else's, opinion was wrong. She never hesitated. Once she made her mind up about something, that was it. She married your dad regardless of what everyone thought about falling in love with a city boy, then she did the same with running this station." Nan squeezed my shoulder gently. "You have that same quality. Do you understand what I'm saying?"

"That I should start listening to people, so I don't end up divorced?" I answered, my sarcasm obvious.

"Hush," she chastised with a laugh. "You know your heart just like your ma did. They weren't meant to be together forever, but if she hadn't stood up to your pops, she wouldn't have either you or Scottie. I can tell you now if your ma could go back to that day knowing what she knows now and remake those choices, she would choose to have the two of you every single time. If you love those boys, then screw what anyone tells you. Choose them, love. Choose your happiness."

"I don't know if I can forgive them." The admission tasted like acid on my tongue. "Or maybe I can forgive Sam, but now I'm scared Craig's going to leave again. I don't know. My head is all messed up."

"He screwed up."

"He did." I nodded. "Epically. Especially after what he and Sam pulled."

"What did they do?" Nan paused, brushing my hair for a moment, her voice lowering in accusation.

"When they first came to work here, they agreed that neither one of them would make a move on me, so they wouldn't hurt each other. They hurt me instead. They took away my chance to decide what I wanted with them. I never even had a say in my own life."

"Hmmm."

"And then Craig ups and nicks off. He didn't even say bye to me. I shouldn't be dirty, but I am. It's stupid, I know." I shook my head but before I could continue, Nan spoke.

"It's not stupid, love. The three of you have been insep- arable for over a decade and suddenly he decided that he was so disgusted by what Scottie and Macca do in private that he was prepared to toss that friendship away. I don't blame you for being upset with him, especially because he ignored you in the whole process."

"He didn't even tell me why he left. Told me he didn't know. What kind of answer is that?" I huffed, frustration boiling over.

Nan ran the brush down my hair, the bristles slipping through the strands unimpeded now. "Maybe he's just not ready to tell you, or perhaps to admit it to himself."

I nodded. "Maybe. Even if I can get over this, Sam told me something else that changes everything and I have no clue what to do."

"Did they ever intentionally set out to hurt you?"

"No." I shook my head. "No, I don't believe they could ever do that."

"And this thing that Sam told you, does it change the way he feels about you? Or the way you feel about him?"

"No, but it does change things between us." I pulled away and turned to face Nan and sighed. "It's not my story to tell, Nan, and I can't tell it because if I do, I could destroy everything, but if I don't, I'm doing the exact same thing that they did to me."

Nan shook her head. "They need to talk to each other. Sam's going regret it for the rest of his life if he doesn't tell that boy he loves him, and Craig could miss out on the most wonderful thing if he can't get his head out of his arse. That's what this is, isn't it?"

I nodded, wide-eyed, and Nan smiled. "I didn't see it with your brother, and it kills me that I missed how miserable he was because he was hiding. But I see it with those two. Have done since day one. They love each other. Craig just doesn't realize it."

"So what do I do? Do I push Sam to tell Craig? Do I pretend I don't know anything? If Craig finds out that I know, he's going to feel exactly like I did. Like I do. I mean, I don't even know if I should forgive Craig for walking away from us. What's to say he won't do it again if he finds out that Sam loves him?"

She cupped my cheeks in her weathered hands. "You can't change your history with those boys, love. You can't undo the hurt. But you don't have to live in the past either. Remember I told you, you'd know when the time is right? Well, now is your chance to choose to start fresh from where you are today. It's not a matter of forgetting the past, but you can put it aside and move on. You can change your future. You can be brave and go for what your heart wants."

"And Sam's secret?"

"I think it's his secret to tell. All you can do is be there to support him and let him know that he's safe here. He'll always be a part of this family no matter what." I nodded, grateful for Nan's insight. She'd said that she was proud of Ma giving everyone the finger and doing her own thing, but Ma had learnt it from Nan. She was the strongest woman I'd ever known.

"What do I do about Craig?" I asked.

"He made a mistake, but he also realized pretty quickly that he'd made it. He came home." Nan smiled gently. "Maybe cut him a bit of slack for making a stupid, reactive decision. Then give him the confidence to be brave enough to accept Sam's love, if that's what he truly wants. If not, be there to try to help them find a middle ground where both are happy."

"I'll be up shit creek without a paddle if I can't."

"You'll do it, love. I've got every confidence that you three will find your happiness together."

"Thanks, Nan." I smiled, wishing that she was right. Only time would tell, I supposed. I got up off the floor, a little worse for wear after six hours on horseback. "S'pose we should get ready for Macca's friend, hey?"

Nan smiled and stood, taking the cleaner out of my hands. "I'll do this if you make the bed." We worked together then, getting the guesthouse ready, my thoughts turning over and over in my mind. Nan was right. I could either hold onto past hurts or look to my future. None of us were perfect. I'd denied myself, holding myself apart so that I didn't rock the boat, just as much as they'd made a stupid decision on my part. Maybe if I'd taken the bull by the horns a decade ago, we would've been in a different position today. But how did I get us moving in the right direction now?

CHAPTER 18

Ally

I was quiet through dinner, unsure of what to say or how to react to them. I could see the looks Craig and Sam were sharing between them. The uncertainty reverberating through the air. Nan's words tumbled over and over in my mind, and I kept returning to the idea that my future would always be the same unless I changed it.

Nan was right. No matter how long I focussed on the past, I'd still never be able to undo what happened. They'd never intended to hurt me. If I didn't let it go, I'd be in this same spot in another ten years wondering why I hadn't done something to divert the course of my future.

After tea, sitting there at the foot of my bed wearing my comfiest PJs, picking at another loose thread on the worn hem, I made up my mind. I had to speak to them. I had to tell them that we just needed to put all the bullshit behind us. I'd had enough waiting and enough debating. I was done with thinking.

Now I wanted to act. To feel. I wanted their touch.

I wanted them.

Regardless of what happened between Sam and Craig, I needed to act for me. It was Sam's decision to come out to him, and I'd be there for him if he did. It was the only way we could do this. Sam wouldn't come out on his own, not because he wasn't brave enough, but because Sam didn't see the two of them together any more than he saw a relationship between just the two of us. It was why we'd waited all these years to do something. I couldn't imagine choosing. Neither would they. It was all of us, or none. We were three.

Fuck waiting.

I was done with that.

I rushed out of my bedroom and Nan called out, "That's my girl." It stopped me short and I smiled, grateful that my family didn't even blink an eye at the idea of me wanting two men. Jogging, I descended the stairs and caught the door before it banged shut. I shoved my feet into my boots and ran to them.

I wasn't waiting another moment.

My knock on the door shattered the quiet of the night, the three raps of my knuckles on the timber reverberating around me. Craig swung it open, standing before me in a pair of low-riding sleep shorts. He looked around bleary-eyed and shook off his sleep. "What's wrong?" There was a hint of urgency in his voice. Rubbing his eyes, he blinked in the lights that had activated when I'd run past. The crease on his face from his pillow remained.

"I need to come in." Pushing past him, I headed straight for their bedroom, stopping short as I saw their beds for the first time—the two singles were pushed apart with a small bedside table between them. Shaking my head, I moved over to Sam's bed and sat down.

"Ally, what's wrong?" He sat up, the sheets pooling at his waist. Sam wasn't wearing a shirt either and being close enough to reach out for him had me clasping my hands together, resisting the temptation of that lean chest and his long muscles.

"We need to talk." I waited for Craig to sit opposite me before I continued. "I'm done waiting. I want to be together."

"Huh?" Craig scratched his chest and yawned.

"I want to have sex. With both of you. Now. I wanna start now."

Craig's head snapped up, instantly awake and the furrow in Sam's brow had disappeared as the emotions flitted across his face—first shock, then surprise. He opened his mouth, but no words came out, and I laughed self-consciously. I hadn't considered that they might change their minds. Craig tilted his head assessing me and I rubbed my neck, not enjoying the scrutiny.

Sam spoke first. "Um, Ally? Are you serious?"

"As a heart attack." I looked between them and waited, wishing they'd realize I knew what I wanted. The dim light being cast by the moon shone through the window, highlighting their faces in both shadow and light. But neither of them moved. They didn't speak. I'd waited too long. They didn't want this. I went to stand, getting halfway up off the bed when Sam stumbled forward, lunging out of bed and Craig jumped up. "It's okay—"

They crashed into each other, the thunk of their heads knocking together drowning out the rustle of their clothes and the bedsheets. Grunts of pain and curses muttered under their breath sounded as Sam's momentum sent them crashing to the floor. Another oomph and a hiss and Sam was on his feet.

"Sorry, man. You okay?" Holding out his hand, he helped Craig up.

"Yeah, mate." Craig rubbed his forehead, gingerly touching the lump already forming. "Ow, fuck." Sam gently gripped his chin, turning his face into the moonlight.

"You'll be right. You didn't split the skin."

Craig sat back down on his bed and Sam reached for the lamp, turning it on before pulling me down again and taking my hand. I looked around, not able to meet their gazes. The walls were the same cream that we'd painted them twelve years earlier in anticipation of their arrival. An old *Lethal Weapon* poster was tacked to the wall, slightly out of square. It was the only change they'd made—the same curtains were still hanging, even the original plastic laundry basket stood in the corner.

"It looks like a bloody dorm room in here," I remarked, self-consciously. Crossing my arms over my body, I noticed for the first time how ratty my PJs looked. They were as old as the hills, one knee almost worn through, and the other torn. The spaghetti strapped singlet had seen better days too, with holes along the hemline where I'd been pulling apart the seam. But they were the most comfortable ones I had, and I needed comfort far more often than I needed sexy. I'd been stuck in a funk for so long that my care factor had been hovering at zero fucks. Until tonight. I definitely wasn't going to win awards for style or sex appeal.

Sam leaned forward, his elbows on his knees. "So you want to sleep with us? You're ready to take this further?"

My hands shook and my nerves ratcheted up. This was what I wanted. Why was it so hard to talk about it? Aside from my less than stellar pickup line asking for sex, my tongue was tied, and my face was hot. Embarrassment warred with my bluntness and for the first time in my life, I knew what real inner conflict meant. Not the "will I or won't I" kind, but the one where I knew I should be strong and able to say what I wanted and yet, feeling the pressure to conform to what I'd seen them expect in a woman. Or maybe it was what I'd imagined that they expected. I had no real idea what they'd want, and that frightened me more than anything.

Taking a deep breath, I gathered up my courage and looked at them. "Yes, but I... I'm not getting passed between beds and the three of us aren't going to fit in one."

The boys smiled and without any words, Craig held out his hand and pulled me up while Sam guided me to the corner. The moment I was out of the way, they moved into action. Like so many times I'd seen before, they worked seamlessly. Barely a word was spoken between them. Sam switched off the lamp and unplugged it while Craig moved the bedside table out of the way. They shifted their beds into the middle of the room, pushing the two metal frames together until there was barely a gap between them. The look between them was the same they shared with one another the first time I thought they were together. It was one filled with adoration. With heat. This time I hoped it was because they were fantasizing about me.

Craig tossed Sam's belt to him and wrapped his own around the two closest legs. Sam fastened the simple pipe headboards together and tested the strength of the fixing by shoving at the bed frames. "That'll do it." He turned to me with a smile.

"You wanna come here, Ally?" He held out his hand but I hesitated.

I watched as Craig moved onto the bed, kneeling on his side of it. "Let's talk first."

"Um, okay?" I hesitated.

"Why don't you take your boots off and hop up." Sam patted the bed between them. "There's no pressure."

I kicked off my boots and looked down at myself, wishing I had more to offer them than just me in my shitty old clothes. I smoothed out my singlet, making no difference to the creases in the cotton. "Zero fucks," I mumbled, kind of disgusted in myself for not even having thought to get changed.

Eyes twinkling with a wicked smirk on his lips, he taunted, "Zero fucks, huh?" Craig chuckled when my gaze shot to his. "I love the look you've got going on, Al."

"Shut up." I pulled the straps up to show a little less cleavage.

"They're cute." Sam snickered.

"If you're gonna hang shit on me—"

"Nah," they answered in unison and I huffed out a laugh. I was back to not knowing whether to be excited or mortified. My heart was beating like a band of wild horses galloping across the plains, my hands shaking with nervousness.

"I wasn't exactly planning on getting laid when I got dressed tonight." I knelt at the end of the mattress. "Right, how's this gonna work?"

Sam choked out a surprised laugh. "Ally, honey, come sit 'ere." He patted the bed between them. "We wanna talk for a second."

I bit back the nerves and shuffled forward. I was between them facing their expectant gazes. Sam shifted, tugging on his loose boxers, unsuccessfully covering himself up while Craig reached for my hand, threading our fingers together. He brushed his lips, whisper soft, against my knuckles, murmuring all soothingly, "Thank you, Ally. It means everything to me that you're here. After I left, I never dreamed…." He shook his head, his shoulders falling.

"I know." I squeezed his hand.

"We're glad you came." Sam paused. "Just so we're straight though, can you walk us through what you want?"

"You want me to give you instructions?" I squeaked, horrified. "On how to have sex?" Jesus, if that's what they wanted, I was screwed. They'd better not be the kind of blokes who couldn't find a clit between the two of them. I hadn't waited years to finally touch them only to be bitterly disappointed.

Sam choked out a laugh while Craig snorted. "We're still catching up on your thoughts here, Ally, but believe me, we can find a clit."

I clapped my hand over my mouth and felt every millimetre of the flush staining my skin, heat crawling up my throat and over my cheeks. "Oh, God." Mortification sent a rush of heat through me and I was sure my skin was flushed a bright red. "I said that out loud?"

"I didn't mean instructions for sex." Sam smiled, running his fingers through my hair before tucking a stray lock behind my ear. "This isn't a one-time thing for us, Ally. We don't just want a one and done."

"Yeah." Craig cleared his throat after his voice cracked. "We want everything. Is that what you want too?"

I looked at Craig, trying to discern if he understood just how far Sam and I wanted "everything" to go. My gaze bounded to Sam, hoping he understood how I would support him. *I'll keep your secret, but I'll be there when you're ready to tell him. I want you to be happy too. I want you to be able to love him too.* "I do," I whispered to Craig, before turning to Sam and adding, "I really do." The smile he gifted me with was everything. Small, but it lit up the room, and I knew that he understood what I was trying to tell him. "I don't want to get bogged down in the past anymore. We all fucked up. Let's move on and change our future, yeah?"

"I could kiss you right now." Craig bit down on his lip.

The rush of confidence and desire hit me hard, emboldening me. "Why don't you?"

He shuffled forward on his knees, until I was sitting between his legs, and wrapped an arm around me. He smiled and leaned forward, pressing his lips to mine. A soft touch. A gentle tease.

"So, the three of us, yeah?" I blurted. "In a relationship."

"If you'll have both of us." Sam sat on my other side. He'd shifted too, moving in so he was nearly behind me. His arm around my waist and his lips nestled against my throat, he inhaled, running his nose up into my hair.

I nodded, my heart pounding as I thought about exactly what it would mean.

"Good." Craig smiled and ran his fingertips up and down the back of my arm, his soft touch a tease before he leaned in and kissed me again, slow and deep and toe-curlingly sexy.

"You guys are gonna have to work at it though." I sucked in a breath, dizzy with desire. Barely able to string a sentence together, I struggled to form the words. Need pulsed through me as I floated on a haze of kiss-drunk eagerness. "I want orgasm for orgasm with you two. There's no way I'm giving BJ after BJ without my own orgasm."

"I wouldn't expect you to." Craig choked out a laugh and I glared at him. "That's the beauty of having two of us. We can both look after you."

"That's good." I sighed, not knowing whether I was referring to our conversation or Sam's licking, sucking, and kissing the column of my neck.

"I should have known you'd be as blunt as you normally are." Craig shook his head, smiling.

I straightened, pulling away from Sam. "If you've got a problem with me being sex-positive and expecting give and take, you know what you can do with your relationship."

"Ally," Sam cooed, pulling me back into his arms, back against his solid chest and his rigid dick. "The whole point of this is to make each other feel good. Let's do that. I want to enjoy making you happy as much as we want to be. Tell me, tell us, if you're not into something. We've had enough of not communicating with each other."

"Yeah." I paused, gathering the courage to speak as Craig kissed a line up the other side of my throat. My hands in their hair, their bodies close, but not close enough and my need ratcheting up, I gasped when Sam moved his hand under my shirt. He ran his fingers up my belly, my muscles quivering as he walked his fingers up to my breasts. Agony and ecstasy warred for dominance and I was a slave to the sensation. Craig pulled back, desire pooling like the deepest oceans in his gaze as he watched Sam brush his thumb over my nipple. "Fuck," I panted. "I need you guys to make me come. Like yesterday."

They were silent a moment, then Craig reacted, shifting backwards so he could uncross my legs as Sam pulled me back against his chest. "How many times can you handle in one night?" he whispered, his voice sultry in my ear.

"Oh, fuck." I breathed hard as he nipped my lobe and Craig ran his calloused palms up my legs. Curling his fingers under my pyjama pants, he tugged them down, exposing me to them. They'd seen me naked once before, but this was different. This was everything. Fingering the strap of my shirt, Sam flicked it off and Craig watched hungrily as it slid down my shoulder. His hot breath on my neck, Sam hummed and laid a trail of kisses up to my ear, tracing the shell with his tongue.

"Kiss me, Ally." His voice rumbled through me and I turned to him. He tilted my face to his and my eyes fluttered closed, imagining the two of them together too. Sam's kiss was the opposite of Craig's soft possession. Sam dived forward, enveloping me in a whirlwind of desire. Every ounce of his pent-up frustration and want had me melting into a puddle of quivering need in his arms.

His kiss seized me. Breathing hard, our tongues touched for the first time and I whimpered as Craig spread my legs. Open to them, their sure touches and hums of appreciation mixed with a constant stream of words telling me how beautiful and amazing I was showed me just how deep the love that had built between us over the long years of our friendship was. I wasn't sure who tugged my top down, but it was Sam's hands that cupped my small breasts, my nipples pebbling in the cool of the room.

"You're so fuckin' sexy." Craig blew out a breath, slowly moving up my leg and peppering me with a line of kisses as he got closer and closer to where I really wanted his mouth. His fingers grazed my pussy gently and my core clenched as I fisted my hands in both their hair and tugged them where I needed them both.

Craig circled his tongue around my clit, delving deeper into my folds as his fingers opened me up, first rubbing before pressing inside me. His thick digits stretched me, lighting up my nerve endings as he crooked his fingers searching for my G-spot. I gasped and pressed down onto him as he hit it and his tongue connected with my clit, just hard enough to send an electric shock through my body. My hips moved of their own accord as I wantonly rode his fingers, seeking and searching for the orgasm that was so close.

Sam slid his hands over my sides, and I arched into him again as he took my lips and his fingers closed gently over my nipples once more, pinching until they were hardened peaks until I shuddered out, "Oh fuck."

Craig licked me again, his fingers sliding in and out of me as he relentlessly tagged my G-spot. His hot breath washed over me, and I jerked in Sam's hold, desperate for more.

Craig didn't disappoint, his lips closing over my clit and sucking. Fireworks exploded behind my eyelids and my entire core clenched, thrumming with energy. My orgasm hit me, pulsing like thundering waves crashing over me. I cried out and rode the high, Craig and Sam stretching out my orgasm until I was too sensitive to touch. I pulled back and instantly they were hands off, Craig moaning and grasping his dick through his shorts. I slumped against Sam who hissed and the rocked his hips against my back. Their movements had me shifting, lying between both of them. "I wanna see you both come," I begged. "On me."

Craig pushed his shorts down, grasping his cock and pumping hard. It only took three strokes for him to shudder and arch back, his jaw clenched as he moaned and painted my skin with thick white ribbons of his cum. He breathed hard, his head back and his hand still wrapped around his dick. My gaze cut to Sam, who hadn't even made a move to pull down his boxers, instead reaching up the leg, his fingers circling around the base of his cock squeezing hard. He looked pained, as if he was desperately trying to hold off his orgasm. I sat up and tugged his hand away, closing my own around his girth. He opened his eyes and stared at me and I smiled. "Come for me, Sam." I kissed him and whispered in his mouth, "I want your cum on me with Craig's."

That was all he needed to let loose, his movements jerky as he pressed into my hand and ground out a moan before shouting as he came long and hard. Pulse after pulse erupted from him, landing on my chest and mingling with our lover's. Craig reached out and smeared it across my breasts mixing it together and making me hum with his touch.

Sam slumped down next to me, resting his head on my shoulder and laying kisses along the curve of my breast. I lay there, legs still spread, their cum drying on my chest and Craig kneeling over me. "Ally," he breathed before lying half on me and capturing my lips with his kiss. I tasted myself on him and in the slow swipes of his tongue. I wished that he would share it with Sam. He nipped my lip and I grinned at him while I ran my fingers through Sam's hair. We stayed like that, both of them with their arms wrapped around me and comfortable in each other's presence until the sticky mess on my chest was dry and pulling my skin.

"Stay here, I'll get us some washcloths." Sam shifted and adjusted his boxers covering himself fully before padding into the bathroom.

"I didn't take you for a snuggler." I poked Craig in the side, teasing him.

"Never been with someone I wanted to do it with before." He paused and lowered his voice. "Is Sam okay? Kinda looked like he was uncomfortable."

"I think so." It was the best answer I could give. How did I tell him that I was guessing Sam was so worried about touching Craig and Craig's reaction to it that he was having to literally put me between them? I knew Sam's feelings for me. I knew he'd never use me to get near Craig. What worried me was how long he would be able to keep holding back before he broke. Before he just couldn't keep doing it. Would he be the one to run this time? "I hope he is."

Sam walked back in and tossed Craig a wet facecloth. He knelt next to me and wiped my chest down, refusing to look at either one of us, and it broke my heart. How was it fair that I had everything I wanted, but Sam didn't?

CHAPTER 19

Craig

The three of us shared a bed every night for a week. Every night we collapsed after hours of stroking and licking, sucking and fucking. And making love. It was a new feeling, wanting to go slow and merge together, to share Ally with Sam and for us to cherish her. It hadn't been awkward either. Much. Sam was holding himself back. He would wait to position himself. He'd withdraw every time my hand got near. It was as if he couldn't bear to touch me. It wasn't like we were jacking each other off, but a brush of a hand wouldn't kill either one of us. I knew it was my fault. I knew I'd been the one to poison us by walking away, but with Ally coming around, I thought we'd be okay.

I wasn't sure we were.

We sat round the bonfire in the yard, each of us perched on a cut log. Sam was late arriving and there was only one spot left—next to me. He'd hesitated and it'd ripped me to shreds. I hated being the one who'd fucked up our relationship, but I didn't know how to fix it. The dream I'd had the night before didn't help things either. The three of us were back in the shed at Hayes Horse Farm. I held Sam close and kissed him, telling him that I wanted him. Ally did the same and much like we'd been worshipping Ally's body, we wrapped Sam up and loved him.

I'd felt the haze of sleep gradually lift while I rocked into the mattress until Ally's playful slap to my arse stunned me awake. Sam was fast asleep, his knee bent and his own cock hanging soft across his hip. She'd whispered, "I'm hungry," and rolled over, presenting her arse to me as she shifted between Sam's legs. When she took Sam into her mouth, I'd barely had the condom on before sinking into her tight heat. Sam's eyes flew open, scrambling to hold onto something as Ally worked him over. Then his gaze had locked on mine and I was done for, coming long and loud in her.

Ally had groaned as I pulled out, a sound I now knew as frustrated. I'd urged her up on top of Sam, tossing him a rubber and mumbled a request for him to look after her. He'd suited up, rolled over her, hitched her leg over his elbow and thrust hard and deep into her until she was crying out in ecstasy. Hearing the two of them together—seeing him with her—had flipped a switch in me, reilluminating a dark corner in my head that I'd always put down to teenage hormones.

But I couldn't deny it anymore. Watching the muscles in his back and the firm globes of his arse contract as he thrust, had me wanting to climb in behind him. I wanted to touch and taste him like I'd done to Ally countless times in the last week. I'd wanted to blurt out the words none of us had said, but we all knew to be true. Except this time, I wanted to tell

Sam too, and not just in the "love between mates" kind of way.

I wanted to finally admit that I wasn't as straight as I'd always persuaded myself I was.

I just didn't know how.

It was mid-afternoon when the Beamer pulled up. Macca was jumping out of his skin at breakfast knowing his mate was on the way. It wasn't excitement though. He was worried. Pacing back and forth, looking at the clock on the wall, his lips were pursed and he wore a deep frown in his forehead. Apparently, something had gone down at this Phoenix bloke's job, and at Macca's insistence, he'd caught the train home, packed a bag, and driven out of the car park to come straight here. It was a nineteen-hour drive, impossible to do on his own in one day. So, Scottie had insisted he stop for the night and then make the rest of the trip that day.

When he stepped out of the dusty blue sedan, the guy looked defeated. Shoulders bent and head hung low, the bloke looked like he'd been beaten down and was barely standing. Evidently still in the same clothes he'd worn the day before—rumpled grey suit pants, black shiny shoes, and a pale pink shirt with its sleeves rolled up his forearms. His jet-black hair was messy, and shadows darkened under his eyes and his cheeks where his day-old growth was showing.

I was in the veggie patch up a ladder reattaching the split pipes on the overhead watering system, so I didn't hear what was said, but Macca was hugging him fiercely after a moment and his mate was nodding and rubbing his eyes. There were no introductions made. Instead, Macca led him into the guesthouse and let the door close after him. Macca had said his mate was in dire straits. Hopefully, he could help him sort things out.

Phoenix had been with us for a few days. When Macca had come out of the guesthouse twenty minutes after his mate had arrived, he'd gone straight up to the Beamer, pulled out his jacket, tie, and backpack from the passenger-side seat and taken it all back inside with him. It wasn't until teatime that we met Phoenix, but even showered, shaved and rested, he still looked like he was teetering on the edge.

I couldn't help but notice the air of sadness that hung around him. Whatever had driven him to the edge, it wasn't the only thing going on. I could see in the way he looked at Macca that he was spewin' that he and Scottie were together. I kind of felt sorry for the bloke.

He was quiet most of the time. But being out here seemed to be good for him. He'd smiled at Nan the day before and laughed at something Ma had said. It was the first time either of those things had happened, and the relief on

Macca's face when it did was palpable. It was kind of nice seeing Phoenix come to life again.

If only the same could be said for Sam. I hadn't seen him smile for days. It was uncanny how one person could be finding themselves again and the other pulling away before my own eyes. I had no idea how to fix it.

The bonfire we were sitting around didn't hold the answers, but it sure was fascinating when everyone started walking away, and I couldn't bear to watch them leave. It wasn't a big deal when Ally hopped up. She just followed Scottie into the house to sort out some paperwork for the new supplies being delivered. Everyone else kind of petered away too. But it was Sam leaving that was like a kick to the guts. He just stood and walked away. Didn't even look at me when he left, and another piece of me shattered when he did.

Phoenix hadn't moved in long minutes, his gaze never leaving the fire licking away at the logs piled into the bonfire. I shifted over, sitting on the log closest to him. "You wanna talk about it?" I was unsure whether it was the right thing to do. I wasn't exactly known for my sensitivity, but this shift inside me made me want to reach out and clutch at anything to steady myself. Even a good-looking stranger.

I froze, then blew out a quick breath. Apparently when you pulled one brick from the foundation of a lie you'd built around yourself, everything collapsed. A month ago, I wouldn't have even looked twice at Phoenix, never mind thought he was good-looking. But today... yeah. Not that there was any competition between him and Sam. Sam was... beautiful, if you could describe a bloke like that. Long and lean, with perfect hair and lips that turned up just so when he smiled.

Phoenix swung his gaze to me, then around the fire, surprise lighting up his expression. "They all went their own ways while you were thinking." I motioned to the empty seats. "Dunno if I'm the right person to talk to, but I'm listening if you want to try me."

He nodded and gave me a small smile. "What's the deal with you, Ally, and the tall bloke? Sam? She seems to be close to both of you."

"Yeah, Sam. We're together, in our own way."

"Huh." He was thoughtful a moment, nudging at a rock with his shoe. "You guys are pretty progressive for country bumpkins." He smirked at me, laughing at his own backwards compliment. "How'd it go down when Pete and Scottie came out? And for you guys I suppose? Having a gay couple and being poly isn't exactly run of the mill out here I wouldn't have thought."

I huffed out a laugh filled with shame. "There were two problem people when Scottie came out. Bob, the co-op owner, and me. I've been here for twelve years and my first reaction was to get the hell outta Dodge when I saw Scottie kiss Macca."

He looked at me and seemed to see straight through me and into my soul. It was as if he knew exactly how it felt. "You wanted to run, hey?"

"You have no idea." I picked up a stray twig on the ground and snapped it in half, tossing it into the fire.

"Packed my shit and got a lift into Longreach. Realized pretty quickly that I'd fucked up."

"And you guys are still together? You're lucky, man."

"We weren't together then." I shook my head, rubbing a hand over my buzzed hair. "We're pretty new. Still trying to work my way back to what it was like with Sam, but things have changed a bit. It's not straightforward anymore." I sighed, wishing that we were back to normal. Or maybe a new normal. "You seeing anyone?"

"Nah, I did have a girlfriend. More of a friends-with-benes type arrangement, but there was a certain redhead that I couldn't stop thinking about." He motioned to the house where Macca had gone to check in on Scottie and Ally. "When all the shit went down with work, he was the only person I wanted to talk to." He shook his head. "He talked me off a ledge I wasn't sure I could come back from. Then when he invited me here, I felt like I could breathe again. Being back in the country was exactly what I needed."

"Where are you from?"

"Bit west of the Gold Coast. The 'rents own a small farm. They used to be pretty self-sufficient, but now that they're older, they rent the barn space out for weddings and parties, that kind of thing. I hated it. Moved away from the Coast as soon as I could. Straight to Sydney so I could be a judge by the time I was forty and hang out on Oxford Street in my spare time." His laugh held no humour, and his grimace told me that things hadn't quite gone to plan. "As if I'd have spare time." He shifted, resting both elbows on his knees and looked at the ground. "Had a position with one of the best firms in the country learning the ropes in court with plans to do an internship with a top QC—a barrister. It all went to shit when he busted me in bed with his son while his daughter-in-law watched us."

I sputtered out a shocked cough. "What? How?"

"They arrived unannounced for Sunday brunch." Even though he wore a flippant smirk, I could see the pain that lurked below the surface. He wore a sadness like I'd recognised in Sam. There was a healthy dose of disappointment too. "I worked hard for that position, but it wasn't supposed to happen that way. That one night was worth it though, even if I did have to divert into another field." He looked off in the distance and bit his lip, hiding a smile that was more genuine. "She was beautiful, and he had a dick that hit my tonsils when he topped me. I had no idea who his crusty old dad was. We didn't exactly exchange family names when we met."

I cleared my throat, the picture forming in my mind all too vividly, my dick instantly more than interested in where this conversation was going. "So, what, you're into both guys and girls?" I desperately wanted him to keep talking so I could try to understand how he was so okay with himself.

"Yeah, I'm bi, like you."

"Ah…" I hesitated. I wanted to scream no, but there was a whisper in the back of my head saying "yes," and I couldn't bring myself to say the words. To deny it. Because for once, I'd met someone who might have the answers I was looking for.

Attending a boarding school as kids, we'd soon learnt that any sign of weakness was defined as gay, and gay was lesser. It was "other." On Sam's family farm, while the atmosphere was better, there was never a hesitation in using gay as an insult. I thought I was fine because I liked girls too, so I'd buried any attraction to boys—to Sam—and convinced myself I fit in that little straight-edged box that everyone apparently wanted me in. But a week of seeing Sam move inside Ally and hearing him moan her name as he came, of clashing gazes and resisting the temptation to shower him with love in the same way I did for Ally had rocked my foundation so solidly that the cracks in the walls I'd erected were irreparable. "How did you realize?" I asked, my voice sounding strangled.

"Same as you, probably. I didn't want to mess around with just the cheerleaders on the field when I was watching the footy. I wanted the players too." He chuckled. "There were a few who were surprisingly receptive to that too." The heat that washed over me made my face burn and a self-conscious laugh burst free from my lips. He wiggled his eyebrows. "There's nothing like giving a blow job when you know exactly how good it feels."

If he'd said that a week ago, I would have knocked him for six. But it would have been out of fear—from disgust that I'd been taught to feel. I was realizing I'd been internalizing my insecurities all along. Now? Well, I closed my eyes and thought back to that morning and the way I'd had to hold myself back from reaching for Sam and running my hand down his back to his arse. How I'd imagined touching and tasting him everywhere. I sucked in a breath. Yeah, I didn't just want the stockwoman, I wanted the stockman too.

"Might not be as obvious out here, but being bisexual is pretty common," he continued probably oblivious to the growing understanding of what I was. "Why not experience the best of both worlds, hey?" He smiled and playfully punched my arm, but that same tension, a sadness hovering in him just below the surface, had resurfaced. "I had to tell myself over and over that it's nothing to be ashamed of, but I'm still not out to so many people. Pete thought I was straight, and we lived together for years. His sister—one of my oldest friends—has no idea. Work doesn't either. I don't understand why people think that liking dick makes you less of a man, but it'd be career suicide in my firm. Look at Scottie. Same with you and Sam. You're all the epitome of masculine." He shook his head. "I can't imagine what you all went through as teenagers though. Realizing you were different, especially with Scottie being gay. He probably thought he was the only gay farmer out here—"

"Station owner, not farmer. Stations are bigger than farms."

"Oh, okay." He nodded. "Still. Wouldn't have been easy."

"No." I thought back on what Scottie was like before Macca. "He was much quieter. Didn't laugh anywhere near as much as he does now. He's lighter now too. It's as if he's no longer carrying this weight on his shoulders anymore. It was holding him back and none of us even knew. Now he's more confident in himself."

"I'm glad Pete's been good for him. He's a good bloke. I miss having him cluttering up my apartment." He became serious again, the heaviness he was holding back, seemingly overtaking him with the expulsion of his breath. "I dunno if I can go back there. Every time I think about getting on that train, or even going back to my apartment, I have a bloody anxiety attack. I was nearly hyperventilating trying to figure out how to get my job back."

"Why do you need it back?"

He raised an eyebrow at me. "Do you have any idea how expensive Sydney is? You can't just keep an apartment there and not work your arse off."

"So, give it up. Move somewhere else. Go home. Stay in Longreach. Whatever. Why do you need to live in Sydney if you're not happy?"

"Because…" He paused and looked at me like I'd given him the answer to the questions of the universe, but the fight soon left him again. "It's expected. It's what I am."

"Okay," I conceded. He knew himself better than me. It just didn't seem like that was what he wanted, but what did I know?

"Anyway, I don't want to think about that now." He dismissed the topic with a flip of his wrist. "Tell me more about your little trio. How long have you known Sam for?"

"All our lives." I smiled. "We grew up together."

He sighed and clasped his hands together. "Childhood sweethearts. That's so romantic. Urgh, the sweetness is killing me. You two are especially adorable around each other. You try to hide that you're madly in love with each other, but it's so obvious."

I startled, shocked that he thought he saw something between us. "What? How is it obvious?"

Phoenix laughed. "Are you kidding me? Sam looks at you like he wants to carry your baby and the way you watch him? It's as if you can't drag your eyes away from him. From both of them. You watch them like you want to protect them with everything inside of you."

He was right, I did look at both of them like that. At least, that's how I felt when I looked at them—I wouldn't hesitate to step in front of a charging bull if it meant protecting either one of them. It's how I ended up playing basketball with Blond to begin with. Ally tried helping get him in the trailer, but he was being stubborn. Not moving at all except to paw the ground and snort. I thought he was going to charge. I didn't even think. I'd jumped that fence with the ball and distracted him just to get Ally out of the way. I couldn't risk her being in there with him.

I'd done it with Sam too, catching a brown snake as long as I was tall when it lunged for Sam on our summer muster. Ally had lopped off its head and gutted it. We'd eaten the bastard that night for dinner. But I never thought for a moment that it was reciprocated. That there was any hope of Sam being into me.

The years of denying that part of me reached a crescendo, the wave breaking over me and washing away the remainder of that wall I'd constructed around me. Had Sam gone through the same thing because of me? Is that why he was constantly pulling back when the three of us were together? Was it because he couldn't bear to touch me for fear he'd shatter, just like I had felt that morning?

Damn it, what had I done? Why had I been so blind? Why had I bought into the propaganda so much? Why was the façade I'd erected so sharp, that whenever I repeated the hatred a shard had broken off and stabbed him?

The absolute certainty that that's exactly what had happened almost drowned me, the churning whitewash dragging me under. I needed to fix it. I needed to show Sam that he was perfect.

"I've gotta go, man." My words came out fast and I stood quickly. "Night." I didn't wait for him to answer, taking off in a sprint to the cabin.

CHAPTER 20

Craig

I barged through the door, letting it bang against the wall as I pushed through. Sam was on his feet in a split-second, upending the footstool in our makeshift lounge-room as he jumped up.

I sucked in a breath, the pounding of my heart reverberating in my chest like the vibrations from the big bass drum I saw one of the kids in our school orchestra play. "We need to talk," I spluttered. "I..." I groaned, frustration getting the best of me. How did I say the words? I looked at Sam, at his weary gaze and his arms crossed over his chest like he was shielding himself. My gaze flitted to Ally who'd come to stand beside him, one hand on the small of his back like she was supporting him.

I reached for Sam and he flinched. It was as if he'd sucker-punched me to the gut, but I didn't pull back. I forced myself to reach for him again, to take his hand in mine. I threaded our fingers together and held tight when he tried to pull away. Sam looked down at our hands and then up to my eyes. I couldn't read the expression on his face. Some unnamed emotion—fear, anguish, hope maybe—flickered in his eyes and I stepped forward into his space. "Sam," I breathed, before cupping his face with my free hand and brushing my lips over his, as gentle as the brush of a butterfly's wings. "My Sam," I whispered again. "Our Sam."

I hovered there, breathing his air, our lips a hair's breadth apart, waiting for him to move. To give me some indication, anything at all, that he wanted this. Instead, he shook his hand out of mine and pulled back, shrinking away from me, and moving into the farthest corner of the room. My legs didn't want to hold me up anymore. My whole world shifted away with him and I reached for the back of the couch to steady myself.

"What are you doing? Why?" His voice shook when he spoke.

"Craig, what's going on?" Ally asked, her tone brooking no argument.

"I…" I blew out a breath gathering my courage. "I've been lying to myself for years. I'm… Jesus, why can't I say it?" My breaths were ragged, my vision blurry. It was as if the room was spinning, the floor falling away from me. I was teetering on the edge. My heart raced and panic overwhelmed me. Fear flooded my veins. I must have looked like a wild animal ready to bolt.

"Craig," Ally said gently, stepping close. "You can tell us. You're safe here. We won't hurt you."

"But I've hurt both of you." I ran my fingers through my too-short hair, failing to grip the ends. "I've been so blind. I ran instead of facing up to who I am."

"When you left?" I closed my eyes and nodded, trying to calm my breathing. "Who are you, Craig?"

"I'm the man who's in love with you." I smiled at her and reached out, cupping her cheek. Sam had stepped closer and I reached for him too, holding out my hand and waiting for him to take it. Hoping he would.

"Craig, do you love Sam too?" she asked, and I nodded.

"Yeah, I love you too," I pledged to him, begging him to understand that I meant as more than friends. "I want to love you like I love Ally." His face crumbled, tears filling his eyes. In one stride he was in my arms, and I held on tight as he buried his face against my shoulder, fisted my shirt and cried silently.

"I've loved you for a lifetime," he whispered against my throat, his breath ghosting along my skin as he shuddered. His words made me shiver too, made me hold onto him tighter.

"I'm sorry, Sam. I'm so sorry for not understanding how I felt sooner. All those years I thought we were just mates. I didn't get it. I didn't see how much I loved you."

"What made you see it now?" Ally ran her hands over Sam's back, comforting him too.

"I've been dreaming of you both, and this morning, I wanted to touch you, Sam." I kissed Sam's temple and he slipped his arms around me. "I wanted to kiss you and hold you. Then I spoke to Phoenix. He asked about us, and when

I said we were together, he assumed it was all of us. His words...." I shook my head. "The walls I'd built just crumbled and I saw everything clearly. I can't explain it. He said he could see how in love we all were. I'd never seen it before. I'd buried those feelings but when he said he saw that I meant something to Sam too, I just... I had to get here."

"Craig, kiss him. Please," she urged. "Show him." Ally stepped back and Sam turned to her. Reached for her. Speaking to him, she smiled. "Let Craig show you, Sam. You've wanted this for so long."

"I want you too, Ally."

"And you've got me. Both of you do. But right now, you two need to connect with each other." Sam nodded but looked down, away from me.

"Sam, baby, look at me." I tilted his chin up with my finger and brushed my thumb over his stubbled cheek. His hairs were rough. Prickly from the day's growth. I brought my lips down to his. Soft lips met mine, trembling in my hold. That first touch, the first gentle press of his lips stole my breath. When he opened to me and I licked into his mouth, our tongues brushing ever so gently, his moan gave me life.

I held him close, cradling his body in my arms. I kissed him like he was water and I was parched from a lifetime of being without. I tasted him and caressed his face, touching him in the way I realized I'd wanted since I was old enough to understand what love was. I kissed down the column of his neck and licked into the divot at the base of his throat.

He tilted his head back, giving me more room and clutched onto me. I needed to prove to him I wasn't going anywhere.

"Ally," I breathed. "Help me show him." She was behind him in a second, lifting his shirt up and over his head, pressing kisses to his back and my knuckles as I mapped the muscles of his back and kissed him again. "I love you." I took Ally's hand in mine and squeezed gently. "Both of you."

She came behind me then and pulled my shirt up and over my head, dropping it onto the couch and slipping between us. "Nothing makes me happier than seeing the two of you together. For years I was happy knowing you had each other and now… now you really do." I leaned down and kissed Ally before Sam did the same.

Pressing my lips to her forehead again, I whispered, "Thank you. For being okay with this."

"I'll always be okay with you loving each other. Now, go back to making out. I wanna watch." She winked, slapped me on the arse and stepped back, waving her hand between us. "Proceed."

I laughed and cupped Sam's face again, hugging him tight with my other arm. "S'pose we better put on a show for our lady." I swallowed. "Um, do you know what you're doing?"

He shook his head and shrugged his shoulders, grinning. "We can practice. On each other."

The same line he used as a teenager. I'd brushed it off then. I wouldn't do it again. I'd been wrong to say it didn't mean anything because we weren't poofters. "As long as you know how much it means to me." I pressed a kiss to his lips. "I'm in love with you, Sam."

"I love you too." He laughed, a carefree sound. "That takes a load off, doesn't it. Fair dinkum, never thought I'd say that out loud to anyone except Ally."

"Can I touch you?" I murmured, licking and nibbling at his pulse point.

"Fuck yeah."

He moaned as I ran my hands down his back to his arse. His muscular cheeks were more than a handful. They were perfect. I kissed him again, our tongues tangling in a slow glide as I slid my hands into his jeans grasping under his jocks, then up, along his abs. Gentle touches mapping every inch of his torso soon wasn't enough. I hesitated, my fingers at the button, waiting for him to say yes.

"Please," he begged. "I need you to touch me."

It was all I needed to hear. Flicking it open, I tugged the zip down and let his jeans slip down his legs. Nerves pulsed through me. What if I wasn't any good? I palmed him, curiosity burning through my apprehension, moaning as my palm connected with his cock. He was hard and long. Not as thick as me, but easily an inch longer.

"Oh God." His whole body was wound as tight as a frog's arsehole. I rubbed his length, cupping his balls on the way down and brushing my thumb over his head as I came back up. He shuddered and hissed, and I wanted nothing more than to taste him.

I swallowed.

Fuck, how did I do it? "Ally, can you teach me how to suck Sam how he likes it?"

"Oh, hell yeah. Both of you get naked."

We did, Sam kicking off his jeans as I tugged my boots off, hopping from one foot to another to ditch them before losing everything else. Ally took my hand, wrapping it around Sam's cock and she pumped, adding a twist of her wrist at the tip. "This is how he likes it. Firm but not too hard. Not too fast unless he's on the edge." She did the same for Sam, wrapping his hand around my girth.

"See how thick he is," she hummed to Sam. "He'll feel so good inside you." I thrust into their grip, needing it tighter. Ally huffed out a laugh. "So needy. Craig likes it tighter than you. Just like this." She tightened Sam's grip and I choked out a cry. God damn, his hands were magical. Big and strong, he squeezed me just right.

Sam cried out and kissed me hard, forcing his tongue into my mouth and taking the kiss he needed. I gave him everything I had, jacking him in exactly the way Ally was directing me, except now, Ally had swallowed half his cock. She slipped her hand down and moved to his balls while I kept sliding my fist up and down his solid length. It was overwhelming. Sam's tongue in my mouth, my hand on him and his on me, Ally at our feet. I was liable to come apart at the seams.

Sam pulled back and heaved a breath and I shouted, a full-body shudder racking me as Ally went down on me. She swirled her tongue over my crown and I nearly came on the spot.

"Oh, bloody hell."

I jumped back, wrenching myself from my lovers' grips and raised my fist before the voice registered. "Scottie, what the fuck?"

Scottie turned on his heel and walked out, the door banging closed behind him. I snatched up my shirt covering my bits and ran, following him into the night. Sam was on my heels too. "Scottie," I yelled as he strode away. "It's not what it looks like."

He whirled on us, coming to stand chest to chest, fire in his eyes and his voice a menacing growl. "Oh yeah? What did it look like?"

"We love her. We aren't using her."

"The three of us are together," Sam added.

"My sister is more than capable of looking after herself, but know this. If you hurt her, I'll castrate you both with the rustiest piece of metal I can find out in the shed. And that's after she's through with you. Make sure you treat her how she deserves to be treated." He looked between us, his chest heaving and his jaw ticking. Scottie angry was a force to be reckoned with.

"We will, mate," Sam promised. He gripped Scottie's shoulder and shook him gently. "This is Ally we're talking about. We'd do anything for her."

"Craig?" Scottie turned his glare to me.

"Anything and everything."

"Okay." He shuddered, a pained look crossing his face. "Next time, shut your door. Lock it in fact. I never ever want to see my sister having sex. Ever again." The grimace on his face made us both laugh. "There's not enough brain bleach in the world for that."

He turned on his heel and strode away, leaving us in his wake, laughing at him. Sam ran his hand over my shoulder and down my back, turning into me and resting his head on my shoulder. I pulled him against me, holding him tight. "Hey, Scottie," I called. "What did you need?"

He paused and turned to look at us. "Came to make sure you weren't planning on jumping Phoenix in his sleep. He was shitting bricks when he told Pete you were bi, and he saw Pete's reaction. S'pose he got it right."

My skin flushed hot and I was sure I was blushing like a fool. "Yeah, tell Phoenix I said thanks for making me see straight. Or, maybe not so straight."

He motioned, wide-eyed, between the two of us. "To-night?" When I nodded, he shook his head, a look of disbelief lighting up his features as he ran his hand through his hair. "Damn. Look after my sister."

CHAPTER 21

Sam

"We just ditched Ally to chase after her brother," I mumbled against Craig's throat.

"Let's get back to her then, hey." He smiled at me and ran his thumb down my cheek whisper soft. It was intimate and tender. Lovely. "Why didn't I see you before?" He paused for a moment, his brow furrowed. "No, that's not right. Why didn't I acknowledge what I saw? Why was I scared stupid? I've wasted so much time."

"You weren't ready, and that's okay." He rested his forehead against mine and threaded his fingers through my hair. "The important thing is that we live now. No more fearing what anyone else thinks. Now, we love each other, and we love Ally."

He nodded and smiled, his lips tilting upwards softly. "I'd like that."

We turned and saw her standing in the doorway, leaning against the door jam. "You guys gonna stand there starkers all night?"

Craig nudged me inside and took her into his arms. "No, honey, I'm gonna bury myself in you." Craig's words were just loud enough that I could hear him. He dropped the tee he'd been holding at his groin. "Oh look, I'm already naked."

"Convenient." I laughed.

"Yeah, and look—" He snatched the tee I was still holding in place and tossed it over his shoulder with a grin. "You are too." We were barely inside, yet he fell to his knees and nuzzled my leg. The laugh died on my lips, replaced with a moan. "Now, these lessons, Ally."

Bloody hell, I'd fantasized about this for as long as I could remember. Wishing and wanting him to see me. To finally notice me as more than a friend. Now that it was happening, I wasn't sure I'd last more than a minute with that intense brown-eyed gaze fixed on me and his hands touching my body.

He reached out and palmed my dick, closing his fingers around my girth and stroking upward before sliding his hand lower, cupping my balls and back up again, repeating the move. I let my head fall back and moaned again when he kissed my leg, getting closer to my cock. "You have such a pretty dick."

I stilled. "Pretty?"

"Yeah, it's all velvety and... long." He smiled a wicked smile, a tease in his voice.

"You realize velvet is furry? You're telling me I've got a hairy dick. Thanks." I laughed, a flush creeping over my skin as they blatantly stared at me, their breaths floating over my overly sensitive sac when they moved in closer. Seeing them there, both of them kneeling in front of me and looking at me like I was their dessert, had me so hard I was going cross-eyed. My cock reached out for them, begging for their touch. "Velvety is such a stupid description."

Craig barked out a laugh and Ally grinned. Apparently, they were all about teasing me now. "How about you've got a sexy love stick?" He wrapped his hand around my length and stroked me again exactly the way Ally showed him. I sucked in a breath, my body shuddering at his gentle grip and the scrape of his work-roughened hands against my skin.

"Mmm, I like a womb raider like yours." Ally bit down on her lip, looking up at me through wide eyes before licking the head of my cock. Unable to stop her laugh, it turned into a graceless snort that had me snickering until she enveloped me in her mouth, my laugh dying on a gasp.

"Raiders of the lost arse." I stared at Craig, breathing hard as his comment sunk in, while Ally barked out a laugh and pulled off me. Jesus, that conjured up all sorts of images, all of which had me sliding inside him. My dick pulsed and I was on the edge, gripping hard to try and stave off spontaneous combustion.

"Weapon of arse destruction." Ally winked at Craig. I knew that laugh. It was relaxed and happy, and I hadn't heard it in far too long. Even that pushed me a step closer. I groaned, gripping the base of my cock. Ally giggled and added, "Oh, I know. His throbbing member was like a seek-and-destroy missile, exploding inside my love cave."

Whatever they continued saying, I was lost to it. My focus narrowed down, tunnel vision enveloping me, except that the only thing I could think about was my cock. I wanted them. Needed them to touch me. Their breaths and their warmth near my skin wasn't enough anymore. Desperation clawed at me, my body begging for human contact—their contact. I jacked myself slowly, pre-cum pooling at my tip and dripping down. When Craig reached out, scooping up the clear liquid with his finger before sucking on it, I hissed, squeezing my cock harder. Through gritted teeth, I begged, "Suck my dick, please."

"Aww, Sam's not playing along." Craig's exaggerated pout had me laughing.

I pulled my thoughts into something coherent, albeit ridiculous and concentrated on enunciating the words. "My fucking meat skewer is gonna paint both your lips with my special gloss in a minute. Suck me, please." I was torn between laughing at their antics and my brain imploding from the need pulsing through me. It wasn't something I'd experienced before. Laughing in bed wasn't exactly foreign, but it wasn't common for me on the rare occasions that I gave into the need for intimacy with a stranger. Never again though, and the relief of that knowledge had me staggering.

Craig batted my hand away and took me in his, looking up with wide eyes. Nerves danced in their dark depths, uncertainty flickering through them. I ran my fingers over his short-cropped hair and cupped his cheek. "Tell me if you hate it." His whispered words were serious, even fearful.

"You could do almost anything and I'd love it." He nodded and closed his eyes, baring his teeth.

"Woah." I pulled back, alarmed, and he cackled before gripping my arse and hauling me back to him. He opened his lips, tentatively touching his tongue against my tip, licking along my slit. He grimaced and I brushed my hand over his head again. "If you hate it—"

He swallowed me down, taking me so deep that he gagged before pulling off. "Fuck, you make it look easy, Ally." He kissed my slit, leaving his lips pressed against me in a move that was more loving than tease.

"Go slow." She stripped off her shirt and bra, then reached for Craig, running her fingertip over his lips. With her top half naked, her jeans undone and her hand in her pants, she was a sight made for sinning. "Lick him like a lollipop and use your hand. Twist your wrist like you did before." Craig tried again, his lips closing over my cockhead while he swirled his tongue over my slit, his eyes burning into mine. There was vulnerability there—for a man who'd only just admitted a same-sex attraction, he was pushing himself hard—but there was also that bloody-minded determination and grit that Craig had shown me over the years. He'd made up his mind and he was no doubt going to perfect the act of sucking cock. I couldn't wait to be his test subject.

"Fuck." I breathed through gritted teeth, trying to stave off the inevitable as Ally buried her face in my balls, licking and nipping the soft skin there. I was coming undone, fraying apart at the seams. My insides were coiling and twisting and turning, ready to detonate. The moans and sharp breaths were loud in my ears, and I knew I wasn't the only one of us making them. Craig pushed Ally's jeans down over her hips and slid his hand until he was cupping her mound, his thick finger pushing into her.

She cried out, bucking into him and she closed her hand over his cock, jacked him harder and faster. Craig slipped his mouth off me and rested his head against my leg. "Ally, I need to be inside you."

"Fuck, yes." She moaned, her eyes closing as if she could picture it in her head. "I want both of you to take me. Together."

Craig was on his feet in an instant, hauling Ally to him and tugging me along with them. We stumbled into the bedroom, all three of us landing in a pile on the bed. I shifted, trying not to elbow either one of them and helped Ally, all smooth skin and long hair, straddle Craig. She was beautiful. Lean muscle and curves, strength radiated from her. I loved her hair, the smooth brown strands so fine and shiny. Her eyes—the lightest blue I've ever seen were almost the colour of an iceberg. Her skin was tanned, all the work we did outdoors leaving all of us with stark lines of contrasting skin tones, but where Craig and I had darker arms and pasty white legs, Ally seemed to have a natural bronze all over.

They kissed, and Craig's hands on her arse encouraged her to rock against him, sliding together. I wanted in on it too. I yanked open the drawer and reached blindly for the condoms, unable to look away from the sensual dance they were performing before me. When Ally's hand landed on my arm and she shook her head, I paused.

"No. We're committed. None of us has been with anyone since our last test and we were negative for everything."

"What about birth control?" I asked.

"Would it be such a bad thing? I mean, I know it's early days, but I'd love a couple of kids." She shrugged, but the hope in her eyes betrayed how much the possibility meant to her.

"A couple of little tackers running around would be perfect." Craig sat up, Ally still perched on his lap. He tucked a lock of hair behind her ear and kissed her gently. "And this change to our relationship may be new, but we know each other. We're not going anywhere. We're in this together now."

I nodded, but fear poked its ugly head up. We were new and I had no doubt that we'd work long term, but there was one question I needed to ask. "What happens if you don't like what we do together? Can we keep going in some way or another?"

He held his hand out and when I grasped it, he brought my hand to his lips, kissing my knuckles softly. It was such a contrast seeing Craig with a lover—seeing the change in him with me. He was so gung-ho in everything else. He dived into things without even seemingly pausing to think. He was a loudmouth and had a personality that people often thought of as prickly, but he was loyal and loving and gentle where it mattered, like now. "We'll do what works for us. I can't guarantee that I'm going to love getting my arse played with or that I'll enjoy doing it to you, but being on my knees for you—" He flushed, his eyes full of heat. "—I liked that."

"It was incredible."

"Sexy and beautiful. I love seeing the two of you finally acting on your feelings." Ally took my hand in hers and held onto Craig with the other. We were connected, a circle of three. Our lady and her two blokes. "We agreed?"

"Hell yeah." I wanted to be bare in her more than anything I'd ever wanted before, but it wasn't just that. As Craig said, we weren't going anywhere and the chance to have a couple of kids with the two people I loved more than life itself... well, that'd be perfection.

I pushed Craig back, making him laugh, and straddled his legs behind Ally. Ghosting my fingers over her sides, I gripped her hips and ground against her, my half hard cock perking up again at the contact. I reached for Craig, stroking him to hardness again and sucked on Ally's neck. I'd waited for this for a decade—probably more—to get my hands on them, my mouth, and finally my dream was coming true.

"Lie down, honey." I nudged Ally and she quickly moved, Craig capturing her lips as soon as she got close enough to him. I scooted down until my face hovered near Ally's entrance, as she rocked, sliding her pussy along Craig's shaft. I licked, the tip of my tongue teasing her labia. As I sucked gently on the skin there, she moaned and thrust back against my face. My stubble rasped against Craig's sac and his hiss had me exploring him too. I moved my tongue, my lips and my hands getting to know my lovers. What they liked, what they loved. What had Craig bucking his hips forward and arching his neck until the thick muscles of his body were vibrating hard enough to worry that I'd make them snap. The burst of his taste onto my tongue, mingled with Ally's essence had me reaching for myself, stroking my cock as I alternated preparing them. Finally, when I thought Craig would lose his mind and Ally would smack me sideways, I helped Ally slide down onto Craig. Her breathy moan and Craig's growl were a temptation that I couldn't resist.

I slid back down, tonguing the place where they connected, sucking his balls into my mouth and sliding first one, then two fingers into her channel alongside Craig's length. I was careful stretching her. Taking Craig's thick cock was enough of a challenge, never mind having the two of us in her, but her demands and Craig's gravelly moans removed all my hesitation.

"Sam, fuck." Craig groaned. "I'm gonna blow like a fucking firework before you get in alongside me if you don't hurry the hell up."

"Now, Sam," Ally ordered.

Sliding my fingers out of her, I shuffled back up and positioned myself, watching intently as I pressed forward in time with Ally rocking her hips. The stretch of her skin enveloping both of us was the hottest fucking thing I'd ever watched. Tight heat surrounded the mushroom head of my dick as I stroked along Craig's turgid length. I rocked slowly, pushing forward into her until I was fully seated. It was a symphony for my senses, touch at overload point, the taste of my lovers on my tongue and the sight of my cock burrowing into Ally's heat worthy of any porn movie.

The sounds of Craig's incoherent curses and grunts, and Ally's moans mingled with my own harsh breaths and choked out pleas, combined with the smell of sex heavy in the air, sent me on a collision course to supernova. My eyes connected with Craig's and held as Ally arched up and rested her head on my shoulder as I tunnelled into her again.

He spread his legs, bending his knees and propelling his hips up, taking away my ability to think. I was a mass of bones and flesh, cells and fibres chasing the same thing that Craig and Ally were—release. With one hand on Ally's breast, playing gently with her nipple in the way she loved, and the other buried between her legs rubbing her clit, while Craig and I worked together to power us towards oblivion, I was on the edge. When the ripples in Ally's walls began, the gentle contractions growing stronger with every second, I lost it, my moan more of a hoarse curse. Her walls milked the cum out of me as Craig rammed his hips forward. His cock sliding alongside mine becoming impossibly hard as he shouted, breaking the quiet of the night. Ally's cry was silent, but her whole body stilled and yet vibrated at the same time as she squeezed us like a vice.

She fell forward, Craig catching her as I tried to drag in a breath, my vision going hazy in the blood rush. Pitching to the side, I dislodged my softening cock, making Craig hiss and Ally moan. My head landed on the pillow next to them, and I reached up with shaking hands to wipe Ally's sweaty hair from her forehead. I didn't know what to say. Words escaped me as I watched her eyes drift closed and a sweet smile lift her lips. Craig reached for me, tilting my head in just the right way that he could capture my lips.

Kissing me slowly, he explored every part of my mouth, his tongue dipping in and out as he made love to me with his kiss. When I pulled back for a breath, Ally was there, meeting my lips with her own.

CHAPTER 22

Sam

Brekkie was always going to be weird, what with Scottie finding out about Ally and us. But I had no idea how strange it'd be until we sat down. Ma had her arms crossed over her chest and one eyebrow raised. Nan took one look at us and cackled. The others' gazes were bouncing between us, smiling like they were all in on a secret.

"What?" Ally finally demanded.

Nan grinned wickedly "Well? Do you need something to take the sting out of the beard burn the three of you have?" My cheeks flushed hot and I touched my hand to it before I could think twice. "Yeah, right there, Sam." If I'd been red before, I was beetroot by that stage. Mortified was an understatement.

Macca snorted and I shot him a look, only for Scottie to laugh harder. The others around the table grinned, and I knew that there was no hiding our secret. Before I could open my mouth, Jono cleared his throat, and all eyes turned to him. "I'll say the same thing I said to all of youse when we found out about Scottie and Pete—if anyone has a problem with you three being together, then you can leave right now."

"Back then it was only me who had the problem." Craig's tone was serious. He looked around the table, and I saw Ally reach for him, resting her hand on his thigh. "I was running. From myself, mostly. So, um... I understand that you might be thinking I'm a hypocrite—" Craig reached over Ally's shoulders and clasped mine, before continuing— "and you'd be right. But Sam and Ally stood by me a long time while I worked it out for myself. Phoenix said something last night and it woke me up. I finally saw what I had in front of me and just so we're clear, I'm with Ally *and* Sam. I hope no one has a problem with us because of me, but if you do, I'll understand."

My heart leapt, somersaulting in my chest as a kaleidoscope of butterflies took flight in my belly. I couldn't help the grin that split my face and barely bit back the excited giggle. I wanted to reach over and kiss him until he forgot his name, but I settled for kissing the hand he still had resting on my shoulder, nuzzling into him. That he'd admitted our relationship to Ally's family—our family—meant the world. Never in a million years did I expect that he'd advertise we were together. I'd hoped one day it'd just be a badly kept secret, but this acknowledgement, this confirmation from his lips was everything.

"I won't," Ma said bluntly, dragging me back to the conversation, my thoughts jolting back to the rest of Craig's comment. "We're a family here. We stand by each other, no matter what. Craig, you needed to accept yourself as much as you needed to see that what Scottie and Pete have is a blessing. Sometimes that's not easy to do. We're thrilled you've found your way to each other."

"Cheers to that." Nan lifted her teacup into the air.

"Hear! hear!" Scottie raised his mug too. "I'm happy for you guys. But no screwing around where I can walk in on you again." He shuddered exaggeratedly and added, "I don't ever want to see my sister naked," before grinning wickedly at us.

Ally threw the crust of the toast she'd been eating at him. "Try knocking next time! And I wasn't naked!"

"Do I need to fight you for my lady's honour?" Craig asked. Ally paused mid-chew and looked to him. He choked out a laugh and pulled her forward, kissing her forehead. "I know you don't *need* anyone. I was just offering."

She swallowed her mouthful before turning to me. "Well? What about you? Are you set on defending my honour too?"

"Oh, hell no. I'll hold your beer while you sort it out."

"Better." She nodded and turned to Scottie who was still sniggering. Ally rolled her eyes but became serious. "Thank you, everyone. We appreciate the support. We know we're not exactly conventional but it's real. We love each other."

"Love is for sharing. You three have got a little more to go round," Phoenix added from his spot next to Macca.

"Thanks, mate. For everything." I could never thank Phoenix enough. What he'd done with a simple conversation had revolutionized my world. He'd been pivotal in giving me everything I'd ever dreamed of.

"I'm glad I could help in that small way, but really it was all Craig, not me."

I would be forever grateful to Phoenix. As if she knew exactly what was running through my head, Ally squeezed my hand and I held tight never wanting to let go. To let either of them go. And now, thanks to Phoenix making an innocent assumption which finally opened Craig's eyes, I didn't have to.

"So, talk to us, boss. What needs doing?"

When Scottie launched into his plans for the day's work, I sat back and enjoyed my family surrounding me. It'd been a while since I'd spoken with Ma and Dad as well as Craig's parents. I wondered, not for the first time since getting together with Ally, whether we should clue them into what was between us. I'd been hesitant before, especially because one woman sharing two men wasn't exactly "normal," as Craig had said, but I was heartened by Ma's, Nan's, and Jono's reactions after announcing that we were together.

Loading up the ute after brekkie, I broached the subject with Craig and Ally. "What do you think about visiting the parentals? Or maybe even just letting them know we're together?"

"I'd love to meet your folks." Ally smiled and laid a hand on my forearm. "And I'll respect whatever you and Craig decide on whether you'll tell them about the two of you." I

nodded and she left the shed, going out to grab some supplies from the smaller one.

"Whaddya think?" I sat down on a hay bale.

He shrugged, but I could see straight through the
feigned calm. "I dunno how they'll take it. They'll either be
shocked as shit, ropable, or be expecting it. S'pose the question is whether you'd be prepared to walk away if they don't
approve—"

"There's no chance in hell I'd be walking away." I stood
and moved to him. "I wouldn't give you and Ally up just to
satisfy them."

"Good thing too." He smiled, pushing me back down
and bracketed my legs with his own. He cupped my face in
his warm hands and leaned down, pressing a soft, lingering
kiss to my lips. "I was talking about walking away from
them. Would you rather keep them in the dark in case they
don't agree? Because, Sam, I'm not giving you up."

"If they don't like our relationship, it's their loss. They'll
be the ones giving up the chance to meet our lady and one
day their grandkids." He kissed me again, slowly and thoroughly until I couldn't bear to have a sliver of distance between us. Pulling him onto my lap, I palmed his arse cheeks
and tasted his lips again, never wanting to stop.

"Can we just text them?" He pulled back a fraction while
he rocked against my hardening dick. "That way we can just
stay in bed."

I hummed. "Mmm, I'm good with that. Think Ally will
mind?"

"Will I mind what?" She came up behind Craig and slipping her hands into his tee, lifting it off him and tossing it aside. I leaned down, licking his nipple and making him arch into my touch. With his hand holding my head against his chest, I nibbled on his skin as he thrust his hips.

"Fuck." His whispered words were ragged. "You've got to stop, or I'm gonna come in my pants.

"Want a blow job?"

"God, yes. But not here." He groaned, releasing my head. When he clambered off me, he stumbled, nearly falling over his own feet. Ally gripped him, steadying his balance until he righted himself while I lurched forward, grasping onto him too. He pressed the heel of his palm against the bulge in his pants, pushing his shaft down. "Later." That one simple word was a cross between a promise and a plea. I had no idea when or where it would be though; we were about to head off on a two-day trip to the north-western paddock, ready to create our environmental sanctuary.

"Can I watch?" Ally winked and kissed Craig quickly before doing the same for me.

"You guys almost ready to leave?" Jono called from outside the shed as he sauntered in.

"Yeah, mate." I stepped back from Ally and adjusted myself.

"Scottie's got the tractor, and the trailer is already loaded with the tank and all the other equipment we need. We just need to hook it up to the ute."

"The shovels were the last thing we needed, and they're in there now." Ally hopped in the ute, reversing it out of the shed.

The tank on the back of the trailer was big—oval-shaped—but shallow. The bore drilled into the Great Artesian Basin fed water into the cattle troughs, which in turn would drip into the tank we were fitting. The shallow watering hole would be low enough for the smaller native animals to drink from. The project, if it worked, would make the north-western paddock the beginning of an environmental reserve. Scottie wanted to close it down to help rehabilitate the desert from the impact of generations of cattle grazing on the land. Erosion and loss of topsoil would hopefully be slowed by reducing concentrated grazing and a regeneration of the ground cover, at the same time minimising compaction of the land. The science behind it was complex, and Scottie, Jono, and I had poured over reports from the CSIRO and information from agricultural advisory bodies.

Waru and Yindi had helped choose which bore to set the tank up at. Scottie had wanted to close off a paddock that contained land with cultural significance for their tribes. Helping their people stay connected with the land was another important thing he was trying to achieve. I respected the hell out of him for doing it too.

We got the trailer connected and the gates opened. It was going to be a bumpy ride, and a long one—four hours over paddocks going at a snail's pace. The river feeding the billabong we'd swam at years earlier was dry. The billabong itself was just a hole in the ground with hard-packed dirt and a few quartz boulders lining the ledge on what used to be the deeper end. It had been devoid of water for almost as long as I'd known it as a watering hole. The drought had ravaged the land and all its animals. We were trying to make a difference, and while we all felt helpless at the loss of native wildlife, we were also struggling. Water availability was at an all-time low.

Finally pulling up to the bore, I slid out from between Craig and Ally. Back aching and my legs tight, I stretched, trying to loosen up. Den and Scottie were already walking the site, measuring out in strides where to place the tank and pipework. I went over to the trough, which would be feeding the tank, and peered inside. Dry as a bone. It didn't surprise me at all, and it meant that the animals were wholly reliant on morning dew and the hardy vegetation for their water. No wonder they were struggling.

We worked as a team, levelling out the dirt, building a pad for the tank to sit on and heaving it into place. By the time we wrapped up, we were ready for a good feed, a cup of tea, and toasted marshmallows by the campfire Phoenix and Macca were building. Both were twitchy at the possibility of coming into contact with a snake—Macca didn't have a great track record with them and Phoenix was just shit-scared, but they managed it without incident. Before we knew it, we were cleaning up, readying ourselves for a cup of Nan's chilli beef and damper baked fresh in the coals.

CHAPTER 23

Ally

I t was hard work, and I was wrecked. But after a day of driving and then a whole lot of physical work, I was glad to be sitting around the crackling fire. Spring was the perfect time of year. Warm enough that we weren't sleeping in freezing conditions at night, but not so hot that it was dangerous to be outside for more than a few hours. Luckily, the bore we were working near was surrounded by a copse of trees. The bore had been sunk in the early days of the station, when they'd just run continuously, water spilling from the pipes and going to waste. Gramps—our great grandfather—had started capping them. Pops had finished the job, but the water had been running long enough to have established trees with strong root systems growing around the bore. An open tank situated here was good for the wildlife. While predators could wait in the cover of the vegetation, their prey could escape into it too, and it mimicked a desert oasis nicely.

For now, I was enjoying sitting cross-legged on the ground between Craig's legs with Sam next to us and a small part of my family surrounding us. Scottie was curled up with Macca, both of them whispering conspiratorially together, and Den and Phoenix were toasting marshmallows and passing them around. Jono had sat this one out, his old bones not liking sleeping rough much anymore, and Waru and Yindi were looking after the poddy calves while Ma and Na were looking after them.

"How long do you think you'll stay?" Sam asked Phoenix.

The other man looked up at the night sky, a million stars lighting up the blanket of darkness floating above us. "Got a message from my supervising partner demanding that I be back before the end of the week." He poked the fire with the stick he'd eaten his marshmallow off and watched it catch fire, burning slowly.

My gaze clashed with Phoenix's. "As in the day after tomorrow?"

He nodded, sadness hovering over him like a dark cloud. "I'll be leaving when we get back. If I get a move on tomorrow, I'll be back in Sydney early enough to stop in at the office before my boss heads off for the day."

It occurred to me that I had no idea what he did for a crust. "What do you do?"

"I'm a lawyer." He sighed, a frown on his lips and a crease marring his brow.

"You don't look too happy about it." Craig held up his hand and shook his head. "Sorry, I've already said that to you."

"Yeah, but that's what I am." He tossed the stick in the fire and clasped his hands together. "It's just the nature of the job. We work long hours and are under a lot of pressure. But you've got to put up with it if you want to get promoted."

Sam reached up and twisted my hair around his hand, playing with the strands in the way he knew I liked, and I sighed, melting into his touch. "That's pretty shitty if you ask me."

"Yeah, but it's par for the course. Every one of the elite firms expect it. If you can't handle the stress, you don't deserve to be partner."

My alternative future—the one I thought I'd wanted years ago—flashed before my eyes and I realized how lucky I was to have come home. I didn't understand it at the time. I thought of myself as a failure, not even mature enough to stave off homesickness, but that wasn't true. I was glad I hadn't gotten stuck in that hamster wheel. Those sliding-door moments in life may not have seemed like a big deal at the time, but the choices I made led me here.

Sitting by the fire on a quiet night, wrapped in Craig's arms with Sam sitting close, I knew that there was nowhere else I was meant to be. I wanted to grow old watching the sunsets and wake up in the morning listening to Hinchey, our rooster, crow. I wanted to live among the stars and see the blue of the sky every day instead of the four walls of an office. I wanted to have babies and love and be loved by the two men I was sitting with. I wanted to watch our kids learn to ride on ponies and swim in the billabong like Scottie and

I did as kids. Life was like a revolving door in some ways. I'd come full circle, right back to the place I'd wanted to leave, except now couldn't imagine ever being anywhere else.

I cleared my throat and spoke quietly, "You know, you could always walk away. Make an alternative future for yourself." I looked back at Craig and smiled. "Maybe you left because you needed to see your truth reflected back at you before you could see your path." Craig leaned down and pressed a kiss to my forehead and I rested my hand on his knee.

Phoenix shook his head. "Yeah, don't know about that alternative path option for me. This is the only real way for me to get to the top."

Conversation petered out and we laid down as the night wore on. It was the first time we'd camped out since we'd moved past being friends. Craig and Sam insisted I sleep between them, except, unlike in their cabin, we weren't sprawled out naked after a night of exploring each other. Still dressed in our clothes from that day, minus as much dust as we could shake off us, we slid into our swags and cuddled close. They kissed me and kissed each other, the three of us settling in just as nearby howls made Phoenix jump up. "S'okay," Macca said around a yawn. "They're just dingos." I smirked. He'd come a long way in the months since our winter muster when he'd been scared of getting eaten by them. "If you hear barking, wake us up. They're wild dogs or a mixed breed, but as long as we've got the fire burning, we'll be right."

"Should one of us stand guard?" The panic in his voice rose it by an octave or two.

"Nah, Pete's right," Scottie answered. "We aren't their food source. But I've got the rifle here just in case they start causing trouble."

"I better not get bloody eaten by one of them." Phoenix huffed and slid his swag a little closer to the fire.

Saying goodbye to Phoenix the next afternoon was strange. The friendship we'd struck up with him in such a short period was unexpected, but more than welcomed. He'd left his mark on this station—especially on us. He'd helped Craig finally work out his feelings and had been nothing but supportive when everything came to light. But now he was heading home to a job that made him miserable and an empty apartment he'd be alone in. He'd watched the man he'd crushed on find the man of his dreams. I was hurting for him; his life was a steaming pile at that moment. But it was also his decision to make.

As we stood on the driveway waving off his blue BMW, I hoped he'd find his happiness.

CHAPTER 24

Craig

I was obsessing. Plotting and planning and bloody scheming. It was all Scottie and Macca's fault. They'd not seen me in the shed when they stole in and Macca pushed Scottie's chest up against the horse stalls, ripping off his shirt. Gripping his hands, he'd guided them to the post and ground down on him, mimicking giving Scottie a thorough fucking. With his hand down Scottie's pants, the slick sounds of a hand job echoing through the shed, I heard Macca murmur the words that'd created a picture in my mind's eye I couldn't unsee. "You want me inside you?"

"Yes. Always. Fuck, I need you." Scottie had begged Macca with both his words and his actions, his chest heaving and his hips moving fluidly against Macca.

"Now? Here?" Macca had taunted. "Right where anyone could walk in?"

"Tack room." Scottie moaned and my heart stopped. I was standing in that room, only a couple of metres away from them. I crept out, but not before seeing Scottie sucking on Macca's fingers, pushing his arse back into Macca's groin.

I'd been curious before, but I'd been fixated on it since.

Desperate to now know what it felt like.

If Scottie liked it—loved it—would I? Was I man enough to try?

The hours until we were safely ensconced in the cabin dragged, each one lasting a week. I wanted this. Wanted Sam to take me. Needed him to.

I closed the door behind me and paused in the hallway. Ally was already in the loungeroom while Sam was at the doorway leaning against the jam, facing me. His brow furrowed and his lips in a thin line, he looked worried. "You okay? You've been quiet today."

"Had a bit on my mind," I admitted. He pushed off the door and took the two steps towards me, sliding his hands up and down my arms comfortingly.

"Want to talk about it?"

I nodded, then changed my mind. "No." Then changed my mind again. "Maybe?"

Ally came to stand next to me, wrapping her arm around my waist. "You can tell us anything, Craig."

I closed my eyes and sucked in a breath trying to fight through the nerves and fear lacing my very bones. Sam laid his hand on my cheek and bent to look in my eyes. "You're scaring me."

"I don't mean to. I'm sorry. I don't know how to talk to you about this." It was a hard admission to make, but I needed to get over myself. "But I want to try."

Sam reached for my hands and laced our fingers together. "Okay."

"I know I said that…" I shook my head and started over. "I want to have sex." I looked to Ally, silently pleading with her to read me the way she'd done the last time, but her gaze was wary, the crease in her forehead matching the one on Sam's. Her lips were pressed in a tight line too and I knew I had to push my way through this ridiculous fear on my part.

I blew out a breath and looked back at Sam. "With you. Not with Ally. I mean, with Ally but… but with you." I groaned, hating how the words were getting stuck in my throat. My body knew what it wanted. My cock was pressing hard against the zip of my jeans, but my head was all over the place. "Inside me." I huffed out a laugh, the relief hitting me like a cool breeze in summer, lifting the fear away and leaving freedom and light and an adrenaline buzz in its wake.

Sam opened, then closed his mouth, and his gaze flicked to Ally before settling back on me. "You want me—" I nodded, and he let go of my hands, reaching for my face with both of them. Cupping my cheeks, he lifted my face to his and pressed soft lips to mine, demanding entry with his tongue a moment later. Pushing me back, my arse hit the door, and he crushed himself to me, our lips never parting. He kissed me like I'd never been kissed, possessing me and at the same time leaving me in no doubt he was on the same page. "Say it again," he demanded.

"I've been imagining it. Picturing you inside me, pumping in and out. I keep thinking about what it'd feel like with you inside me. I need to know."

"Where do you want me? Tell me where you want me to be inside of you." He captured my lips again and slid his tongue against my own. He ground against me, his engorged cock steely hard against my own.

"Inside my arse. I want you to just fuck me."

He stilled and sucked in a breath but shook his head. "It'll never be *just* fucking between the three of us, Craig."

"Then give me everything. Please."

"Come into the bedroom," Ally directed. Sam took my hand again and led me up the hall, following her. She patted the bed where she'd turned down the covers and placed the lube on the pillow. I stopped at the side of the mattress and reached for Sam, needing him close.

"Jesus, you're shaking." Concern laced Sam's voice. "You sure about this?"

"Never been surer. Just nervous." I smiled, but I was sure it looked more like a grimace.

He cupped my cheek gently again and pressed a kiss to my forehead. "We'll look after you. But you tell us to stop or give you a sec and we will, okay?"

"Yeah." This time when my lips tilted up, I knew it was more genuine; the corresponding smile Sam gave me lit his eyes up. The whole room if I were being honest. He kissed me then, soft and slow. He made love to my mouth. Ally's hands under my shirt, lifting it, made me shiver. Goosebumps rose on my skin as Sam kissed along my jaw and down my throat, humming as he licked at my pounding pulse point.

"I've loved you a long damn time, Craig. I can't believe that you love me too," he whispered, kissing a line along my collarbone. He shifted me until the backs of my knees hit the bed and guided me, hovering over me as I laid down. My feet hung off the end of the bed, and Ally slipped off the thongs I'd worn to the main house for tea. She fitted herself behind Sam, pressed against my legs. I heard the clink of his belt and the rasp of the zip of his jeans sounding before Sam wiggled above me. I knew he was trying to kick off his clothes, but it was awkward as fuck. My lips turned up in a smile and he pulled back, gazing down at me.

Kiss drunk with wet lips and glazed eyes, he looked fuck-ing sexy. I'd never wanted him more. Reaching up, I pulled him down to me, but not before Ally's deft fingers had my jeans unzipped and yanked down over my arse. Sam shifted, connecting our lips again and straddled me.

Cool air hit my body, then a warm breath. Ally. A hot tongue swept out, licking over my balls. But then it was gone. Sam moaned from above me and I knew she was play-ing with both of us. Sam dropped his weight down, sliding our shafts together and my back arched, every fibre of my being needing to get closer to him. His fist closed around our cocks, gripping them tightly. I tore my mouth away from his, needing to look down. To see us together. The purple head of my dick leaked a drop of pre-cum onto my belly, a thread of the viscous liquid holding until Sam swiped his fin-gers over our tips and stroked downward, as he thrust forward. I sucked in a breath and moaned when sensation shot through me with Ally sucking one of my balls into her mouth, tonguing the sphere.

The flick of a cap sounded, and cool, slippery fingers touched the strip of sensitive skin behind my balls. I gasped. Trailing down, featherlight swipes as she teased me, I couldn't help but thrust into those deft fingers. Sam moaned. "Oh yeah, do it again."

Ally ran the pad of her finger over the tight ring of muscle and I clenched, a full body shudder passing over me. I dragged my mouth away from Sam and panted as Ally circled and nudged me. I'd never wanted anything more in my life, the need spiking in me whited out any other thoughts. I needed the penetration. I needed to know. Bending my knees, I opened myself to her, and Ally stopped teasing, slipping the tip of her finger into me. My shout was muffled by Sam's kiss.

"Okay?" she asked, pausing.

"More."

She slid deeper, pushing past the muscle and inside me. The stretch was foreign, like my body wanted to eject it and yet suck her finger in deeper. Sam's teeth grazed my jaw and I arched up into him, then collapsed back as I drove my dick into his fist. Ally fingered me, her movements slow and gentle. "Ally," I begged, and she responded, going deeper and faster. My body bowed off the bed as she hit something inside of me that had every nerve ending lighting up like a Christmas tree. My prostate. "Oh fuck," I gasped. "Harder, deeper."

Instead, she pulled out and I cried out in frustration only for it to end on a moan as she pushed against me again, the stretch more intense and the lube cool once more. She crooked her fingers and my arse lifted off the mattress. My cock slid through Sam's fist and he sat up and looking behind him. "Oh fuck, that's the sexiest thing I've ever seen. I wish you could see how your arse is swallowing Ally's fingers, Craig. Jesus, you love it, don't you?"

I moaned again as Ally moved, unable to form a coherent thought, never mind words. When she pulled out again, I clenched, trying to keep her there, but there was immediate pressure again and more burn.

"Let me in, Craig. Just relax." It was intense, even though she moved slowly stretching me. My erection was flagging, and there was no doubt in my mind that Sam could feel it. He shifted, pulling away from me and spinning on his knees until his mouth was hovering over my dick. Ally curled her fingers and hit that bundle of nerves again, driving me insane with the electrified jolts moving through me. Sam licked me from base to tip, then sucked my cock into his hot mouth while Ally stretched me, rotating her fingers and tagging my P-spot with every pass.

The tingling at the base of my spine hit me faster than I expected. With my hand on Sam's shoulder, I squeezed, rasping, "Stop," before I hit the point of no return. "I'm gonna come."

Sam pulled off with a pop and Ally slowly dragged her fingers out until she had just the tip of one in my arse, taunting me with more. Still playing with my rim, Ally turned

Sam's face to her with her free hand and kissed him, humming, "Mmm, the two of you—my two favourite flavours."

"Think he's ready, beautiful?"

"Why don't you see for yourself?" She flicked the cap on the lube again. I watched, seeing my chest heave as she drizzled lube on Sam's fingers and he reached down, painting my balls, my taint and my hole with it. I sat up in a partial crunch, desperate to see him slide his fingers into me. The breath gushed out of my lungs as he pushed all the way inside me in one slow move. His gaze never left mine; our eyes connected over the distance.

"Never in a million dreams." The awe in his voice stoked the burn of desire and love inside me into an inferno. He pumped in and out before curling his finger and hitting that spot inside me again. I scrambled on the bed, my legs slipping as I fucked his fingers, needing more of the press against that bloody spot. Fuck me, it was so damn good. There weren't words for how fucking stunning it was.

He pulled back and must have added another finger, the burn of the stretch making me moan. With a hand on my dick, I pumped, riding the edge of an orgasm again. "Now," I breathed.

The flick of the cap sounded again, and I licked my lips as he slicked himself up, running his fingers over his length. I hissed with the drip of cold lube on my cock, grateful for the extra slide it gave me.

Ally held out a pillow. "Shuffle up and put this under you." She slid it under my arse after I'd moved into place and Sam crawled between my legs.

"Maybe this would be better if you rode me. You want to do that?"

"Not yet. Just get inside of me," I begged, not too proud to let him see my neediness now. One hand on my arse cheek spreading me and the other holding my leg out wide, he pressed his broad head against my hole.

"Push against me if it hurts." He nudged forward gently. I'd just had three of his thick fingers inside of me, but it was still a stretch accepting his cock. I hissed out a breath and gripped my shaft, stroking it to distract me from the burn. "That's it," he moaned when he popped past my resistance and I shouted out, my hoarse cry one of fulfillment. "Fuck. Fuck, fuck, fuck." His words were said on a hoarse whisper, as if he was praying while he waited.

"Move," I demanded, desperate to feel more.

A buzz and a soft moan had me opening my eyes and what I saw nearly made me come on the spot. Ally was kneeling on the bed, watching where we were connected, a vibrating wand held against her clit. She'd come hard when we'd used it on her, me in her tight pussy as Sam slid into her mouth.

Sam bent me almost in half, my knee getting damn close to my shoulder as he pressed me down and slid nearly all the way out before rolling his hips into me in one smooth glide. I choked out a cry, overwhelmed by the motion. Over and over he pumped into me, until he leaned down and kissed me. When our lips met, his hips stuttered, and I sucked in a breath. I was so close already.

"Roll over."

He pulled out of me, letting me flip onto my belly and spread my legs, tilting my hips up and inviting him back in. Lube dripped down onto my hole before Sam climbed on top of me, straddling my hips and nudging my legs closed. He thrust against me, his cock fitting between my cheeks and making me moan as he rubbed himself all over me. We were locked together from head to toe, his arms curled around my shoulders and his legs tangled with mine. A few more of those sensuous glides and I was pushing back against him, silently begging for him to come inside me again.

Fisting the sheets, I arched my spine shoving my arse back and grunting when he slowed his movements. He shifted slightly, his hand pressing down on his cock as he guided himself into me again. This time he hit my prostate dead on; the rush of electricity through my veins making me shout out. I was expecting him to slam into me, rough and ready, but instead, he lay down, pressing every inch of our sweaty bodies together again, curling around me and holding me close. We weren't facing each other, but it was more intimate than before. His movements were a slow grind, more a roll of his hips than a slap and pump.

The sensuous puff of breath in my ear as he trailed his tongue around the shell and bit down gently on my lobe made me moan. The line of soft sucking kisses down my throat to my shoulder had me shuddering. My sense of touch was magnified, like every nerve ending was connected to Sam, singing in exaltation as he made love to me. My body absorbed every movement, every breath, every moan as ecstasy. The stretch of my arse around Sam and the press of my dick against the sheets had me moaning. My balls slid along the cotton, my toes curled, and my hands grasped for purchase as Sam thrust long and slow inside me.

I needed more. I needed everything.

Reaching over my shoulder, I pulled Sam closer and turned my face to his. Our lips met and our tongues tangled. I rocketed toward the edge, about to come for the first time in my life without a mouth, hand, or pussy around my shaft. On stimulation overload, I shuddered again, my arse tightening around Sam's cock.

"Oh fuck," Sam choked, shuttling his hips harder. He bit my shoulder and blinding rapture flew through my body. I shouted out my release as jets of cum shot from me. With every tunnel of his dick into my hole, Sam lit me up, reigniting my orgasm. It went on and on until I was slumped against the mattress unable to move.

Sam lifted up, and all I could do to keep him there was let out a pitying whine and hold as tight to his nape as my gelatinous muscles would allow me.

"Come inside me, Sam. I want your cum inside me." My voice sounded like I'd swallowed gravel, raspy and hoarse, but Sam reacted like I'd struck him with a cattle prod. He cried out, buried his head against my shoulder and thrust once more, stiffening above me as he shot his load deep inside my body.

The press of his lips to my neck, the nuzzle of his nose along my spine and his weight on me was everything and more. Ally shifted and snuggled into my side, resting her head on my forearm and I closed my eyes, savouring the quiet. The only sound permeating the night was our ragged breathing.

Sam pulled out of me slowly and I hissed at the sting. The emptiness from his retreat left me in no doubt that we'd do that again. And again. He slid off me to the side and wrapped his arm around my waist, his head on my shoulder.

Face down on the bed, lying in a wet patch, with my two lovers curled into me, I couldn't move. But I didn't even want to try. I took every second of love that they'd given me and tried to telepathically communicate to them how much I loved them too. Ally, for her strength and compassion. For her unending love. Sam for his perseverance and determination to find his home. For his willingness to lean on me when he needed it.

I could finally say that I loved myself too. It'd taken me half a lifetime, but I was finally proud to say the words. "Hey," I murmured, exhaustion dragging me under. "I'm definitely bi."

Sam chuckled and Ally snorted. She leaned in and kissed my sweaty forehead. "And we both love that you can say it now."

EPILOGUE

Sam – A year later

The days preparing the station were going to be worth it. High winds and strong rains were predicted, but none of us were holding our breaths. The station was bone dry. The ecosystems were hanging on by barely a thread. We hadn't seen the wet stuff for years. Just like twenty years earlier as a teenager waiting for the rain at our farm, we were back here, waiting for it. And like then, I wasn't even sure if I remembered the sound of it hitting a tin roof.

Change was eternal though, and we knew the drought would, one day, come to an end. It seemed like a lifetime ago since we'd been able to run more than a litre or two of water for a wash. I could barely remember the feel of fresh water surrounding me as I swam in it. When we'd made the trip to Sydney to meet Ally's dad, it'd been utterly foreign having the waves crash around us at Bondi Beach.

We were relaxed, finally slowing down after days of non-stop work. Roofs had been checked, every nail hammered down again, every gate latch secured, and the animals tended to. We'd staked and tied all the plants in the veggie patch and shifted furniture out of the way so we could quickly move the chairs and swing inside if the winds picked up as predicted. Cyclones didn't hit this far inland, but we did get a taste of the winds that went with them.

But for now, we waited.

Macca and Scottie sat curled up on the swing under the veranda and Nan and Ma rocked on the rocking chairs, Jono never far from the love of his life. He'd finally confessed his feelings to Ma and they'd stopped dancing around each other. When Scottie had asked Jono about retiring, he thought he was being asked to move on. Devastation had clouded his features. But Scottie hadn't meant that. He'd asked him to slow down, enjoy his home—which he'd never be ejected from—and Ma. Scottie and Jono were training me up as lead stockman.

It was the push Jono and Ma had needed. Now we saw them holding hands or smiling softly at each other over a cuppa in the afternoons and he'd not long ago vacated his cottage in favour of the main homestead.

We'd shifted too, taking up the family's offer of the guest house. Ally had been reluctant at first, not wanting to reduce the station's income, but Ma was insistent. Scottie gave us the opportunity to do things right, so our next job was to begin renovating the two old staff cabins into guest accommodations.

I scratched my blunt fingers over Craig's buzzed hair as he sat between my legs on the stair below, his back to my chest. Ally was perched on his lap, cuddled in close.

We watched the angry clouds roll over the horizon in the distance, jagged flashes of lightning illuminating the darkening skies. Thunder boomed long seconds later, like the crack of a whip and a low rumble. The storm was still too far away to do anything except provide us with an afternoon's entertainment as we sweated it out. Waru and Yindi had prayed to the spirits of the land to ask for the storm to reach us and all the other stations in the dry red interior. I prayed that their ways would work.

Time ticked slowly by and we watched quietly as the storm rolled closer and closer. This year had been one to forget. We'd experienced so much heartache as a nation, but in some ways, we were so incredibly lucky too. Now all we needed was rain.

The cool breeze reached us first and Ally sat up straighter. My heart rate notched up and I felt Craig breathe in deeply under my hands. I could smell the rain in the air. The storm churning in the metallic grey-blue clouds above us was close. The air was heavy, and shadows stretched across the land. It was dark and ominous to the inexperienced, but to us those clouds meant hope. Life. I held my breath waiting for Mother Nature to give us her greatest gift.

Another gust of wind brought the smell of damp soil to my nose. My breath caught in my throat and Ally stood, taking Craig's hand, then mine. She smiled at us, her gaze full of excitement. Love.

The first drops on the iron roof were like an orchestra in a Disney movie, when the hero defeats the villains. It was the sound of hope. The drops sped up as the rain washed over us, beginning in earnest. I lifted my face, letting the cool drops kiss my skin. Not one of us spoke. Instead we held each other close.

Laughter sounded and we saw Scottie and Macca kissing in the rain. Their hats lay discarded on the ground and they whooped, happiness radiating off them. All around us, our family danced and cheered as the water soaked through our dusty clothes. Tears of joy fell, and our spirits soared. We were one with this land, and the two people in my arms gave me more love than I'd ever thought possible.

I'd been blessed in this life. My rocky path had finally calmed, and before me were cool, clear waters.

I had it all. Or I would in about six months.

Puddles formed around us, the rain falling in sheets as I dropped to my knees and pushed up Ally's shirt, kissing her belly. A bump had started to appear, but we were yet to tell anyone except Ma and Nan, who'd helped Ally with the never-ending morning sickness.

I grasped Craig's hand as he kissed our lady and I nuzzled her belly again, whispering to our plum-sized baby how much they were already loved.

"Ally," Scottie called, his voice pitched high with barely contained excitement. I looked up to see her nod at him and rest a hand protectively on her tummy. Scottie was pointing, open-mouthed. She lifted a hand to her mouth and nodded again, tears tracking down her cheeks and her wet hair plastered to her head. She'd never looked more beautiful than in that moment. Scottie charged forward, slowing only to scoop her up in his arms, lifting her and spinning her around. "Oh my God, you're gonna be a mum?" She nodded again as he put her down and he hugged her tight again. "And you guys are gonna be dads!"

"Yeah, mate." Craig helped me up off the ground, every part of me soaked to the bone. He wrapped his arms around me, and I leaned down to kiss him softly.

Grinning, we reached for Ally, but Macca was on us, hugging us tight. "I'm gonna be an uncle?" He was practically jumping in the puddles in excitement. "Oh, man, I can't wait to spoil this kid."

All around us there were hugs and congratulations and animated conversations about babies and due dates and excitement on whether we'd have a boy or a girl. It didn't matter to us—we just wanted a healthy baby.

With Craig's arms wrapped around me, I watched as our lady moved back towards us and we enveloped her in our embrace. I savoured the security of having the two people who I loved more than life itself in my arms. Our baby was already adored just as much.

Little bean was a celebration of our love. Our baby would grow up with a family who loved them unconditionally, and supported whatever life threw at them. We would protect them with our lives. We'd guide them and watch them grow up to be as strong as their mum, as loyal as their dad, and as loving as me—Daddy.

We'd found each other a long time ago. It may have taken us decades to move past our friendship into something more—something unbreakable—but we were finally there.

None of us had any idea what happiness was until we accepted ourselves and understood that we were simply meant to be. The three of us together, forever. Craig still blamed himself for taking so long to see things clearly, but I wouldn't change a thing about our lives or our love story. All the hardship, the decades of wandering rudderless across the land. It led us here, to this very moment. To each other's arms and to this life that had given us so much. To the land of red dirt and big blue skies. To droughts and sacrifice and now, pouring rain. To hope and life and love.

To Pearce Station.

To home.

The end.

NOT READY TO LEAVE PEARCE STATION?

Outback Treasure I

A city boy in Australia's outback? He won't even last two weeks.

Pete is geeky-cute and sweet. He's also way too young for me. But he's so much like me too. He loves this desolate land, and he fits right in with station life. My family. Me.

There are a million reasons why we shouldn't be together. But I keep forgetting them when he's near.

If only he'd told me why he was really here...

Outback Treasure I is the first part of the Pearce Station duet. Pete and Scottie's story concludes in Outback Treasure II.

Available on Amazon

Outback Treasure II

A city boy in Australia's outback. Who would have thought I'd last longer than two weeks?

My station owner may be older but he's as beautiful and rugged as the red dirt that flows through his veins. Scottie deserves better than me too. I lied to him. But he encourages me. He helps me follow my dreams.

Scottie has warned me a thousand times though. It's not easy. The desert is as unforgiving as the people. We've each got a fight on our hands. For our happiness. For our survival.

Outback Treasure II is the conclusion to Pete and Scottie's story.

Available on Amazon

About Ann Grech

By day Ann Grech lives in the corporate world and can be found sitting behind a desk typing away at reports and papers or lecturing to a room full of students. She graduated with a PhD in 2016 and is now an over-qualified nerd. Glasses, briefcase, high heels and a pencil skirt, she's got the librarian look nailed too. If only they knew! She swears like a sailor, so that's got to be a hint. The other one was "the look" from her tattoo artist when she told him that she wanted her kids initials "B" and "J" tattooed on her foot. It took a second to register that it might be a bad idea.

She's never entirely fit in and loves escaping into a book—whether it's reading or writing one. But she's found her tribe now and loves her MM book world family. She dislikes cooking, but loves eating, can't figure out technology, but is addicted to it, and her guilty pleasure is Byron Bay Cookies. Oh and shoes. And lingerie. And maybe handbags too. Well, if we're being honest, we'd probably have to add her library too given the state of her credit card every month (what can she say, she's a bookworm at heart)!

In 2019 she was an Award-Winning Finalist in the Fiction: LGBTQ category of the 2019 Best Book Awards sponsored by American Book Fest for her story In Safe Arms.

She also publishes her raunchier short stories under her pen name, Olive Hiscock.

Ann loves chatting to people online, so if you'd like to keep up with what she's got going on:

Join her newsletter: http://anngrech.us8.list-manage2.com/subscribe?u=0af7475c0791ed8f1466e7fd9&id=1cee9cdcb6

Like her on Facebook:
https://www.facebook.com/pages/Ann-Grech/458420227655212

Join her reader group:
https://www.facebook.com/groups/1871698189780535/

Follow her on Twitter and Instagram:
@anngrechauthor

Follow her on Goodreads:
https://www.goodreads.com/author/show/7536397.Ann_Grech

Follow her on BookBub:
https://www.bookbub.com/authors/ann-grech

Visit her website (www.anngrech.com) for her current booklist

She'd love to hear from you directly, too. Please feel free to e-mail her at ann@anngrech.com or check out her website www.anngrech.com for updates.

ANN GRECH'S BOOKS

UNEXPECTED
Whiteout (MM)
White Noise (MM)
Whitewash (MM)

MY TRUTH
All He Needs (MMM)
In Safe Arms (MM)

PEARCE STATION DUET
Outback Treasure I (MM)
Outback Treasure II (MM)

GOLD COAST NIGHTS
Delectable (MMF)

MV DREAMCATCHER
Dance with Me (MM)

STANDALONES
Home For Christmas (MM)
The Gift (FMMM - free for newsletter subscribers)
Take Two (MM – free for newsletter subscribers)

M/F TITLES
One night in Daytona

Ink'd

www.ingramcontent.com/pod-product-compliance
Lightning Source LLC
Chambersburg PA
CBHW020259120726
47904CB00001B/271